WHIRLWIND

THE WWII ADVENTURES OF MI6 AGENT KATRIN NISSEN

BOOK THREE

A NOVEL BY
KAREN K. BREES

Black Rose Writing | Texas

ISBN: 978-1-68513-454-9
PUBLISHED BY BLACK ROSE WRITING
www.blackrosewriting.com

Printed in the United States of America
Suggested Retail Price (SRP) $24.95

Whirlwind is printed in Book Antiqua

*As a planet-friendly publisher, Black Rose Writing does its best to eliminate unnecessary waste to reduce paper usage and energy costs, while never compromising the reading experience. As a result, the final word count vs. page count may not meet common expectations.

To my Family

Acknowledgements

To (in alphabetical order) Bill, Colleen, Denise and Cherry, Jeanne, Mike, and Millie. Here you go! Hope you enjoy your characters. It was fun writing you!

Thanks to Cate Perry, developmental editor extraordinaire. You always find a new direction for me to explore.

And a big, heartfelt thanks to Reagan Rothe, Creator of Black Rose Writing, and his team. You are nothing short of phenomenal and the best publisher a writer could ever hope to have.

WHIRLWIND

July, 1940

CHAPTER ONE

Berlin

We are creatures of habit. There is a sense of order in habits—a certain familiarity, a calming reassurance. If one is engaged in matters of treason, as was Admiral Wilhelm Canaris, Chief of German Military Intelligence, his habit of a morning stroll through the *Tiergarten* with his aide, Martin Brunner, provided the perfect cover. The former wild game park was now a peaceful respite from the hectic pace of wartime Berlin and a place for reflection and planning. *Alles ist in Ordnung,* he thought. Everything is in order, or at least it would appear that way to the casual observer, and Admiral Canaris was most certain he was observed. Everyone was observed at all times in this glorious Third Reich, from the minor civil servant to those closest to der Führer. Especially those closest to der Führer.

"Let's turn here," Canaris said, moving away from the main path and onto a side trail that wound through the forest. The *Tiergarten* was a large park frequented by lovers, families with children, office workers on their lunches, and anyone who needed an escape. Wilhelm Canaris and Martin Brunner fit the last category quite well. "The dream has become the nightmare," he said to his aide, "and something must be done before it destroys us all."

Physically, Canaris and Brunner, separated by only ten years in age, were total opposites. Wilhelm Canaris was not an imposing figure. Slightly under five foot four inches and slight of build, his intelligence was his strength, and except for one regrettable lapse, his keen mind had served him well. He'd joined Hitler at the beginning, believing this was Germany's only way out of the debacle of The Great War. God knew, Germany needed something to believe in. Unfortunately, as it turned out, God hadn't been consulted and Germany had cast her lot with the devil. The future looked as bleak as the past.

Canaris was a soldier. A career man. In a legion of thugs, sycophants, and sadistic psychopaths, he was a man of honor in an organization that neither understood nor honored the concept. Honor is the creed of righteous men. The last straw for Canaris had been the slaughter of Polish civilians and the defense of that crime by the higher ups. They'd left him no choice. Whether he lived or died was up to the Fates, but he swore from that moment on that he would do everything in his power to stop the madman from Austria.

Brunner had also joined Hitler at the beginning in 1923 at The Beer Hall Putsch, when Hitler had stormed onto the world stage. Brunner's tall, muscular frame had allowed him to manage the crowds with ease, so Hitler could move among them, casting his spell. It had been his first assignment for MI6. With a German father and an English mother, both of whom insisted on remaining in their separate homelands, he'd been shipped back and forth as the mood suited them. He'd had two homes, until first his father, and then his mother had died. Two homes but nothing to go home to. Seventeen years was a long time to be away.

Brunner glanced at a young couple seated on a bench, engaged in conversation. He looked more closely, then frowned. "Sir," he began, but Canaris called his attention to a pair of swans that had left their pond and were now wandering about the grass.

"I see them, Martin," Canaris said. "And they see us." He gave a mirthless laugh. "It's their job to see us, after all."

The two men walked on, until, satisfied they were not being observed, Canaris resumed their conversation. "Well, Martin, who will I find to put up with my incessant orders and mountains of typing, now?"

"Sir, I expect it won't take long at all for my space to be filled." Brunner's tone grew serious. "I've only been with you three months. If you don't mind my asking, Sir, why…?"

Canaris held up his hand. "Martin, I could say because you are an excellent aide and loyal officer, but we both know the truth, don't we?"

His brow creased, Martin searched his memory for the one mistake he surely must have made to have brought him to this moment. Complete allegiance and obedience to the Party had marked everything he had done for the past seventeen years. Rising in the ranks and delivering total loyalty, Martin Brunner's record was impeccable. "I don't understand, Sir."

"Don't look so concerned, Martin. You did nothing wrong. Nothing at all." He took a medal from his uniform pocket and closed his fist around it. So small the object was. Strange that Hitler's intentions to create such massive destruction and loss of life could be reduced to something hidden so easily in the palm of one's hand.

"Yes, Sir." Martin's words didn't mask his confusion.

"Good. There is a great deal of work to be done, and Churchill needs this." Canaris pinned the medal to his aide's uniform jacket lapel and smoothed the cloth back into place.

"Sir?"

KAREN K. BREES 5

"Please give him my best. He speaks highly of you. And it's time you went home, wouldn't you agree? With this," he nodded at the medal, "you complete your mission with honor. Your first, and only, task now is arriving safely in London, being an accomplice in an act of treason." He shrugged. "We must save Germany from herself, if we can."

The clouds of confusion were releasing their grip on Martin's thinking. "Churchill. You and Churchill."

"Yes, Martin. Somebody has to stop this maniac, and you've been recruited into an extremely small army to help accomplish the goal."

"But, Sir, why not just walk into der Führer's office and shoot him when he's alone?"

"He's never alone, Martin. And while I don't overly value my life, I don't relish the thought of throwing it away on a reckless gamble. The whole cadre must be taken out, and with just Hitler gone, we're left with Goring and Himmler and the rest. No better. Probably worse. No. That is not the way — at least not at this point. There may come a time when it's the only option, but that's not for now." Canaris slowed his pace. The swans had wandered across the grass and were now positioned by an empty park bench, hoping for handouts from the next occupant. "Even they know when biding one's time is the best option," he said. "It is time, however, for you to play your part. The staff car is waiting and your flight will be leaving within the hour. You will not be returning." He turned to watch another man approaching, a newspaper folded under his arm. "They are certainly everywhere, aren't they? It's only going to get worse. Distrust and suspicion breed more of the same. It cannot end well. God speed, Martin."

"Sir? One last thing." There was a mixture of hope and pain in Martin's voice. "Erika?"

Canaris waved his hand as if swatting at an annoying insect. "I had her arrested this morning, and she's being held for interrogation." He kicked a stone from the path. "She's waiting for you on the plane. I've given her new identity papers."

"Thank you, Sir." For Martin Brunner, everything had fallen into place, and tonight, finally back in the arms of Old Blighty, he wanted three things: At least two pints of ale, a supper of bangers and mash, and a night of sleep where he didn't keep a pistol by his pillow with the fear of the door being broken down and him being hauled off to his death. Tonight would bring him all three, and it had been a long time coming. He would be back in England after seventeen long years.

At the next junction on the path, Admiral Wilhelm Canaris turned left, an army of one heading back to the Abwehr and his own destiny. Martin Brunner turned right and found the car waiting for him just outside the park. In slightly under two hours, when they'd landed at Heathrow in London, yet another staff car was waiting to take him to Churchill and transport his wife to his mother's country estate in Yorkshire.

Understandably, Martin Brunner's armed escorts engaged in no small talk with him, and he'd expected nothing else. Still in his SS uniform and bearing a German name, he was the enemy until proven otherwise, and in the years he'd been gone, personnel had undergone many changes. No one knew him, and the photograph in his file of a boy of eighteen bore only a slight resemblance to the prematurely grey thirty-five-year old man standing before them. Fortunately, fingerprints didn't lie, and he'd had his taken upon his recruitment into MI6 — something new that had been added to the screening process. Initially used to identify those killed in service and whose bodies were recoverable but unidentifiable, today it had a different, more benign outcome. Memories fade and the body ages, but one's fingerprints remain the same through life, barring injury or deliberate attempts to erase them. For Martin Brunner, the prints just taken in the waiting cubicle on the main floor of Whitehall, when compared with those taken when he'd joined the Service, left no doubt of his identity. And with that confirmation and being very much alive, he was given a pass and permitted entry to the War Rooms for a private audience with Prime Minister Winston Churchill.

· · ·

The Cabinet War Rooms, from which the Prime Minister directed the war effort, were a group of basement offices in a Whitehall building near

Parliament. Accessed by a long corridor sheathed in corrugated metal, the door leading to Churchill's inner sanctum was guarded by two armed Marines in blue uniforms. Surrendering their charge, the escorts returned to their duties, and the Marines began the identification process anew, studying Brunner's identification papers and searching him for any weapons or other devices that might be employed against the Prime Minister. Satisfied, one of the Marines pushed the button that allowed the door to be opened. Leaving his comrade to guard the entrance, the Marine led Brunner into the inner sanctum, where Churchill, having been notified of the arrival, waited with his habitual impatience. Looking up from a sheaf of papers he'd been reading, Churchill motioned for Brunner to advance and dismissed the escort.

Without ceremony or delay, Brunner unfastened the medal from his uniform lapel, placed it on the wooden table in front of Churchill, and saluted. "Captain Martin Brunner reporting for duty, Sir."

The Prime Minister returned the papers to the massive stack that awaited his attention and picked up the medal. "Well done, Martin, well done," he said, pressing a gold pin on the medal which caused a small compartment to open. He turned the medal over, and a roll of microfilm dropped into his hand. "We'll have this developed," he said. "How is Canaris, by the way?"

"He sends his regards, Sir. He's walking a tightrope."

"Indeed he is. Let's hope he keeps his balance. A fall would be fatal." Churchill's cigar, smoldering in the ashtray, sent up a tendril of smoke. "There's much work to be done, and we'll need to pick your brain. But," and he picked up the lonesome cigar and waved it about, sending the smoke on a different path, "before you meet with the Cabinet, I believe a change of clothing is in order. If this is all you have, I don't believe it will make the best impression this evening." He gave a cursory glance at his agent's attire and pressed a button on the desk next to the lamp. Immediately, one of the Marines outside the door entered the room.

"Captain Brunner requires a change of clothing, including nightwear and toiletries. He is most anxious to divest himself of his costume. Also, orient him to the location of the water closet and the canteen. He'll need sustenance. And then show him where he'll bunk tonight. He'll be with us the next few days, if not longer." He jammed the cigar in his mouth. "And have this developed," Churchill said, passing the microfilm to Brunner to hand to the Marine. "That is all." Churchill turned to Brunner. "Welcome home, Captain. You'll report back here at 2000 hours."

.   .   .

The contents of the decoded microfilm delivered to Churchill within the hour revealed the scope and intensity of Hitler's plans for Britain. Invasion now appeared inevitable and imminent, and there would be no escape. If Britain were to survive, it would require everything in her power. If she fell, Hitler would be unstoppable. Britain was, with no exaggeration, the only hope of the free world, and success or failure rested on the shoulders of just one man, Winston Leonard Spencer Churchill.

CHAPTER TWO

London

I'd arrived in London on June 28, officially on indefinite leave from Yale University, where I was Assistant Professor of Botany in the Department of Horticulture. Lately, it was an intermittent employment. The war, like some sort of psychotic octopus was wrapping its tentacles around every facet of existence, its insatiable appetite intruding more and more into life— mine and everyone else's —with only one goal. Absolute destruction.

My eternal quest for tenure was also on indefinite leave, and I wondered, somewhere deep in the recesses of my mind, if I would ever return to that life that seemed to belong to someone else. Katrin Nissen was a woman without a country for the duration, although I did have a nice temporary residence. John had found us a small furnished flat within walking distance of Whitehall in an older neighborhood. Nothing fancy, unless you counted the black wrought iron fence that marked the boundary of our lodgings from the property next

door. There were three geraniums in clay pots, one
on each step that led up to the small porch and the
front door. Our set of rooms on the ground level
consisted of a bedroom, parlor, bath, and kitchen.
All the essentials. No frills. There was a wardrobe
for the clothes and a pantry for the food supplies.
All in all, it was efficient, if rather sterile, but we
wouldn't be spending much time there apart from
meals and sleeping. I'd bounced on the mattress
and it had passed the test. No sharp springs. What
more could a girl ask for?

John was in the same boat. Well, not actually
the same boat—more like on the same ocean. He
was Full Professor of Law at Yale, as well as full
partner in the law firm of Breckenridge, Bernstein,
and Bertolucci. He was the Breckenridge and also
my husband, although, according to the rules and
regs of MI6, we were merely, close, personal
associates. Quite close, as a matter of fact. I was
lucky enough as it were to be aboard at all, being a
woman. Being openly married would have meant
immediate dismissal. And so, I kept my maiden
name. I was Katrin Nissen, a woman occasionally
living in sin when the occasion arose. Occasionally,
also, John and I worked together as business
associates. That was the case now, and we had
both been summoned to London to await orders.

I'd established a comfortable daily routine. We
reported to Whitehall in the morning, and I
shopped for enough food for supper and the next

day on the way home, so as not to overburden the tiny pantry. Never knowing when we'd receive our marching orders made any long-term stocking of the flat a risky business. Our suitcases remained packed and waiting for us by the door. The other mundane chores of housekeeping, such as the cleaning and the laundry were done spottily, and only when the time necessary for their completion seemed ensured. It was life on the short.

At Whitehall, we received updates on the worsening situation in Europe. It was most depressing. Then, we worked our way through the messages that had been transmitted by wireless radio, decoded by the cryptologists, and processed by the typing staff. We didn't know what we were looking for, so anything that might require dealing with here at home was taken seriously. It was busy work of a sort. We were waiting for the remainder of the agents to arrive from postings around the world, and those who worked in Europe had to deal with numerous obstacles that increased their travel time. As the days wore on, the number of messages increased exponentially, and it took the better part of the morning to work our way through the stacks that never seemed to decrease in height.

Before the war changed everything, the duties of Britain's Intelligence community had been clearly delineated. MI6 dealt with national security issues that impacted Britain and occurred on foreign soil. MI5 operated within Britain, and Scotland Yard handled the homegrown criminal activities of a more general nature. It was all neat and tidy, with everyone knowing the precise parameters of their authority and responsibilities. The war changed all of it. It was as if a kitten had gotten into a neatly wound ball of yarn and had had a field day with it, tangling and intertwining strands until it was a hopeless muddle. So now, duties overlapped and professional boundaries were crossed on a routine basis. It was about the only routine that existed. We worked together, sometimes grudgingly, sometimes amicably, but internal cooperation was a necessity. The heads of the Army, the RAF, and the Royal Navy found themselves in the same situation. We were all in this together. Some days, it worked better than others, human nature being what it is. Nobody likes to share overly much, when it means relinquishing a bit of one's authority. And that meant for tense meetings in the War Rooms, as attested to by the scratches gouged by Churchill's fingernails on the arms of his wooden desk chair at the head table. A testimony to Churchill's barely contained anger and tension, each day, it seemed, new marks appeared.

There was order in the midst of chaos. And quiet, as well. Churchill detested extraneous noise. A sign in the tunnel leading to the War Rooms, *There is to be no whistling or unnecessary noise in this passage*, was a reminder how seriously the Prime Minister enforced the rule. Even the typists were silenced. Noiseless typewriters manufactured by Remington and sent over from America, transformed the typing room. Instead of the clicks of the keys as they struck the ribbon and the ding of the bell signaling the typist had reached the end of the line, requiring the carriage be slammed back so the next row could begin, an eerie silence hovered over the room—the typists had been transformed into pantomimists. The only thunderous noises came from Churchill, himself. And his volume was legendary. If decibel level equated with power, there was no question who was in charge.

Each day moved along in the same way. Until today. It had been a long day, running down leads and sending off what we'd learned to the next level of the bureaucracy. After a brief lunch at the canteen, we were notified our presence would be required that evening. Throughout the course of the afternoon, the tempo picked up in the work rooms, and the change in the atmosphere was palpable. There was no longer any idle conversation. The presence of the military noticeably increased, and the grim set to most of the faces couldn't be dismissed. Something was afoot, and it wasn't a good something. I was curious, and having to wait until the evening to learn what that might be, made the afternoon drag on. Finally, it was evening, and I was glad I'd snagged some extra food at the canteen. I was sure there'd be no dinner.

· · ·

There were a dozen of us seated around the central table. Crammed was more like it. John had taken an end chair to give him more leg room. He's a tall man, and I'm a tall woman. I hadn't had the foresight to grab an end seat, and so I was resigned to dealing with the inevitable leg cramps that lay ahead. The setting reminded me somewhat of departmental meetings at the university, although there wouldn't be any after-meeting lunches or drinks at the bar. Everything began and ended in this room. I recognized a few faces, one in particular, and Margo Speer and I exchanged brief looks.

The presence of MI6, MI5, and Scotland Yard at the briefing didn't augur well for what Churchill would have to say. The agencies may be required to work together, but the truce didn't extend to the eating arrangements, and we still kept to ourselves, as much as was possible. The tension in the room was pervasive and oppressive. The air, already sullied by Churchill's incessant cigar smoke, was a dusky blue. As the door opened and closed to admit more operatives into the crowded chamber, tendrils of smoke drifted towards the

KAREN K. BREES 17

ceiling and wafted back down, seemingly at a loss to find an escape. They, like us, were trapped, waiting. Conversations were muted. Something big was at hand, and speculation was running wild. Privately, I hoped it meant that Hitler had been assassinated and this whole bloody mess would soon be over with. I couldn't have been more wrong.

This was my first briefing with the Prime Minister, and to say I was a combination of nervous, excited, and slightly in awe would be a fair estimate of the way I was feeling. There were three manila folders in front of Churchill, an ash tray overflowing with ashes, and a glass filled with a brownish liquid that I guessed was some sort of whiskey, judging by the measured sips he took from it. Of one thing I was sure. It wasn't tea. A slight rustling of papers signaled the beginning of the meeting, and Churchill wasted no time laying out the specifics of what Hitler had planned for us.

It seemed that each day, Hitler grew bolder and more powerful, and Europe was falling like a stack of dominoes before him. There was no end in sight to the carnage. Hitler was unstoppable on the Continent, and the only roadblock in his quest for world dominion was the man at the head of the table, Winston Churchill, Prime Minister of Great Britain. The room grew quiet as he launched into the meeting, without preamble.

"When I addressed the House of Commons last month, it was apparent that Hitler had us in his sights. We had rejected his terms of a so-called orchestrated peace that would have spelled the end of Britain as we know her." He paused, shifting the cigar's position in his mouth and slammed a chubby fist on the pile of papers, disturbing the arrangement and causing a few to flutter to the floor. He stared at them until the Chief of the Air Staff, the head of the Royal Air Force, bent down to retrieve them. Satisfied, Churchill continued. "Britain will not suffer the fate of France and become a bastardized shadow of her former self."

The huge map of Europe that hung on the wall behind his chair showed the reality of Hitler's successes. Pins had been stuck into the map, and the cord that connected them showed the unabated advance of the German military. There were no pins marking any retreat. It was a frightening visual reminder of what we were up against.

Churchill gave a brief nod of recognition to a man in military uniform, seated front row and directly opposite the head table. "Captain Martin Brunner has returned from an extended assignment in Berlin. As a result of his efforts, we now know precisely Germany's timetable and what Hitler's plans entail. Captain Brunner, your country is most appreciative of your efforts."

Churchill then deposited his cigar in the overflowing ashtray and took a sip from the glass. Yep. Whiskey.

"The invasion, *Operation Sea Lion*, is planned for mid-September, but it is contingent upon them first having control of the Channel, control of the skies, and good weather. For once, Britain's foul weather might actually be her salvation."

There was a bit of coughing and snorting after the last item on Churchill's list. Churchill continued. "The Luftwaffe is insisting there be decent weather before they'll take to the air, and we find this indicative of squabbling amongst the various branches of Hitler's military. Everything hinges upon the Luftwaffe being able to soundly defeat the RAF in the skies over the Channel, destroying as much of our aircraft as possible and demoralizing us. Their Kriegsmarine has refused to sail against us if this is not accomplished." Churchill's voice had been low but now it thundered. "It is our task to ensure this is not accomplished! They will never set foot in Britain! Hitler will not conquer our island. He will not possess our soul!" Churchill retrieved his cigar and waved it in the air as if it were a battalion pennant. "The responsibility of the defence of Britain and ultimate victory has now fallen upon your shoulders."

In the silence that followed, the enormity of the task was the central thought in everyone's mind.

It's difficult to think of Britain as an island. It fits the definition, of course. It's a body of land surrounded by water. I wondered, though, if any other island in history had ever been the heart of an empire that stretched around the world. "The sun never set on the British Empire" was an old and true saying. Somewhere in the world, the sun was shining on a piece of land that Britain had conquered and claimed. It was apparent if Hitler wanted this island, it wouldn't be gotten easily.

"Countering Operation Sea Lion is the responsibility of our armed forces," Churchill continued, moving folder number one to the side and moving folder number two to center stage, "but at the same time Operation Sea Lion is underway, Operation Lena will begin. The latter will be a contingent of twenty-one Nazi operatives who will infiltrate Britain—arriving by boat or parachute. Their mission will be to continue the attempt at demoralizing our population and preparing them to accept Hitler's *inevitable* victory." His emphasis on *inevitable* produced the intended result, and righteous anger was evident on every face.

"You are charged with apprehending each and every one of them, along with any advance members that have been positioned here to receive their comrades. Coordination with the defence volunteers to monitor the coast and other civilian defence groups to watch the skies will be essential."

There was a faint murmuring from the assemblage. The official view was that all German agents had been arrested and dealt with. Privately, we believed this scenario to be highly unlikely. Those already here had eluded capture at least once before and wouldn't be easy prey. We didn't know who they were or where they were. No, it didn't make sense that no foreign agents lurked in our midst, and now, the actuality had been confirmed. German agents had been dispersed throughout Britain and had effectively settled in, without capture. They were doing what they had been sent here to do—observe and report to Germany using wireless radio. Additionally, they would attempt to demoralize the population, paving the way for first, resignation, and then, acceptance of Hitler's victory over the Crown.

Churchill's gaze moved about the room, meeting everyone's eyes. It was a moment unlike anything I had ever experienced. It was, for want of a better word, a sealing of a compact. "We have one thing operating in our favor. We have information that these operatives will have been rushed through the training process in order to meet Hitler's timeline. Their inexperience may be their downfall. Time will tell."

Placing the second folder atop the first, Churchill glanced at folder number three, and there was a brief, barely noticeable headshake. Some sort of internal argument had been decided. "You will report at 0700 hours tomorrow morning. Further information will then be given to you concerning your assignments. That is all." He rose, collecting his folders and the nearly empty glass which he drained in one final swallow. He added the cigar and ashtray that dumped a goodly portion of its contents on the desk and floor in the process and returned to his bedroom office next door, heavily laden in both body and mind.

I rubbed my calves, trying to wake up legs that complained at the treatment they'd been given. The cramps finally released their grip on my leg muscles and I stood. It was late, and the day had caught up to me. Apparently, it had caught up to others, as well, and we filtered silently out of the room to seek our own lodgings and beds.

.   .   .

We'd entered Whitehall in the damp coolness of morning, and the remnants of the oppressive heat and humidity that had collected during the day and still lingered in the air was a shock to the system as we exited the building and rejoined the world outside. The silence we'd been surrounded by all day also vanished. A siren pierced the night. A police vehicle, an ambulance, perhaps a fire engine. I still had difficulty distinguishing one from another. Regardless, somewhere not too far away, an emergency was playing out. This time it wasn't playing out in silence. Fires don't stop in wartime. They become a daily occurrence when bombs seek their targets. Crime doesn't stop in wartime. If anything, there's an increase. The criminal mind seeks opportunities, and with people's minds distracted and less aware of what's going on around them, there's an inevitable upsurge. Accidents and illnesses don't stop, either. Everything continues. War is just the overlay: demanding, incessant, and merciless. Sirens would soon not be an occasional alert but a normal occurrence. I was depressed. Not a good way to end the day, so I forced my mind in another direction.

"What do you suppose that third folder contains?" I asked my husband as we wended our way back to the flat. "Did you see how his expression changed when he touched it? Anger. No, more like rage. He looked ready to explode. That can't be good for his blood pressure. He's a bit overweight, to put it gently. And those cigars. He is never without one."

"Don't know."

John's voice was heavy with fatigue, and his normally brisk pace had slowed to a walk. I almost said something but had the good sense to keep my thoughts to myself. The constant need to be at the top of our game is often at odds with the body's need for rest. Too many long days and short nights take their toll. Experience comes with age, and we were both closer to forty than we cared to admit. Still, lessons learned and remembered are what allow us to keep on breathing, and those lessons come over time.

It was nearly midnight when we hauled ourselves up the stairs to our flat. I was almost beyond hunger, but just then my stomach growled. Actually, it was more of a bellow and a demand for food. I sighed. Feed the beast, I muttered. It was obvious that we wouldn't be keeping anything close to normal work hours for some time, and adapting to the current situation would be the only way to survive. "Breakfast or supper?" I asked, standing in front of the refrigerator, scanning the limited contents.

"Don't care."

"Snap out of it, John. You're not the only one who's tired. And," I wagged a finger in front of his nose, "you had the end seat. I was packed like an oversized sardine in an undersized tin."

"Sorry."

I frowned. This wasn't like him. He was never overly communicative, but this was pushing the limits. "You need food. Go collapse in the recliner, and I'll feed you. There's bread for toast and some jam. I'll fry up some eggs and reheat the potatoes."

"Bacon."

I smiled. That was more like it. "All right. Just give me a minute." It would be a strange breakfast, if that's indeed what it was. But first, whiskey. If Churchill could drink his whiskey wherever and whenever, then by God, so would we. I sloshed some Jameson into two glasses, added the necessary ice, and handed John his glass on my way to my own chair with mine. Five minutes later, soft snoring from the recliner spared me the effort of cooking. I took John's empty glass and my own to the sink, covered him with the Afghan and trudged off to bed. Tomorrow would be time enough to adapt to this strange, new world.

CHAPTER THREE

Port Hope, England, on the English Channel

A stand of mature birch and oak trees not far from the main road was Denise Pritchard's destination this sunny, July morning. Digging spade in one hand and pail in the other, with Cherry trotting along at her side, Denise was on the hunt for truffles. This site she had previously scouted had seemed promising, and its location, past the overgrown garden behind the abandoned home, looked promising, as well.

On the signal, Cherry bounded away. Still a pup and in the early stages of her training, she had an exuberance difficult to rein in. Shortly, sounds of furious excavation reached Denise's ears, and she grimaced. Cherry needed work on not destroying the truffles, but at least she'd gotten her mind around the general concept of locating them. Training a champion-level truffle dog took time. By the time Denise got to the site, Cherry had ceased digging and was now tugging at whatever she'd located. Her entire head was engaged in a furious tossing about that seemed a bit of overkill for a truffle. Mangling the prized fungus wasn't the object of the exercise, and Cherry wasn't having anything to do with Denise's commands to cease and desist. Denise sighed. She'd thought the pup further along in her schooling than this. Soon, however, whatever had been anchoring Cherry's treasure finally released its hold, and the dog gave a final shake of her head, loped up to her mistress, and dropped a human hand at her feet.

. . .

"Sit down and have a cuppa," Colleen said to her friend who was pacing the confines of the kitchen while they waited for the police to arrive.

Denise, however, was looking at her dog with concern. "I should wash her mouth out. I don't want her to get sick." Cherry, unimpressed with the fuss and bother, had stretched out on the mat by the back door for a nap.

"She's probably been into a lot worse that you've never known about." Colleen paused to give the dog a critical look. "Well," she added, "maybe not a whole lot worse. Still, she's going to be fine."

"Unlike me."

"You'll be fine, too. It must have been unsettling, though, to say the least. One doesn't normally find that sort of thing just lying about."

Denise shook her head. "That's the problem. It wasn't just lying about. Somebody took pains to make sure it wasn't. Why on earth would somebody bury a body in the garden when there's a perfectly good cemetery on the other side of town?"

"I have no idea. Most likely not for a good reason."

"I don't know how deeply it was buried, but it took Cherry a bit of digging to uncover it. It wasn't in very good shape. And the color was definitely off." Denise shuddered and took a sip of her cooling tea. "Do you suppose the rest of the body is still there?"

"We'll find out soon enough," Colleen said, looking out the kitchen window at the bicycle pulling up outside. "Here's Jim."

. . .

"I covered it with a pail, just in case a cat or something else hungry came by." Denise turned back to where the officer was negotiating a bit of boggy ground and beckoned for him to quicken his pace. "If you keep moving, you won't settle in quite so much," she said.

"Right." Detective Sergeant James Aldercroft managed a weak smile and plowed on. After taking Denise's statement, collecting the hand from under the pail, transferring it to an evidence bag, and giving a cursory glance at the presumed burial site, he cautioned the women not to touch anything or disturb the site until he returned with the forensics team later that afternoon. He then reclaimed his bicycle and pedaled back to the station to file his report.

"Why don't I have a whole lot of confidence?" Colleen asked.

"Because Port Hope is low priority. What's next?"

"Next? After they send a team out here to dig up what's probably the rest of the corpse, destroying a perfectly good truffle patch in the process, and remove the body to the morgue, they'll fill out a respectable number of official forms, and we'll never hear another thing about John or Jane Doe."

"Nobody's gone missing from hereabouts," Denise said. "If anything, we've gotten a bit of an influx of new people."

"Still. Somebody's gone missing from somewhere."

The morning, which had begun much as any other day, had turned fickle. The temperature was rising and with few clouds in the sky, it was going to be beastly hot by noon. Colleen was rethinking her plans to putter about in the gardens. Actually, she was feeling a bit at loose ends, and judging by the way her companion was staring off into space, it appeared Denise was feeling much the same.

Finding a body, or part of one, wasn't something that happened every day, and it would take a bit of time and effort to move on. "What makes someone kill?" Colleen asked, thinking out loud. "It's not the usual means of concluding an argument, after all." She looked at Denise. "Could you kill someone?"

"I suppose so, given the right circumstances." Denise shrugged. "I've never given it much thought. And even though the idea has occurred to me from time to time, it's more a figure of speech. You know, when someone's done something irritating and keeps at it, you get the urge to throttle them. But to actually do the deed? No. People just don't do that sort of thing."

Colleen nodded, digesting what Denise had said. "That's true for the most part. But I think we're all capable of it. What would push someone to cross that line?"

"It would help to know whether we're looking for a man or a woman. I mean, men and women handle things differently."

Colleen smiled. "We've had three suspicious deaths in as many weeks, and I don't think Colchester or even Ipswich can boast of such a record. Something is going on here. You know that as well as I do. Aren't you just a tad curious to find out what that something is?"

"I'm curious if we've seen the end of this. What have the police done about it?" Denise asked, then answered her own question. "Nothing."

"That's not fair, Denise. Bill's been working on the cases, but there hasn't been a lot to go on."

Denise pulled a face.

"All right," Colleen said. "Let's start with the body count." She got up to fetch a notepad and pen from the kitchen drawer. "Let's start at the beginning." She sat down and rubbed her hands together in anticipation. "Who's first?"

"Until we find out how long the body's been in the ground, we can't be sure."

"Right." Colleen made her first investigative entry on the blank page. *1.Body?*

Denise gave a skeptical glance. "We're going to have to do better than this if we're to discover anything at all. Let's put that to the side and start with Dave."

Colleen crossed out *body* and wrote *Dave* in its place. "I think once we get going this will get easier." Her tone was dubious. She set the pen down and pushed the pad aside, then her expression brightened. "We only have three people to consider. What did they have in common? We need to approach this the way they do in the mystery novels."

"Slow down, Colleen. You're getting ahead of yourself. The investigation method varies considerably, depending on who you're reading.

Christie, Sayers, Wilke, and a host of others, if you consider the Americans. And besides, novels are fiction. They're not real. Most of the time, those murder mystery writers work backwards, from what I've learned. They know who the killer will be at the onset. And they know the motive and the means, as well. And they know it long before the reader does. It's entertainment, not reality. We don't know anything, except that at least three people are dead. That's how life really works. It's not all tied up in a neat package before it all begins. It's messy and confusing and sometimes impossible to sort out."

Colleen tapped her pen on the notepad. "I understand, but we have one advantage. We're real, and so are the victims and the murderer or murderers. And," she raised an index finger to hammer her point home, "regardless of real or not, those authors used the same tools we can use. It's all about analysis, logical thinking, and sequencing. Those are relevant. And the police, and they're as real as it gets, work to find out means, motive, and opportunity." She pulled the pad back and started over.

"All right," Denise said. "*Means*. We don't know anything about the mystery corpse, but Dave was run over by a car or truck or whatever, and Alese was hit in the head by a spade." She pursed her lips. "They're different. We've got a car and a shovel. If that means anything, I sure don't know what it is. *Opportunity.* I don't know anything there, either. Seems rather spur of the moment? Murder by whatever was at hand?"

Colleen frowned. "Where were they when they were killed? Dave was bicycling home from the post office. Alese had been digging by her roses. That much is obvious, but she wasn't found there. She was across the yard by the stone wall. The police said she'd possibly been kneeling over a flower bed."

Denise tilted her head, considering. "But there was no flower bed by the stone wall. And Dave was..." she paused, searching for the right word. "It would be helpful to know if he knew he were being pursued or if he died unaware that someone was about to run him down."

"He was a bit of a busybody. Always interested in everyone else's business," Colleen said. "More than once when I stopped at the post office, I saw him close a key on the switchboard as soon as he saw me. They say he liked to listen in on conversations. Definitely not ethical. Perhaps he overheard something and that something got him killed?"

"And Alese was much the same. She loved to gossip."

"All right," Colleen said. "We're making progress, of a sort. They both snooped and gossiped. And that," she finished triumphantly, "leads to motive."

The rhythmic ticking from the grandfather clock seemed loud in the silence that followed, while both women considered the *why*. "I think I'll go to the library tomorrow. I've read almost every mystery novel ever written, and if I spend a bit of time there refreshing my memory, I may be able to chart out a list of motives that will have some bearing on our situation," Colleen said. "Meanwhile, off the top of my head, I'm thinking they were silenced because they had seen or heard or said something that wasn't meant for public consumption. So, all we need to find out is what that was." She drew a firm line on the notepad. "What's happened here in the past three weeks that they weren't supposed to find out about?"

"When we find out the *what*, then we'll learn the *why*, and then all we have to do is find out the *who* and we've got our killer," Denise said. "What could be easier?" She snorted.

Denise helped herself to a biscuit, and Cherry, her ears perking up at the familiar crunching sound, opened her eyes, stretched, and padded over to the table to collect her treat. "All right. First, there's the mystery body. The hand by itself doesn't give us a lot to go on," Denise said, waiting for Cherry to sit before she handed over the goods. "First, we need to establish whether it's a man or a woman. Then, what was the body — sorry, person, doing here. There's also the time factor to consider — how long the body's been in the ground. After that…" she shrugged. "What do you think? Accident or murder?"

"It's murder, all right," Colleen said. "Why hide a body in the ground if it isn't murder? An accident would be reported. Although Dave could possibly have been an accident." She rested her forehead on the kitchen table and exhaled in frustration.

"We just don't know, that's true," Denise said, "but the corpse and Alese were definitely murdered, and whoever killed them is still out there. It's not just the Nazis we have to worry about. There's enough evil grown at home."

Colleen set her teacup aside. "Don't be so sure about that. That 'recent influx' of people coming to live here? I don't trust Hitler. I wouldn't be a bit surprised if a little digging turns up more than a stray hand. I'll wager we'll ferret out some worrisome details about our new neighbors." She nodded. "Only one way to find out. We didn't have unexplained death here until the new people began moving in." She got up from the table. "All right. We have to start somewhere, while we're waiting for lightning or inspiration to strike. I need a ruler." She walked over to the kitchen drawer by the sink that held all the odds and ends that accumulate and don't seem to have a place of their own. The ruler, grimy and a bit sticky from waiting for years in this limbo for its moment of glory, cried out for a washup, and she obliged by taking it to the sink to give it a bath.

Back in her chair, and with the ruler in hand, waiting for direction and poised to fulfill its destiny, Collen hesitated. Sometimes, what seems to be a simple task turns out to be more involved. "How far back should we go for a starting point?" she asked.

"Good question," Denise said. "I don't exactly know. What about Bernice and Aldred? They're the oldest of the new people that I can think of, but they've been here since after the Great War."

"They're no spring chickens," Colleen said. "Besides, they came here from Scotland, not Germany."

"That's what they say," Denise said, her brow furrowed. "How can we know for sure? I say we write them down. And that Miranda Hainesworth and — what's his name?"

"Douglas. Douglas Hyde-Stuart."

"You know," Denise confided, "I don't think they're married. They don't act like it."

"What does that mean?" Colleen set the ruler down on the pad.

"I can't put a finger on it, but you just get a sense about people. Anyhow, that's four."

Colleen nodded and the list began to take shape. By the time they'd conducted their census, they had eight names, having added the new postmaster, the desk clerk at the hotel down by the wharf, and the Taylors — Gerry and Anne. Apart from Bernice and her husband, the remaining five had moved to the area over the past ten years and resided in the area extending from Ipswich to the north, Colchester to the east, and Port Hope at the southern end.

"What about the Italian? He's back," Denise said. "At least his boat is. I was talking with Mildred at bells practice last night at church, and she said Jeanne told her she saw it down at the marina."

"When the parties start late and go on all night, you'll know for sure he's here," Colleen said. "Good thinking, though. The Italians are in it with the Germans. I'll add him to the list."

"If I had this much of his money," Denise said, holding up her thumb and index finger and pinching them together, "I'd buy myself a fishing boat. I like to fish." She sighed. "At least you've got the rowboat down at the pond. Oars and everything. That puts you in the League of the Rich."

"Then, maybe I should paint a name on her bow," Colleen said, "like all the rich boats have."

Denise propped her elbows on the table, her chin resting in the palms of her hands. "You need an exotic name."

"Exotic? In Port Hope? Get a grip, dear." Colleen chewed on her lip, thoughts not coming easily. "All right, then. *Pollywog.*"

Denise pulled a face. They took their tea out to the back porch where they had a good view of the newly christened *Pollywog* bobbing on the pond.

"Donald loved that boat. Funny how we get so attached to things."

"I don't think the Italian is that attached to his boat. At least, not in the same way Donald was to *Pollywog*," Denise said, patting her friend's shoulder.

The women finished their tea, each absorbed in her own thoughts, and finally, returning to the task at hand, reviewed their work. "We've got nine names on our list," Colleen said, setting down her pen. "Nine is a lot." She sighed. "Now what do we do with it? Snooping about without raising suspicions is going to be difficult."

Denise nodded. "You can run it by Bill and see what he thinks of it. In the meantime, let's keep our eyes and ears open. When, or if, we find out who the dead body is—was—that might help us get a start."

"I'll let you know what Bill says. In other matters, what are we going to do about Alese's rose?"

Denise removed Cherry's training harness and set her free to wander around the back yard. "I'm not blaming the Land Girls and their dungarees and work boots, but they've been rather aggressive in pushing their Dig for Victory campaign, and quite frankly, I'm sick of it. Vegetables are important. Don't misunderstand me. Of course, we have to eat. But flowers, for heaven's sake. Are we supposed to give up everything we love to fight that horrid man? Alese pampered that rose for half a century. It deserves better than to be uprooted for a turnip or whatever. There's got to be something we can do." Exhausted from her tirade, Denise got up from the table and plunked herself down in the rocker by the fireplace and fanned herself with Cherry's neck scarf.

Truly. It was a bit of a problem. Alese had nurtured her Tudor rose since her grandmother had entrusted its care to her before she'd died. With no living relatives, the cottage would eventually revert to the Crown, and God knew what would happen to the gardens then. In the midst of major tragedy unfolding across the Continent, this minor tragedy seemed to mirror what Britain would face should the Nazis win.

"You're spot on, my dear. We must do something about Alese's rose. Perhaps that woman from the Horticultural Society will be of help." She looked at her friend. "We're not the only ones who want to keep our precious things safe." Pushing back from the table, Colleen stood and stretched, then walked back to the kitchen drawer to return the ruler. Glancing out the window, her eye was drawn to the sky, and she spotted an interesting cloud formation passing slowly overhead. The cloud had changed its shape into something resembling an elephant. Odd formation. There was a whole world up there, but people were so besotted with things on the ground, they never looked up. She shook her head and was about to join her friend in the parlor when a low drone coming from somewhere overhead caused her to turn back.

"Denise! Come with me!" she called and threw open the screen door to get to the back yard and a better view of the sky. "There!" She pointed to a faint white cloud, smaller than the rest that seemed to be moving away from the elephant.

"What are you looking at? What are you talking about?" Denise stood on the threshold of the screen door, her hands in the air.

"There! See it? Come on! It's going down! We've got to follow it! Move!"

The two women took off at a respectable pace, Cherry running along with them and barking furiously as they raced to the field where they had an unobstructed view of a parachute directly overhead. Off to the right, a small airplane continued on its final path, unmanned, and crashed into the churchyard.

The pilot, either by planning or accident, had escaped the crash, but his landing wasn't going to be so good. In an entire field of grass and small shrubbery, he'd avoided the copse of trees but was heading directly for the rock pile the tractor had made when clearing the field. Colleen winced, Denise cried out, and Cherry barked, but they were helpless to prevent the parachutist from making contact with a sharp boulder. He connected with a thud and then lay still.

Colleen gave a quick look at the body, crumpled on the ground. "Dear Lord, he's a child. He can't be more than fifteen or sixteen, if that."

Denise had reached the young man and was checking his limbs for breakage. "His right leg is broken, that's for sure. I'm not sure about the left. Maybe the ankle. We've got to get him out of here before they find out where he's crashed."

Colleen looked at Denise, concern etched on her face. "They? Denise, we've got to notify the authorities, and we've got to get this boy to hospital. There's no wiggle-room here. We're at war, and he might be the enemy. We don't know where he came from." She looked at the boy. "Perhaps not much of an enemy, but able enough to have caused us harm if he'd so chosen."

"But he didn't, Colleen. Don't you see? He was escaping. Look at his clothes. That striped shirt and pants. And he's nothing more than a skeleton, he's so thin. All he wanted was to get away from Germany. We can't turn him over. We can't." Desperation colored her words.

"I know. But he's not a lost pet you can take home." Colleen frowned. "You stay with him. I'll get Bill." She rested a hand on her friend's shoulder. "I know. I know." She left Denise, cradling the boy's head in her lap.

.   .   .

Half an hour later, when Colleen, Bill, and the ambulance arrived at the crash site, Denise hadn't budged, but the boy had regained consciousness and gotten himself into a semi-sitting position and was talking a blue streak at her. Unfortunately, it was not an English blue streak, and Denise was doing quite a bit of nodding and smiling.

"*Hallo, mein Junge. Wir haben ein kleines Problem, Ja?*" Bill said, as he took a seat on the ground.

"*Polski,*" the boy said, shaking his head, fear in his eyes.

"What the…?" Denise sputtered, then narrowed her eyes at Bill.

Colleen took a deep breath and held up a hand to Denise to stop her before she got started.

Denise, however, was on alert mode and had grabbed a rock from the pile and was making noises as if she was prepared to launch her own counter-offensive.

"Denise, for God's sake, put that bloody thing down. What the hell do you think you're doing?"

All Denise could do was point at Bill and sputter.

"Oh, for Christ's sake. You need to work on your memory. Bill spent two years in a German prisoner of war camp in the Great War, or have you forgotten?"

"Oh." Denise looked at the rock, returned it with care to the pile, and managed a weak smile.

"Sorry."

Bill motioned for the ambulance attendant to move in and then stood. "I'll be going with him to hospital." He gave Denise a serious look. "The boy isn't German. He's Polish. He may have valuable information for us. You've done well, Denise. Don't worry. I'll notify London about the plane."

Denise nodded. She called to Cherry who had behaved perfectly during the encounter, gave a tentative smile to Bill, and set out for home with Colleen right behind, leaving Bill to deal with their young refugee, the enemy plane, and the killer or killers in their midst.

Late that night, in the stillness, Colleen once again took up her notepad and the ruler to pick up where she'd left off. *I've never encountered such a thing in any novel*, she thought. *If someone had written about a Polish boy fleeing the Nazis by stealing an airplane and flying across the English Channel, parachuting into the field behind my home while the plane crashed and burned, nobody would believe it.* But it had happened, and she knew in her heart as well as her mind, that the war had come to her doorstep, and she'd been recruited into the homeland defence because of it. She set down the pad as the enormity and responsibility of what that meant washed over her. She walked back to the window and gazed at the stars, pinpoints of light so far away. And she wept.

CHAPTER FOUR

New York City

"Mr. Jameson, if you would be so kind as to direct your attention away from Miss Finarelli and join the lecture, I would be most appreciative." Professor Adam Franta, Ph.D., Fellow of the Royal Academy, world-recognized expert on Medieval documents, art critic, and author of eleven volumes of academic critiques, treatises, and not coincidentally, the textbook for this graduate course, *MDVL 5742 Medieval Manuscripts and Literary Forms: Towards a Critical Historiography,* had reached the end of his patience. Granted, Miss Finarelli was one of five female students in this field of males and, as a consequence, a highly sought-after companion, but there was a time and a place. And this, Franta muttered, was neither.

The bus ride from New Haven with the group of fifteen graduate students from Yale University had taken over two hours, stopping along the way once for what the driver referred to as a "rest break" at what the professor deemed a less than desirable gas station. It did, however, provide the opportunity for the passengers to exit the confines of the bus and fine tune their relationship overtures, and when the students returned to the bus, several had chosen different seat companions. As a sociological and behavioral study in the mating habits of post-adolescents, Professor Franta found it mildly interesting.

It was a given that students on excursions were more inclined to see the trip as a jailbreak from the regimented structure of academia and an excellent opportunity to seek out sexual partners. In more than a few cases, it was apparent that for several students, and Franta used the word *students* reluctantly, the idea that the outing might have other objectives and actually be a chance to expand their intellectual horizons had never crossed their minds. Not that Franta blamed them. He'd much rather be so-involved, but duty first. However, when he returned to Yale, *if* he survived this jaunt, he'd have a serious conversation with Claude, his graduate assistant and the party responsible for the more mundane chores of the course. As the price for two tickets to the Met, this far and above exceeded the debt owed. His thoughts drifted to more pleasant pastimes than playing tour guide and chaperone, and he pulled himself up short. Letting down one's guard never ended well—a lesson best remembered. Mercifully, the ride ended, as all things must.

Once at the parking facility, and with everyone's belongings safely in tow, the group made its way through the entrance gates of the 1939 New York World's Fair—The World of Tomorrow—and joined the throng of visitors there to see the marvels of technology and consume overpriced hamburgers and hot dogs on stale buns.

Franta and his charges had a different agenda, and they progressed to the London Pavilion and the point of the whole field trip: viewing the Magna Carta on loan from Great Britain and on glorious display behind thick glass. Glorious may have been a bit of an exaggeration. Time marches on, and it makes no matter if you're a human or a document. Age will overtake youth. Case in point was before them. Yellowed with time, written in almost illegible Latin with ink that had faded to brown, a mere sixteen by fourteen inches in size, and kept at a secure distance from the crowd of visitors, it wasn't all that imposing a sight and student interest was waning. To be more accurate, interest hadn't been all that high at the outset, and what little remained was declining at an alarming rate. The situation was dire, and if Professor Franta couldn't reel his charges back in, all would be lost. In one last desperate effort, he called on his theatrical stage training. He spun around and pointed to the first student he saw. Unfortunately, it was the libido-driven Mr. Jameson.

"Imagine that you possess total power! Total! No one can tell you what to do, and if they attempt to, you can have them executed on the spot!" Franta thundered and Jameson smirked. "Every wish you have is granted. Nothing is too big or too small. Everyone must do your will. You are the king. The only entity above you is God. And, sometimes, you may even doubt that to be true. Your ego knows no bounds." Franta's gaze swept over the students, their attention and interest finally secured. Ah, he thought. The eternal power of story time.

"Now, if you will," Franta continued, "imagine the unimaginable. Overnight, it seemed, rumblings of discontent begin among your subjects at their treatment by you, and the discontent grows, much as a stream becomes a river that ultimately flows to the sea, gathering strength and power as it moves on. To hold back the tide is not possible. It is the apex of power. And one day, you are kidnapped by some of your subjects who take you to a field near Runnymede. The date is June 15, 1215." Franta paused as some of the students did some mathematical calculations. "Yes. That long ago. For the first time in your life, you are powerless, and you experience an emotion most foreign to you. What is that emotion? Fear! You suddenly are aware that your safety and your very life are now in the control of those you have dominated and subjugated at your whim. There is no escape unless they allow it. And you are threatened with the unthinkable. You are threatened with civil war — unless you submit to your captors. Suddenly, remaining king becomes secondary to gaining your freedom and saving your life. Then, you learn the price you must pay."

Interest had triumphed over boredom. Pausing to allow the students to wonder what price the king had to pay, Professor Franta then waved his arm towards the document in the case. "This! This was the price for his freedom, and it's one of the four original copies of England's historic 1215 Magna Carta, the foundational document of English law. Let's talk about what that means."

There are times when teaching is exhausting. One has to be prepared for anything, and keeping the body in a constant state of readiness means adrenaline continues to flow without respite. This is draining. Adrenaline was designed for short-term sprints, not a marathon. Fight or flight, short and sweet. With beads of perspiration on his forehead and an irritating trickle of the same dribbling down his back, it was time for the question-and-answer portion of the lecture. While his story had entertained, it couldn't dredge up knowledge that wasn't there, and so the next segment was heavy on professorial questions and light on student answers. Still, Professor Franta soldiered on. "To recap, the copy on display is one of four original copies made in 1215 at

Runnymede, where the nobles confronted King John and forced him to sign the document. Why was this a watershed moment in history?" Franta paused, waiting for someone, anyone, to jump in.

Finally, the object of Mr. Jameson's affections, Miss Antoinette Finarelli, ventured an answer. "It was the first time anybody told the king what he couldn't do," she said.

"Thank you, Miss Finarelli. That's a good beginning." With no one else adding to her rudimentary comment, the tentative beginning was also the end of student input. The professor took a deep breath and attempted once again to engage his audience. "Besides being the cornerstone document of English law, there are also some interesting provisions that we can only wonder about. For example, would you believe it decrees the proper width for the bolts of cloth used for the robes the monks wore? What could have prompted this? Who had so much influence that this would be included in such a document?"

With this last attempt at eliciting interest a failure, Professor Fanta consulted his watch. They'd only been there ten minutes. "All right. Let's continue." Using the collapsible pointer that traveled with him on these excursions, he indicated one of the passages and recited it in Latin, from memory, translating and explaining its significance as he went along. When he reached the end of the line, however, he stopped and stared at the text, a quizzical expression on his face. Bending closer, he studied the parchment in more detail, silently rereading the Latin text. He straightened and frowned. He took one step back, his eyes still fixed on the parchment. He took his camera and proceeded to snap several shots, including close-ups, from various angles. Returning the camera to its case, he gave a final look at the display case.

"That's all for today," he said to his students. "Feel free to explore the rest of the Fair. The bus leaves at seven this evening. Be on it or be left behind." Without another word, he turned and hurried towards the exit, leaving fifteen graduate students to wonder at the circumstances of their sudden, unexpected freedom.

· · ·

Sitting at the counter of one of the cafes scattered throughout the concourse of the Fair, Adam Franta stirred his coffee while he rifled through a mental Rolodex of his associates. He'd rejected his first thought almost as soon as it had entered his head. Wiring R.A. Mitchell, Dean of Lincoln Cathedral which had housed the Magna Carta before shipping it to New York the previous year would profit him nothing and would raise serious questions that he would be unable to answer. This situation called for more drastic measures.

Trust, in desperate times, is a commodity worth more than gold or rubies or diamonds. It all came down to trust, and Adam Franta, having completed his analyses of everyone who might be of assistance in the matter, found no one to whom he could or would entrust the knowledge he had gleaned today, except possibly one man. Franta would need to proceed carefully, that was a given, but conscience wouldn't allow him to let this slide by. It had been a few years since they'd worked together, and finding him would be a long shot, but he'd always played the odds. Sometimes, it even worked.

Franta pushed the coffee cup aside. One decision made, but there was something else niggling at him. Something had been out of place. It hadn't been so long that he'd lost all his instincts, and he decided to do a final check before it was time to board the bus for the return home. This time his surveillance would be thorough. Training had kicked in.

The number of visitors to the Fair had increased markedly as the day wore on, and the slowed pace allowed him to observe his surroundings more carefully on this second visit to the Pavilion. Nothing unusual caught his eye along the way to the entrance. Once inside, he methodically scanned the interior, and it was then that he saw the small cardboard box, unobtrusively placed in the corner to the left of the display case. His first thought was that one of his students had left something behind, but for some reason he couldn't explain then or later, he decided not to retrieve the box and instead, left the Pavilion and notified security of the presence of the box. It turned out to be one of the better decisions of Adam Franta's life.

At seven p.m. that night, other, more-pressing issues having been dealt with, security finally arrived at the Pavilion to investigate another crackpot spotting of a mysterious object. It happened all the time. Security's main job was to be sure nobody stole the Magna Carta. Nobody was interested in articles brought in. Maintenance would deal with lost and found. Grumbling that everybody wanted to be a hero, the four security officers dispatched to dispose of the box were unconcerned. Unexpectedly and unfortunately, however, the box contained a time bomb. Two of the officers removed the box and carried it outside the Pavilion to a back lot where they attempted to disarm the device. They were killed in the ensuing explosion, and the exhibit was closed while the authorities had the bodies removed, photographed the scene, and began an investigation.

·   ·   ·

As Franta had threatened, the bus had just closed its doors, all the passengers being accounted for — including Mr. Jameson and Miss Finarelli who had taken seats together at the back of the bus. The sound of the explosion, muffled a bit by distance, went unnoticed by the students, but Professor Franta, veteran of the Great War, knew that sound all too well. He rested a hand on his camera case. No matter. He had what he needed.

The trip home was interminable. It seemed that every traffic light had conspired to turn red and then go out to lunch before deciding reluctantly to turn green. Eventually, however, the bus arrived back home in downtown New Haven and deposited its passengers at the bus stop on Elm Street. His jaw set as tight as a vise and his right hand gripping the camera case close to his side, Adam Franta strode the two blocks to the Western Union Office. Hesitating briefly, he scribbled *High Noon* in the message box and waited for the operator to send it off. Retrieving the slip of paper, he then hailed a cab to take him home.

If Gene didn't show tomorrow, then what? He dismissed the thought. He'd cross that bridge when and if he needed to. For now, he was counting on Gene's loyalty to his men, however badly they'd been treated.

CHAPTER FIVE

London

The clock meant nothing to Churchill, but it meant everything to the rest of us. It was as if he had recreated the concept of time itself and had become the god of its management. He lived by a strict schedule whether at his country estate in Chartwell or at Whitehall in London, but his bedroom at Whitehall, located next to the Map Room in the Cabinet War Rooms, was his principal office and it was where he dictated, conducted meetings, and slept. It was the only carpeted room on the premises. Far into the night and often the early morning hours, he did as much work as he could in his pajamas and dressing gown, aided and abetted by a constant supply of cigars and whiskey. Or champagne. Or whatever alcoholic beverage was at hand.

The Prime Minister's work habits required major changes in everyone else's. What would have been considered a normal workday by the rest of the civilized world bore little resemblance to ours, and it began early in the day, shortly after breakfast which also came early after a night's sleep, the length of which had become considerably shortened.

John and I had managed about five hours of the precious commodity, and when we dragged ourselves out of bed, in my case, and out of the chair in John's, it was obvious we hadn't had enough of it. The meal I had intended to make when we'd gotten home from Whitehall last night or early this morning, to be precise, now officially became breakfast. Strong coffee and potatoes, toast with jam, and bacon helped take the rough edges off the morning, but it was the bacon that did the trick. Bacon is a powerful motivator. It fills the kitchen with an aroma that tells you life is worth living. Bacon or not, our lives would have decreased measurably in value if we were late to report at Whitehall, so there was no time to dawdle.

We were at our desks promptly at eight. The decoded messages were waiting for us in their trays, and as had become the pattern, each day there were more and more to process. A fair number of them concerned reports of suspicious persons, possible German agents operating in and around London. Some reports were anonymous, obviously based on rumor, or the "I heard it from my brother's barber" type, but buried among these were an increasing number that had the air of truth

about them. Those originating from vital sectors —
the ports, railroad hubs, airfields, refineries,
manufacturing   and   industrial   plants — were
marked high priority. These went into a separate
tray for further investigation. When we would
receive our field assignments sometime in the next
day or two, these would most likely be our target
areas. Every bit of knowledge we had going into
the field increased our chances of success. And
then, I looked up, and out of the corner of my eye,
saw Margo Speer slip one of the messages into her
pocket.

There must be some sort of chemical or
electrical impulse that carries through the air and
even circumvents physical barriers when you stare
at someone. I've noticed the phenomenon while
driving. Glancing at the car in the next lane more
often than not results in that driver looking at you
as you pass. It's strange, and that's what happened
now. I must have stared at Margo a second too
long, because the next thing I knew she was staring
back at me. So now she knew that I knew and I
knew that she knew that I knew, and it was a
problem. There was no doubt but that I should
report this immediately, but then, she raised her
hand, the index finger touching her forehead, then
sliding down her nose until it stopped at her lips,
which she opened and then covered in the
universal sign for "don't say a word". She waited
until she must have been convinced the silent

message had gotten through, before she finally returned to work. I resumed my own tasks, but my mind was struggling, curiosity competing with duty. And, as usual, curiosity won. I'd wait until lunch and then have a chat with her. Action could wait a few hours. I owed her that much.

Margo and I weren't friends. Truth be told, I was a bit wary when I was around her, and it all hearkened back to our first meeting a few months ago in New Haven at Glick's Delicatessen, where we were both having lunch. I was people-watching, appreciating the new spring fashions, and I'd been admiring her outfit. When she looked at me, her expression was less than friendly. Staring is actually an invasion of personal privacy, and you never know when the person you're giving the once-over might turn out to be a danger to your own well-being. Controlling this tendency is something I really need to work on. Curiosity is one thing. Being stupid is another.

The next time I saw Margo, she'd showed up at the door of my room at the women's residence maintained by MI6 in New York City. The building was a safe house, designed to protect us while we were traveling. Scheduled to fly out on the Clipper the next day on assignment to Denmark, I'd just dropped my handbag on the bed when she'd knocked on my door.

After the formalities of establishing who had come calling in a building where everyone minded her own business, I opened the door and let her in. The fact of her presence in this highly secured facility meant she was a fellow agent, and that most likely explained her displeasure at having being watched in the delicatessen. She must have thought she'd been made.

Once we've received our assignments and are out in the field, there's a protocol for checking in. We meet with our handlers if that's feasible. Gene is my handler, and it turned out, Margo's as well. As I learned after a bit, she'd subsequently checked me out with Gene to be sure we were all on the same side. Subsequent to that, and for reasons unknown, she'd decided she'd do me a favor. Maybe as some sort of peace-offering for not trusting me at first, but why would she? I didn't trust her, and as a testimony to that I did greet her with service revolver in hand and kept it there until I was sure she was on the up and up.

Margo Speer was a paradox. That fact made her an extremely interesting person. For reasons she couldn't justify, she'd felt compelled to come warn me about a double agent operating in Denmark, my destination. The kicker? That double agent, code-named Ronin, was her brother. Ronin and I did cross paths in Denmark, and it turned out better for me than it did for him. The last I saw of him, he'd jumped out of a second-story window in my hometown of Sankt Peder, but I'd captured the wireless he'd been using to transport intelligence to Berlin. It was a draw.

The next time we crossed paths, he was working for the Brits. He rescued me from a sticky situation, not to help me specifically, but to repay a debt he owed someone else. In his twisted logic, I guess it made sense, but he left with a warning that next time we chanced to meet, he'd kill me. I believed him. So, with all that history between us, and with Margo, up until now, firmly on our side, the reason she'd stolen the paper was a mystery.

. . .

The lunch menu at the canteen didn't offer a lot of choices, so I settled on an egg salad sandwich on a crusty roll, an apple, and a ginger water. I hadn't realized how hungry I was until I'd taken my first bite, and it was while I was chewing away, Margo set her tray on the table and sat down next to me.

"I appreciate your not ratting on me until I'd had a chance to explain," was her greeting.

I nodded, my mouth still full. We'd be all right with this conversation, given our security clearances, but we were still watched, as was everyone. Spend too long in the loo, and you'd have to explain why. It could be embarrassing for a woman, but it was the way it was. Someone lingering overly long could be flushing information or copying some confidential

KAREN K. BREES   61

correspondence. No one was above suspicion. Even if Caesar's wife came in, she'd be subject to the same rules. We had half an hour for lunch, and that included the time it took to get to and from our offices to the canteen. Actual eating time wasn't all that long, but it wouldn't be unusual to chow down with a colleague. Careful to make the conversation appear casual, we shared a laugh from time to time, along with some head shakes at a presumed joke. It wasn't that difficult. Dissembling is our job. But in the spaces between, she told me a story that rang true.

"This won't take long," she said. "We're going to receive our assignments tomorrow or the day after at the latest. Scuttlebutt is that they've broken up all of Britain into sectors, with each of us assigned one. I'm counting on being sent to Canvey Island and the shoreline in that area. It just makes sense."

"Why?"

"Because that's where the family home is, and I'm known there. It's the perfect cover."

That was logical. It didn't matter to me where I was sent, since I had no ties anywhere in Britain. It still didn't explain why she'd done what she'd done.

"I know what you're wondering. That message concerned a suspicious individual—male—in the area near my home. I don't know why he was considered suspicious, but I need to make sure nobody else gets that assignment. I'm going to handle this myself." She took a bite of her sandwich, although it was more for window dressing than hunger. "My brother is there now. I'm sure of it. And he'll be there until July 15th."

I turned my attention to my own sandwich, but my heart was thumping like a rabbit on the run. "Who's he working for this time?"

"I don't know. I never do, but I intend to find out. Regardless, he'll be in Canvey. No matter, he never misses that day and hasn't for the past twelve years."

Waiting for her to take one more small bite of her sandwich and a sip of water took too long for me, and I asked, "Why?"

"Because it's the anniversary of the day his wife and daughter died. He visits their graves every year, without fail."

I just about choked on my ginger water. Ronin? A husband and a father?

"Yes." Margo saw the incredulity in my eyes. "He was different then. He worshipped Elizabeth and Mary. 'Gifts from God,' he'd say. The sun rose and set on them. They were his life. And when they died, he did as well. He buried them in the family plot on the estate, refusing to leave them in the care of the parish church. He blamed God and cursed Him for what He'd taken." Margo looked around the room, and I saw the tears forming in her eyes. She got up and lifted her tray off the table. "I need to get back." We exchanged another small laugh as a final gesture.

It's hard to watch someone you love disappear. When that person is the only family you have, it's almost more than you can bear. I didn't watch Margo leave. It seemed like an invasion of privacy akin to staring — something I'd sworn not to do — and so I waited another minute or so before I took my own tray to the cart and headed back to work, thinking about my encounters with Ronin. The man I'd dealt with bore no resemblance to the one Margo described. It was his eyes, mostly. They say eyes are the mirror of the soul, and if that is true, Ronin had lost his soul twelve years ago. The man was a shell. His eyes were cold as ice and hard as stone. It explained how he could kill without feeling anything.

We've all killed, but each time, it takes a piece of us, as well. I'd said before, if killing ever became easy, it would be time to quit the job. But for Ronin, killing was the reason he had signed on. Each death was an attack on God. An act of revenge. If he were working for Germany, he had to be stopped. He was a threat that had to eliminated. Tragic figure or not, if our paths crossed, I'd do what was necessary, even if once upon a time, he had loved.

I'd reached a decision, and I had Ronin to thank for it. We'd win the war, that much I believed. With Winnie's confidence in persuading Roosevelt to join the fight, victory would be ours. But when it was over, I would return to America, buy that home in Bethany, raise chickens, and flowers that I could grow just for the pure love of them, without dissecting and cataloguing. Most of all, God willing, I'd have John, and that would be enough. I sighed. Tomorrow. Each today was one more day towards that tomorrow. All we had to do was stay alive long enough to get there.

We worked far into the night, but no longer than Churchill did. The man was a relentless machine, despite the façade he showed the rest of the world. He was an astute judge of people and political entanglements, and his work ethic inspired us to give our all. It sounded like some sort of romantic idealism, but it was true. Churchill wasn't a machine, although he gave a good impression of one. Today, for instance. Day had become night. Again. When Winnie worked, everyone worked, but when he relaxed, so did we — although we were required to relax the same way he did. At midnight, we reported to the film room, and it wasn't just us. The typists, the decoders, the whole staff was here.

I missed my soap operas. I had no idea if Helen Trent had ever solved the case of her husband's murder and learned to love again. I wouldn't find out until this blasted war was over. Tonight, I put Helen aside, consigning her to the fates and settled back. The selection Churchill had chosen was *His*

Girl Friday with Cary Grant and Rosalind Russell. We were a captive audience, but escaping to another place and time for just a couple of hours made all the difference. Laughter filled the room. The war was put to bed for the night, and we rejoined the world of the living. It was a powerful antidote to Hitler's psychological campaign to destroy our minds. Our spirits were lifted. When John and I finally got back to our flat in the wee hours of the morning and fell into bed, we slept well. As for Churchill? I expect he went back to the War Rooms.

CHAPTER SIX

Port Hope

The Port Hope Library was nestled comfortably and privately on the estate of the late Sir Thomas Braithwaite, an eccentric bachelor and twelfth in line to the throne. He'd had a fondness for roses, a philanthropic duty towards abused and neglected horses, a guilt complex over the way he'd treated his mother, an insatiable appetite for books, and an aptitude for wise investing—to the end that his sole problem was finding a way to spend his fortune and reduce his tax burden to nearly nothing. And he'd done it all in the name of the Common Good. An added benefit was that he'd died a happy man (if there can be such a thing), with a clear conscience, beloved by the community that was recipient of his largess. So beloved in fact, was Sir Thomas, that a bronze statue depicting him seated on a bench, reading a book to his horse, Stanley, now stood in the center of town, on a small plot of ground by the butcher's. Possibly not the best choice of location, but the price of the land there was reasonable.

In his Will, Sir Thomas had made provisions for all of his concerns — the roses, horses, his mother, and books, and he'd had the presence of mind to see to it that none of anything he'd owned would go to the government for taxes upon his demise. Everything was to be administered under the watchful and capable eyes of Badger, Croft, Davies, and O'Reilly, a London law firm with more power than Parliament.

Sir Thomas had arranged for a gardener and assistant to divide the vast grounds of the estate into two equal portions. One would produce vegetables to be sold for income that would then be used to acquire roses from around the world to fill the other half of the grounds. The greenhouses, all eleven of them, had been turned over to the community so those who had no room for a small plot to grow their vegetables could now claim a small section for their own use.

The stables became home to a dozen aged draft horses who, he had decreed, were to live out the remainder of their lives in comfort with ample food and care. To this end, he specified that a groom be hired with the understanding that this was to be his sole employment and that he take up lodgings in the carriage house which was to be remodeled into a compact residence complete with cottage garden, where he would be available to tend to his charges and be on call at any hour, should it be required of him. The amount of the salary was to be sufficient for the purpose. Additionally, any horse abandoned or ill-treated would be received without question, and the same level of care would be given, in perpetuity. As a consequence, there were now twenty-seven permanent horses on the estate with room for an additional dozen, should it become necessary.

The manor house had been remodeled into small apartments for the elderly who were no longer able to manage on their own. The kitchen staff who had once served him, now stayed on to tend to the new occupants, with a small stipend in place for each of them to ensure they had sufficient clothing and transportation to medical facilities. All in all, it was a testimony to his generosity and good planning, assuaged his guilt, and not coincidentally, kept his fortune out of the hands of the government. It worked splendidly.

The crown jewel of the estate, however, was the library which was a scaled-down replica of the Tudor manor house that Sir Thomas, an amateur architect, had designed. The exterior was accurate to the last shingle, screw, and nail. The interior was a bibliophile's dream. There were two stone fireplaces and alcoves to provide privacy for those who wished to read without disturbance. There were comfortable chairs, small tables with lamps, larger tables for research or for holding seminars, oriental rugs, mullioned windows that provided additional light on those rare occasions the sun actually shone, bouquets of flowers, and bookcases throughout that held books — thousands of books. It was the repository for the contents of his personal library and had an annual budget sufficient to retain the services of a librarian, periodic acquisitions of new works of both fiction and nonfiction, and the hiring of a woman between the ages of 35 and 60 to dust the collections on a monthly basis. The reasoning behind this last stipulation was never explained and was the subject of much local discussion, but Sir Thomas was a complex man with more than a few eccentricities.

This morning, the librarian, Miss Sarah MacTavish, a heavy-set woman in her mid-seventies, was at her desk, sipping a cup of tea and taking a short break from her duties. Possessed of a keen intelligence and a wicked sense of humor, Miss MacTavish prided herself on her ability to answer any research question put to her. This was the reason Colleen had come calling.

"Good morning, Sarah. I need to know every possible reason a person would commit murder," Colleen said by way of greeting, setting down her handbag on the wooden counter that served as the barrier between the public and the business end of the library.

Sarah moved the cart filled with books to be processed away from her desk, giving her room to squeeze by. "All right, Colleen," she said. "Murder." She motioned to the worktable by the front window. "This is an interesting exercise. Let's have a sit down and consider it. Why, if I may inquire, are you pursuing the topic?"

"There is a murderer among us, and I want to know who it is." Colleen paused, watching Sarah's expression, before pulling the list of suspects from her handbag and placing it on the table, smoothing the wrinkles with the side of her hand. "The police certainly aren't coming up with anything. There's the body that Denise found, for starters. Then there's Alese and also Dave. The police haven't found out who killed them, and each day that passes, the probability that they will, decreases. And, there's something else. We're at war." She threw her hands in the air. "The newcomers. How do we know they aren't foreign spies? What if there's a connection?"

Frowning, Sarah studied the names on the paper, and then nodded assent. "Motive, then. Oft times, motive is as good a place as any to begin. If we first make as complete a list as we can, we can next eliminate motives that don't fit the victims."

The pendulum on the ancient grandfather clock on the far wall marked the passage of the next fifteen minutes as the women's list gradually expanded from the commonplace: *Lust, anger, revenge, accidental* to the not-so-common or specialized:

Hit job
Frameup
Cover up
Mistaken identity
Interrupted crime
Wartime
Diversion
Tying up loose ends- killing an accomplice to prevent betrayal or protect resources
Eliminating someone who had seen or heard something they weren't supposed to

"There's one thing we must consider," Sarah said. "If the murderer is mentally ill, motive is difficult to categorize—a person living in a different reality, perhaps someone who was hearing voices or who believed God was ordering the crimes be committed and felt they were just following orders, doing their duty—you'd need to be a trained psychologist to follow that line."

Colleen looked skeptical. "I suppose so, but if that's our murderer, the means is different for each, and so is the disposition of the body. One is buried, one is left in the middle of the road, and the last is left in the garden. One murder is different."

"Let's start at the beginning and see where it leads us."

"All right," Colleen said.

It didn't take long to eliminate *lust* (Alese was elderly, and Dave was fat and bald) and *accidental* (the murders were deliberate).

"I say we also eliminate *diversion* and *hit job*," Colleen said. "There was nobody around to divert. And *hit job* is usually done by gangs or the Mafia." She frowned. "Of course, we still don't know anything about the corpse person, but those motives don't fit Alese and Dave."

"Agreed. So what's next?"

"I suggest eliminating *interrupted crime, frameup, coverup, and tying up loose ends — killing the accomplice, anger, and revenge,*" Colleen said. "I mean it's safe to assume the murderer was angry, so that's more of a crime of passion."

"All right," Sarah said. "That leaves us with two motives at this point: *Eliminating someone who had seen or heard something they weren't supposed to and wartime.*" She set her pencil down and leaned back. "I can accept that. If the killer is a German agent and killed because one of our people saw something not meant to be seen, that would make sense. Yes, I can see that for Dave and Alese, but our corpse might not fit that motive."

"Still, don't dismiss it prematurely. Once the identity is known, that murder may fit nicely. It was one of the motives Denise and I came up with, and the more I think about it, the more I think it's spot on. One more thing," Colleen said. "Don't rule out sympathizers to the Nazi cause. They're not officially Nazi agents, but they believe in Hitler and they're here, as well."

CHAPTER SEVEN

New Haven

Sally's Apizza, in the heart of New Haven's Little Italy, was a newcomer to the restaurant trade, having opened just two years ago. Located at 237 Wooster Street, it served New Haven-style pizza and Ballantine beer. Today, however, Adam Franta wasn't interested in the best pizza this side of Naples. All he wanted was for Gene to have agreed to the meeting and be sitting in one of the booths that ran along one side wall and down the other. He stood at the doorway, searching for his luncheon companion.

The framed photographs of the owners, Flo and Sal Consiglio, hung crooked on the wall. For unknown reasons, it was forbidden to straighten them. The framed photo of Frank Sinatra, however, hung straight, seemingly listening to his rendition of *All or Nothing at All,* currently playing on the Wurlitzer. The 78 seemed appropriate, given the circumstances. The juke box bore a German name, but it had become a naturalized citizen, grandfathered in. Even in war, allowances are made. Respect. He shook his head. Respect could vanish in a heartbeat, and without it, you were ignored at best, vilified at worst. He'd seen the worst.

The high-backed wooden benches along each wall offered privacy, but they also made it difficult to locate someone waiting for you. He walked the length of the room, checking the occupants of each booth, and felt Flo's gaze fall upon him as she sat in her office, the last booth on the right, the stacks of paper in front of her, totting up each transaction by hand. He nodded at her and she returned to her work. Finally, he spotted Gene on the other side of the room, three booths catercorner to Flo, facing the entry. Slipping into the booth, Adam settled himself opposite Gene and waited. Forced to sit with his back to the entrance was just one more reminder of how much his status had changed.

Italians aren't known for the moderated volume of their conversations, and voices rose and fell and intersected in the air, weaving a tapestry of sound. When you added Sinatra's velvet tones to the mix, eavesdropping on individual conversations became impossible, and for a number of the customers, precisely the reason they were there. It was a good place to discuss business of a sensitive nature.

"All right. I'm here. What do you want?" Gene said, ripping off a generous bite of pizza and shoving the entire thing into his mouth before dropping the rest of the slice back onto his plate.

"Some things never change, do they?" Adam said. "Nice to see you again, too, Gene. And they call that transference." Adam pointed to the brutalized pizza. "You know—anger." While he waited for an answer, he studied his former handler. Gene had put on weight. No wonder, the way the man consumed food. He ate enough for a field hand, which, in a way he was, although his caloric intake far exceeded his physical labor. Regardless, he accepted the rude greeting. There was too much dirty water under the bridge to expect civilities.

"Look. You wanted to see me. I'm here. Let's not spend any more time than needed, all right?" Gene pushed his plate aside. "I repeat. What do you want?"

Adam's eyes bored into Gene's. "London Bridge is falling down—if that's still the correct code." In the ensuing silence, Adam watched a series of expressions flash across Gene's face. The man would never make it in the field. His face was a mirror of his thoughts.

"How bad?"

"Pretty bad. I need to get in touch with Shadow."

"Not possible."

Stage names. They all had them. Actors in a play, although in these productions, death wasn't part of the plot. It was something to avoid at all costs. When one of them died, it was for real. There was no getting up off the floor when the curtains closed. "Gene. I need you to get me to him as quickly as you can. Would you put that goddamn slice down for a minute? Look at me. This is serious. I don't give a shit what you think about me. What do you want from me? Haven't you already taken enough?"

"What the hell were you thinking?"

"A minor indiscretion."

"Major consequences, Adam. My hands were tied."

Adam raised an eyebrow and offered a grim smile. "Love is blind."

"You were one of my best."

"With the emphasis on *were*. Look, we can continue this back and forth until hell freezes over, but that won't change anything. And I'm not going to change, either. Why the hell should I? I couldn't, anyway. I'm honest. That's a hell of a lot more than I can say about J. Edgar. But he gets a pass." Adam leaned forward, his voice a harsh whisper. "One day, and I hope I live long enough to see it, all this will be behind us, and we will look back and wonder why destroying a man's career was considered an act of morality." He sat back. "Will you do what I ask? If I'm correct, and I generally am, you won't want to be the one who threw the proverbial monkey wrench into the works."

Easing himself off the bench seat, he stood, "Your choice, of course. But I need you to put me on a train, plane, or ship and get me to Shadow while there's still time. You know where I live. I'll have a bag packed and I will be waiting."

By way of a reply, Gene pulled his plate back in front of him and attacked another slice of his pizza.

CHAPTER EIGHT

Port Hope

The mirror doesn't lie, they say, but this morning, Colleen was hoping it would be willing to stretch the truth just a bit. She'd spent a little extra time on her hair and was now checking the contents of her wardrobe, looking for just the right outfit to wear. She had been torn between the rose frock and the cream one. The rose had cap sleeves and a slightly flared skirt. The cream one with the scoop neck and bodice tuck flattered her bust. She returned the rose to the wardrobe. Then there was the matter of footwear. Sandals would be perfect — her legs being her best feature, but by the time she'd pedaled the five miles to town, her feet would have gathered enough dust to negate any possible benefit. Frowning, she settled on the brown espadrilles. Finally, a dusting of face powder and an application of her ruby red lipstick, and she was ready.

It had been two days since the corpse had been carted off and there had been no word from the police regarding their progress on the case. These things take time, of course, but time was a commodity in short supply these days. If the body had any connection to the German threat, she wanted to know about it. She blotted her lips, gave a last look at the mirror, tied her scarf around her hair, and set off on her bicycle to interrogate Bill.

. . .

"Colleen, you know I can't discuss the details of an active case." Detective Chief Inspector William Barton was going to play this one by the book.

"Aha! So it is an active case. I knew it!" Colleen leaned across the desk and made eye contact, although Bill's eyes were occupied elsewhere. Advantage, Colleen.

"Come on, Bill. You know you're going to need help on this. And," she tilted her head at the empty desk in the corner, "Jim has his hands full with everything else you do here, and you know it."

The groan was audible and Bill shook his head, a slow side to side movement. His resolve was weakening. She always had that effect on him. Over the past two years, they'd come to an understanding. And while he liked things just the way they were, Colleen was a woman, and women weren't content with that, as he'd learned over the course of his sixty years. He'd remarked on that fact on occasion at the Cock and Whistle, and every man there had nodded solemnly at the wisdom of his words. Now, the object of his affections and the thorn in the side of his investigation was making things difficult. Colleen, widowed early on in her marriage, had managed to raise her children without the help or hindrance of a male figure, and now they were grown and she was not yet fifty. He shook his head again. Damn the woman. All right. If that's the way it was going to be, so be it.

"What do you want to know?" he asked.

"Everything, of course."

She smiled at him, and the last of his resolve crumbled. More than crumbled. It dissolved.

He got up, wheeled the chair from the roll top desk over next to his own chair and motioned for her to have a seat. As she settled in by his side, he caught a faint whiff of her perfume. It was light, not like the stuff the whores down on the docks wore. No. She was a lady. An insistent, opinionated lady. Why he let her wear him down he couldn't fathom. She just did. "Do you want a sheet of paper and a pen to take notes?" he asked.

"No thank you. I'm prepared." Colleen produced a notepad and pen from her handbag.

"All right, then. This is what we know." He opened his top desk drawer and extracted a folder which he opened on the desk. Lifting the first page of a small file, he began to read. "Let me know if I'm going too fast for you," he said.

Colleen laughed. "Bill, we've already had this conversation."

The Detective Chief Inspector cleared his throat and returned his attention to the coroner's report. "Adult male, aged 25-35. Five foot ten inches in height. Weight: 12.5 Stone." He gave Colleen a serious glance. "I assume that's with the addition of the severed hand." He continued. "Advanced stage of decomposition."

"Is that why the hand was such a ghastly shade of purple? I've never seen anything such a color before."

"Yes. If I may continue?"

Colleen huffed.

"Cause of death was blunt trauma to the left side of the skull. Subject was fully clothed. There were lifts in both shoes."

"He wanted to appear taller than he was," Colleen said. "Like the movie stars in Hollywood. Many of those leading men are shorter than their female leads." She gave a disapproving cluck. "Ego. They say women are vain. You know, Bill…"

"As I was saying," Bill gave a slight cough. "Due to the stage of decomposition, we were unable to capture any fingerprints. Photographs were taken of dental work, and the clothing was searched for labels or any possible identifying marks. None were discovered. There was no wallet on the deceased's body. Analysis of pocket contents revealed a soiled handkerchief — I'll skip the details — and a scrap of paper with a telephone number at the bottom, and that's it." Bill set the paper down, closed the folder, and met Colleen's gaze. "We called the number on the list. It was disconnected. That's it," he repeated. "Case closed. We're done. He's a John Doe and headed for the pauper section of the cemetery."

"No."

"What do you mean, no?"

"Fingerprints, Bill."

"Colleen, I told you. There were no fingerprints left to take impressions of. The body is a putrefactive mass of decay."

"Yes, that's true. But there's one thing the coroner overlooked." She gave her words a moment to sink in and was rewarded with a twinkle in Bill's eye.

"The slip of paper with the phone number. I'll be damned. Good work, dear. I'll be back in a few. Wait for me?"

"Of course. But if it turns out our corpse never had his prints taken, and even though the number's been disconnected, is there a chance to find out whose number it was?"

"That's two for you, Colleen. I'll see what I can uncover. I'll make a call to British Telecom directly." He scribbled a notation on the report. "And the crime scene's been cleaned up. You can tell Denise she's welcome to go and check on her truffles." Bill turned up his nose. "Why anyone except the French would eat fungus defies logic."

"I'll tell her you said so."

"Back in a flash."

.   .   .

Police stations have their own measured pace. In a profession that deals with emergencies, crime, and other issues of public safety, there's generally a kind of controlled mayhem, and that was the case today. The phones were all in use, and there was a queue of people waiting to lodge complaints or seek some sort of official help for whatever problem they were dealing with. Colleen scanned the faces and recognized everyone, except for one woman she'd never seen before. She was in her mid-thirties and plainly dressed, with a worried expression on her face. Another newcomer to add to the list or just someone passing through who needed help? Distracted by this line of thought, she didn't hear Bill return and startled when he began speaking.

"I said, is everything all right?"

"Sorry, Bill. I was looking at that woman." Colleen tilted her head in the direction of the queue. "Do you know her?"

"Who?"

"The woman whose turn is next. I've never seen her before."

Bill's eyes narrowed. "There are a great many people who come in here I've never seen before. Why is this a concern?"

"It's not. Not really. It's just…" She opened her handbag and took out the list of names she and Denise had put together and handed it to him. "We are volunteers in service to Britain, that is, we're…" she leaned forward and lowered her voice. "We're keeping our eyes open for possible Nazi spies." She sat back.

"You're what?"

"Bill, you know as well as I that the government has told us to be aware of possible dangers in our midst. This," she tapped the paper, "is a list of newcomers to our area."

Scanning the list, Bill sputtered. "Bernice and Aldred? Good God, Colleen, the man's ninety if he's a day, he's totally deaf, and his wife is in a wheelchair. They've lived here for over, what? Twenty years?" He handed back the list. "Get a grip, woman."

"All right. All right. Don't get your blood pressure up." She returned the list to her handbag. "They are others, though, who are recent to Port Hope. It won't hurt to be aware. Just in case. And speaking of newcomers, what's happening with our young Polish pilot? Have you learned his name yet? Is he still in hospital?"

"He is for now. His leg required surgery. Nasty break. They needed to pin some bone together. But he's got a healthy enough appetite. Eating the hospital out of house and home and finally starting to fill out. It defies morality, what the Nazis are doing to people. Starving children is one of their specialties. Once we found an interpreter, he wouldn't shut up. His name is Jan Wotjkowski. He's definitely a different type of case. London's prepared for prisoners of war, not teenage slave laborers who manage to negotiate such an impressive escape." His eyes traveled back to the woman in the queue. "Excuse me a moment, would you?" He walked to the counter and had a few words with the clerk who nodded in reply.

"Don't look so smug, Colleen. It's just a precautionary measure, that's all," he said, reclaiming his seat. "Not everyone you're suspicious of is a German agent. Anyhow," he said, "back to the Polish boy. If you were a Hollywood film producer, you'd take a second look at his story. His whole family was killed — massacred, just because they were Poles — and he only survived because the Germans needed workers. His father had been an airplane mechanic, and the lad often helped out. So, when the Nazis were sorting their prisoners, the survivors of the massacre, they decided to work the lad to death over time, instead of killing him on the spot. So generous of them. Damn Krauts. They sent him to the Deutsche Luft Hansa repair facility in France, on the coast. Since he was a skilled mechanic, even at his young age, they assigned him to the repair crew. He actually worked at repairing engines! He hauled equipment and washed the aircraft, and he paid attention and he learned how to fly by watching what the pilots did while he carried their gear and did whatever else they required of him. Once he'd figured out how to operate a parachute, he just bided his time until the sortie. The plane's engine was on, and he was inside and gone before they could stop him. He's a smart lad. He could pilot the aircraft. He knew how to take off and follow the other planes, but he hadn't gotten the landing procedures down well enough — hence the exit by parachute." Bill laughed. "And he destroyed one of Hitler's Junker F.13s because of it. Our military's been all over the wreckage. And, there's more. He's an experienced saboteur. While he was servicing the engines of the aircraft at the hanger, he loosened the fuel lines of each plane he worked on. That allowed them to take off, but as they gained altitude, the lines separated." Bill shook his head in admiration. "He's responsible for at least five kills. So, when you told Denise that he might have been a danger to us, you were more correct than you realized. He was certainly a danger to Hitler. Now, we've got a Polish refugee who's already a war hero. He wants to stay in England and fight for Britain. For a fourteen-year-old lad, he's seen more of this war's horror than many of our soldiers."

"Will he be able to stay?"

Bill nodded. "Yes, once he's been fully debriefed, they'll find a home for him here, but hopefully the war will be over with before he's old enough to serve legally."

"If he wants to join the Air Force, that would be wonderful."

"Yes. They'll teach him how to land, I expect." Bill put his papers back in the folder and stood. "I've got to run."

As Colleen was leaving, she saw Bill turn and give the woman, now at the counter, an appraising look.

CHAPTER NINE

London

Winston Churchill, attired in pajamas, dressing gown, and slippers, had grudgingly abandoned his main office, his bedroom, to study the charts that lined the walls of the Map Room. He'd also left behind his breakfast, the magnum of champagne, along with Nelson, his cat, and was, therefore, in a foul mood. More so than usual. It was barely dawn, and all hell had broken loose. If I could have become invisible, I would have. It was evident this morning would not pass quietly into afternoon.

As if he'd been postponing the inevitable as long as he could and must now perform a distasteful duty, the Prime Minister finally turned to the folder on the table. It appeared innocuous enough, but the force with which he'd slammed it there indicated otherwise. His face grew redder by the instant, and his jaw clenched around the hapless cigar wedged between his teeth to the extent that the wounded portion fell to the table and died. All this had been done in uncharacteristic silence, but now he acknowledged his audience.

"This," he growled, waving the folder whose contents still remained a mystery to us, "is what Hitler plans to do with Britain's treasures, should he be successful." The rage in his voice was barely suppressed. He signaled for an aide to pull down the screen that was waiting on the wall above the map of Europe and then turn on the projector. He sat in silence as we viewed the ten slides projected on the screen.

The England Room was what the introductory slide said. From that point on, we viewed slide after slide of architectural drawings of massive buildings and concourses, and finally, a detailed sketch of a large room. This was The England Room, and its furnishings consisted of the throne of the English monarch and took up much of the central space, an accurate rendition of the Coronation Crown resting on the seat. There was a handwritten notation at the base of the throne. "*To be transported with the greatest care from London.*"

On the wall behind the throne were hung the extant four copies of the 1215 Magna Carta. Each had been elaborately framed and the expected museum light was installed above each one. And above all four was mounted an enormous swastika, claiming possession of everything beneath it.

The walls to the left and right of the throne held just two pieces of art. It seemed odd. With all the art in the world, why these two pieces for display? Intriguing question. On the left was Constable's *Burial at Sea* and on the right, Turner's *The Angel Standing in the Sun*, depicting the Archangel Michael victorious over the enemy.

Subtlety not being one of Hitler's qualities, even as an appreciation for symmetry was, the message quickly became clear. It was clearer than clear. It was blatant. The subject matter of the art was there to illustrate the powerlessness of Britain against the powerfulness of the Third Reich. This was the end result of Hitler's psychological warfare game. Humiliation of the vanquished and rubbing it in for the entire projected one thousand years of the Third Reich. It was revenge for what Germany felt had been humiliation by the terms of the Treaty of Versailles in 1918 that had ended the Great War. It was a celebration of invincibility. It was an abomination.

The projector was turned off, and in the silence one could almost hear the thoughts of everyone in the room. What on earth was all this? I looked up to see the same blank expressions on everyone's faces, my husband's included. After we'd all played a silent game of Twenty Questions with ourselves, Churchill spoke. His voice was controlled, but an anger such as I had never witnessed before simmered just below the surface. "Captain Brunner, if you will, please."

.   .   .

Captain Martin Brunner, one of our agents who had been serving in Berlin, and who was now seated at the head table next to the Prime Minister, had the floor. Over the next half hour, we listened, spellbound, as he explained what all this was and what it meant.

"The England Room, as you can deduce, was designed to both showcase the treasures of England and reinforce Hitler's complete authority over his conquests. However, it is just one part of a massive project that is at the heart of a coordinated series of art thefts throughout Britain and Europe. These artworks are destined for display in the Führermuseum, a huge complex that Hitler plans to make the cultural center of the world. The complex is to be located in Linz, Austria, Hitler's birthplace. He has agents operating in every capital city in Europe to accomplish this goal, and yes, that includes London. The building will have two wings, one with 32 rooms, the other with 28. England is destined to receive its own place of honor there." He passed around a diagram, drawn by Hitler, that showed the massive structure. It looked like a mausoleum. "It is incumbent upon us that Britain never receives that honor," Brunner said.

Museums have never appealed to me. They all look like mausoleums. Everything that was once alive is dead, stuffed, mounted, and needs to be dusted at regular intervals to keep up its appearance. After my one trip to the Peabody Museum in New Haven, I swore I'd never enter another Natural History Museum again. Ever. I stared at Hitler's sketch. One more reason not to like museums—hate probably being too strong a term. But still.

"Acquisition of pieces for display in the museum is well underway," Brunner said. "And Hitler's inner circle are actively involved—Goring, Himmler, the lot of them. Whether they appreciate art or not is not the issue. They see a fortune to be gained, and in this sense, Hitler is the idealist. It's the ultimate irony. He's a collector. The rest are in it for the money. Unfortunately," he continued, "they're doing quite well at it."

"Indeed they are," Churchill interjected. "We believe that Germany has a highly organized ring of thieves operating in Britain, working to supply Hitler with the art he requires to furnish his museum. These operatives live among us, work among us, and they will be overseeing the next wave of agents that Operation Lena will bring. And," he added, "not all of them are Germans."

"If you will look closely at the diagram of The England Room," Captain Brunner said, "you will note there are check marks above three of the four copies of the Magna Carta. We believe this means that Hitler has them accounted for. Perhaps he has physical possession of them. Perhaps they are still in Britain. Their location, as well as that of the artwork, is unknown at this time."

It takes a great deal to make an impression on a room filled with secret agents and police detectives. This was that great deal. To say that the crowd was stunned would have been the mother of all understatements. Somehow, Hitler had managed to acquire the foundational documents of British law and nobody had seen it coming. And that was when the shit hit the fan.

Taking over from Captain Brunner, the Prime Minister gave his directive. "Three are missing," Churchill said, glaring at the document with the Magna Cartas hanging on the wall around the throne. "But," he rested a chubby finger on the final document, "so long as one remains out of his grasp, he has not succeeded. I repeat what I said yesterday: "He will not possess our island. He will not possess our soul! The three missing must be found, wherever they are, and returned."

· · ·

I was fishing in my handbag for the key to our flat. The key had snagged on the lining of my bag and was giving me some trouble. I finally managed to free it from the frayed threads and made a mental note to do some mending before the hole got too big to handle. The metaphor wasn't lost on me. It was exactly what our task was now, faced with the ever-widening swath of Nazi destruction on the Continent and the new threat, confirmed this morning, to Britain.

All I said, however, was, "Captain Brunner looked tired."

"You'd look tired too, Katrin, if you were in his shoes."

"I wonder if he still has family here," I said. "I can't imagine being separated from you for so long. How do you even begin to pick up where you left everything?"

"You don't," John said. "You can't. You have to start over."

I thought about that. Even now, having lived in America for so many years, when I visit my sister, Inge, and her family in Denmark, changes are evident. Nothing stays the same, and the longer you're away, the more you're a stranger when you return. Captain Brunner must be feeling that way now.

"Do you think he's in danger? I mean, he worked for Hitler. They've got to be royally pissed at him. Hitler is not a forgiving individual."

"I would expect he's in extreme danger. We have him to thank for knowing exactly what's ahead, and there's not much time until the air attacks begin on the 10th," John said. "But they're keeping Brunner close to home." He smiled at me. "Don't worry overly much. Once he's been thoroughly debriefed, he'll be issued new papers and will carry on with a new identity. That's one way the Brits are different from Hitler's crew. Whether Brunner remains in London or retires to the Cotswolds, it's not for us to know. Just like that Polish boy we learned about from the police in Port Hope. The lad had all kinds of information about the planes the Germans were assembling in France. Once he's told everything he knows, his life starts over somewhere else."

John was right, of course. Intelligence came to us from many sources, but the 10th was only days away, and there didn't seem to be enough time to get everything done we'd been charged with before it hit. "Hitler's timetable has already been pushed back," I said, "but even if he does start raids, I think he'll try one more time to 'reason' with the Brits before a full scale invasion. He can't seem to get it through his thick skull that Britain wants no part of him or his plans to make them a British Vichy. Once that fails, he'll strike quickly."

My handbag finally released its hold from my key. The threads had made a tangled mess around the teeth, and it took a bit to pick the threads from them. "He's got a nasty temper and a short fuse." I wadded up the threads into a ball and shoved them into my jacket pocket.

"Speaking of," John said. "We've got company." He pointed to a male figure on our front porch, leaning against the door and reading a newspaper, which he folded and tucked under his arm as he saw us approach. Two valises waited by his feet. If these contained clothes, it appeared he planned on staying awhile. Or he had laundry to do.

"Adam!" I cried, sprinting the last meter or so to the stairs.

"What the bloody hell!" cried John, also hastening his approach.

Needless to say, a bit of confusion ensued, as we all converged on the postage-stamped front porch, trying to greet each other without tripping over the two valises and a small box our friend had deposited that now blocked our way.

"About time you two managed to show up. I'd just about decided I had arrived at the wrong place. What kind of hours are you keeping these days?" He leaned forward. "If you have plans for the evening, I'll make myself scarce until the morrow."

"Not at all! Not at all!" John said. "Come in!"

Within a few minutes, we had reconvened inside and Adam had deposited his two valises in our small hallway. The box he handed to me with a slight bow. "For you, Katrin. You'll like it. Open it at your leisure."

That was Adam. Never in doubt about anything. And I was sure I would indeed like whatever was in the box, but opening it would have to wait until a multitude of details had been sorted out. I set the gift on the hall table.

"Shall we move this party into the parlor?" John asked. "We're glad to see you, Adam, but you must admit, this is a bit unexpected. Actually, how did you find us and what's this all about?"

"Gene and the Magna Carta, in that order," Adam said, picking up one of the valises and following us into the parlor. Setting his valise on the floor by the sofa, he unlocked the clasps and scooped up an armful of papers which he dumped unceremoniously on the coffee table, scowling at the lot.

John and I exchanged glances, not for the first time this day. Magna Carta was quickly becoming a household word.

"I need more room," he said, looking about our small flat as if an oversized table was somehow lurking about. "The floor," he pronounced and proceeded to transfer his papers to several stacks on the carpet, freeing up the coffee table for display purposes. "I had this developed at the British Embassy," he said, picking up the first sheet from the first pile. He moved to the coffee table and motioned for us to join him. "This is a photograph of the copy on display at the London Pavilion." He looked up. "At the World's Fair," he added. "It's a close-up, obviously. I managed to avoid any glare, which is important to my purpose." He set the paper down and frowned at it.

Adam Franta was one of those people who weighed words with extreme care before sending them out into the world. Each word was evaluated for meaning, and if it came up short, Franta would discard it and search for another. It might be a trait of all great minds. I didn't know, but there were times when it took every ounce of self-control to keep a neutral demeanor and wait patiently, resisting the urge to grab him by the neck and scream '*Just get to it!*' He'd release the tiniest bit of information at a time, and the result was that you had to piece things together — sort of like doing a jigsaw puzzle. Everything was there and all the pieces assembled perfectly in the end, but the waiting was excruciating. The waiting this time, fortunately, was just about over.

"It's a close-up of the Magna Carta," John said, prompting Adam to continue.

"No," Adam said, "it's not." He removed his glasses and stuffed them into his jacket pocket. He then produced a magnifying glass from another pocket, passing it to John, who used it to examine the photos. Shrugging, John passed it to me. I looked as best I could, but seeing nothing worth seeing, Adam motioned for me to give it back to John. I returned the glass to him, and my confusion was evident. This little game of pass the glass was getting frustrating.

"What does that say?" Adam pointed to a line a little more than halfway down the document.

John, magnifying glass in hand, leaned over the picture, searching for whatever Adam was getting at. After a moment, he stood and shrugged. "Adam, please. Don't make this a test. This is in Latin. My Latin is more than rusty; it's corroded. Just tell me what you want me to see." He handed back the magnifier.

"All right. All right. Is your history as rusty as your Latin skills?"

"Depends. I know as much about the Magna Carta as most people — probably more, since I'm an attorney. It's a legal document. It's also a royal charter of rights that a group of nobles forced King John of England to sign at Runnymede in 1215. It's the first limitation on the absolute power of the monarchy and the beginning of the rule of law. Essentially, it's a big deal."

Franta nodded. "What value would you place on it?"

All right. This was going to take forever. I decided to interject my two cents in this male ping pong match. We were playing professor and student. I'm a professor. Not of law — a professor of botany. But still, we were on equal terms, in a manner of speaking, and so I ventured my opinion for consideration. "Adam, we heard all of this at Churchill's briefing this morning. There are four original copies of the Magna Carta. Three of them have gone missing. Each is as valuable as the other. They're beyond putting a price tag on. They're irreplaceable. They're the foundation of our entire legal system. You just can't put a price on that."

"Good thing," Adam said. "Because it's a fake."

For once, Franta hadn't wasted any time finding the right words. For possibly the first time in his life he had cut to the heart of the problem in one stroke.

"What?" John and I let out the question at the same time.

"It's not possible," John said. "How the hell could it be a fake? I think you'd best start at the beginning."

The look he shot at John would have killed a lesser man. "Wish I could, but I don't know the beginning. All I know is this." He tapped an index finger on the photograph. "This is not the Magna Carta. Here. Hold on a moment." He turned back to his paper stacks and rifled through the second one until he found what he was looking for. "I made some notes." He took the two sheets of paper he'd extracted from the pile and placed them side by side on the coffee table. "Compare them," he said.

John and I, heads together, tried once again to see what was so apparent to Adam. I tend to read more quickly than my husband, but the downside of that is that I sometimes miss things along the way. It was that way this time. I scanned the lines too quickly and got to the end as if I had won a race. But Adam shook his head in one of those professorial signs of disapproval and pointed back at the texts, and I accepted the message and started over. The second time through I spotted it at almost the same time John did.

Simply stated, Paper B was a few words longer than Paper A, and it didn't take any facility in Latin to realize that one or the other was the imposter.

de tempore usque ad tempus

I set my finger down on the words. Words that didn't belong, from the nod of approval on Adam's face. He then set two new pages with the text in English on top of the Latin. The first read:

The city of London shall enjoy all its ancient liberties and free customs, both by land and by water. We also will and grant that all other cities, boroughs, towns, and ports shall enjoy all their liberties and free customs.

The second was exactly the same as the first. Except for the addition of *from time to time.*

"What the hell?" John said, and I agreed wholeheartedly. What the hell, indeed.

"It's a clever turn of phrase, and someone was having a bit of fun with this," Adam said. "Obviously, from time to time is neither the text nor the intent of the original document. But," he looked up, "what you should be asking is, 'Where is the real 1215 copy of Magna Carta?'" Taking the magnifier from me, he used a pencil point to indicate a faint dark line that appeared to be something embedded in the parchment close to the edge. "This shouldn't be necessary and it's a bit of overkill, but just in case whoever you report this to remains skeptical, there's this. And there are others." He pointed out several additional lines that occurred randomly throughout the parchment.

"I give," John said. "What are we looking at?"

"These are hairs," Adam said. "They're commonly found embedded in parchment made from calf or goat skin." He set down the magnifier. "Tiny hairs that escaped the scrape, if you'll pardon the slight joke, although there's nothing humorous here at all."

The lines, at first nearly invisible, now seemed to be everywhere, now that I knew what to look for. "I don't get it," I said. "It's parchment, and it's a tad sloppy. Conditions when they made these documents weren't exactly sterile or even all that clean, for that matter. Why is it important?"

"It's definitive," Adam said, "even without the textual alteration." His tone left no room for argument or discussion. "The original copies were made on sheep parchment. There's a world of difference in the texture and shape when you compare these different hides. Without scientific analysis, of course, we can't prove our theory, but there's no doubt. That would just be a formality. The bottom line remains the same. The copy on display at the London Pavilion is a forgery."

CHAPTER TEN

London

"Lists. Maps. Charts. Calendars." I was clearing space on the kitchen table, since the coffee table didn't have room for one more sheet of paper. As it was, each time one of us walked by it, the draft was enough to threaten an avalanche onto the carpet. "Maybe if we can cut off Hitler's supply source for paper we can put an end to this miserable war," I muttered.

It was the day after Adam's bombshell announcement. The three of us had reconvened in the parlor and were deep into a discussion of the who, what, when, where, how, and why. All we had determined so far was that the *what* was the Magna Carta, and I knew without a doubt we were going to need more paper. That is why I had availed myself of an entire ream from the supply cabinet at Whitehall this morning and hauled it back to the flat. The easiest way to successfully pull off a minor theft, and probably a major one as well for that matter, is to do everything out in the open and as brazenly as possible. Act as if you belong….

"John?" I rested my hand on the still-wrapped ream.

"Hmmm." My husband had taken the paper with *who* at the top and was busily doodling a line of rectangles across the page. We all approach problems differently.

"I've been working on the *when*. I know it's down on the list, but if I'm correct in my thinking, it narrows our search area by a substantial amount." I picked up my pencil, ripped open the wrapper, and took the first sheet of my stolen goods to make notes as I spoke. I looked at my companions. "Like an entire continent and the Atlantic Ocean narrower. Everything is happening here. The art thefts. The three Magna Carta thefts. Why think that the fourth Magna Carta was stolen from the World's Fair? That's just where the theft was discovered. It makes more sense if we consider that the theft occurred here, before the document ever left England. It wouldn't have been difficult." I set the paper down and tapped the pencil on it, sort of a contrapuntal accompaniment to my thoughts.

I'd grabbed John's and Adam's attention, and that reinforced my conviction. "Look. Before bad things begin happening, nobody is expecting anything to go wrong. It's only afterwards that people get their guard up. Last year, the hope was that by sending the Magna Carta to America for display at the Fair, people would start to empathize more with the Mother Country, and Congress would decide that helping Britain was the right thing to do. Britain didn't send off its most prized legal document on a whim. It was a gamble. High stakes, I might add."

John and Adam hadn't jumped into my little speech to offer their opinions and arguments against what I was saying, and I took that as a good thing. "What we need to consider here first is," I continued, "did Britain knowingly send a forgery to America, thus safeguarding the original back at home? They would have risked discovery." I nodded in Adam's direction. "And that would have compromised the sincerity of their appeal. I'm wagering not. It's more likely that someone stole the document at the British Museum, before it was crated up and shipped away. My money is on the second scenario. Much simpler. And, if it had been nicked here, so much easier to add it to the ever-growing collection of stolen art." I sat back, folded my arms across my chest, and waited to be shot down. It didn't happen. In fact, there was silence. Finally, John spoke.

"I'll buy it," he said. "It makes sense."

"Definitely," Adam said.

From Adam, that was high praise. "So," I said, "are we lumping the Magna Cartas in with the stolen art, or are we dealing with two separate issues? Personally, I don't believe in coincidence, but it's possible with all that's going on that there are two different agendas here. Maybe three. Or more." It all seemed hopelessly tangled.

Adam sat back in his chair and returned his paper — another *who* sheet — to the table. He looked at me and nodded. "It was hotter than hell the day the Magna Carta arrived in New York. There was no inspection. It came all crated up. We took it to the Pavilion and the workmen installed it. All we were concerned with was its safety — nothing else. Why would we be? And it was secure. Thick glass and barriers to keep the public at a distance. There was no breach."

"Timeline, then," I said. "That's next. If we assume it was stolen from Salisbury Cathedral, it had to have been last year." I tossed my pencil on the table. "That hasn't shortened our timeline. It's actually lengthened it by what?" I did some mental calculations. "Six months, minimum. Hell, it could have happened any time in the past. It could have happened years ago. We have no way of knowing. No way at all." Discouraged, I got up and wandered over to the window. "We know less now than when we started." I rested my forehead on the windowpane. The glass was warm. The day had been hot and had been slow to cool down.

"You're right to a point, Katrin," Adam said, "but we most definitely have a date for the beginning of our timeline. I authenticated the document myself here in London at the Cathedral two days before it was crated up and shipped off to the States. I came over with it on the Queen Mary as an official chaperone and stood by as it was delivered to the Fair. In fact, I even have a photograph of myself with the mayor, the police commissioner, Britain's consul general, and another fellow with an official British title at the docks in New York City. So, Katrin, we know a great deal more than we did. If we accept that the documents were switched here in England, it was done between April 12th and April 14th of last year."

So, we had a beginning. All we had to do was travel the path ahead and bring everything to a successful conclusion. Shouldn't be too difficult. No, not difficult at all. It would be downright impossible. I wanted to bang my head against the window, but that would just have given me a headache. However, one does what one must. Somewhat encouraged, and with the mood noticeably lighter, we pressed on.

"*Who, where, how*, and *why* remain," John said, "and I believe that when we find out *how*, we'll have some good information on *who* and possibly, *why*. All criminals have a *modus operandi*. If our thief is a career criminal, he'll have some favorite methods. It's difficult to believe an amateur would be involved. This case is bigger than petty theft. There's more involved and we haven't even scratched the surface." He stood and stretched. "I'll pay a visit to the Cathedral and do some checking on anything that might have been out of the ordinary on those two days. It's a longshot. People have short memories and we're talking a year ago."

"There are at least two in the *who* category," Adam said, "unless you believe the forger is also the thief. We're talking about two distinct skill sets here. Just off the top of my head, I can think of three men. Sorry, Katrin, but most forgers are men. As I was saying, I can think of only three men with the expertise to do this. Well, make that two. One died last year. It's a narrow field. There's an American by the name of Roger Prince. He's quite good, but he works mainly in Oriental art. No. My money is on Angelo DeMontana. He has the ability without a doubt, but I don't know if he's still active. He's always been adept at defining ethics as it suits him. Mostly he's quite full of himself. The man's ego is boundless."

Adam looked at John and then at me, almost daring us to reply. I was thinking that this was a case of "it takes one to know one". Adam shared the same trait as our quarry. When he and DeMontana met, there'd be a collision.

"I think that's my line of inquiry. I don't know where he is, but I still have some contacts. I'm up for one last go round, John. I've submitted my resignation to the university, and I have no doubt

KAREN K. BREES   111

that my students will be relieved, possibly overjoyed, to find that I've abandoned them to a younger, more approachable instructor. The last field trip was my final academic undertaking." He took a sharp breath and busied himself straightening the papers on the coffee table. "I've already packed up my office, don't you know. It didn't take all that long. A few cardboard boxes filled with photographs, diplomas, awards—you know the sort of stuff one accumulates over a career. And what do I do with it? Who would want it? It's just a collection of paper and glass. Soon forgotten." He turned to John. "Why do we have to memorialize forever the actions of the moment? No one cares. It's over and done."

"So, what did you do with it all?" John asked.

"Walked away from it. Too cowardly to toss it in the trash. Left it for the janitor. It's actually rather liberating. I'm no longer fettered to my past self." This time, his smile was sincere and he seemed to stand a bit taller. "I've given myself permission to…to walk away without regret. Too many of us hang on when there's damn little to hang on to. You have to know when it's time to break free and leave the past where it belongs. And so, I have." He cleared his throat, preparatory to his request. "How about one last caper, old friend? Might I tag along? I promise to keep a relatively low profile."

John looked at me.

I nodded. Old times.

"Not terribly convinced about the low profile aspect, Adam," John said, "but you're already knee-deep in this mess. Might as well finish what you've begun."

"All right then," Adam said. "I'll begin the rounds tomorrow."

We all need purpose. Without something to fix on, life becomes a series of routines, filling what time we have with mundane, meaningless detail and drivel. I could see the change already taking effect in our friend. He straightened his bow tie that had been a bit askew, and the decisive manner in which he now moved the papers about reinforced the image of a man who had found that purpose. One door closes, and another opens, as they say.

"I'll work on a calendar," I said. "We're going to need dates and times for the reported art thefts. And locations," I added as an afterthought. "This stuff is being gathered and held somewhere prior to shipping out to Germany. That's our *where*." I laughed. "Our *where* is *somewhere*. Now, all we have to do is find it! Tomorrow is our final briefing at Whitehall and we're scheduled to pick up our specific assignments. We saw the map today. England's been cut up like a pie. We're each to have a slice as our home base with the freedom to move about from there as necessary."

John hauled himself out of his chair and went to the kitchen where he opened one of the cabinet drawers. Producing the box of toothpicks, he took two, broke the tip off one, and put both behind his back. I could see the movement of his arms as he shuffled them about. Puzzled, I waited for an explanation. I didn't have to wait long.

He returned to our makeshift War Room and stood before me. "Tomorrow, one of us has to inform Churchill that the fourth copy of Magna Carta has also been stolen. Short straw gets the dubious honor." He straightened to his full height, and not to be intimidated, I also got out of my seat and stood before him.

At five foot eleven inches, I am not a short woman. Still, John had a good two inches on me. I took a breath and tapped his left arm.

John brought both arms to the front and opened his hands. The left arm held the intact toothpick. I touched his shoulder. Fate had spoken, and I didn't envy his task tomorrow. Given Churchill's propensity for thundering when angered, I made a mental note to bring some earplugs to prepare for the outburst that would be loud enough to rupture a few eardrums.

CHAPTER ELEVEN

London

There are no certainties in warfare, that's a given, but the situation wasn't looking good for Britain. Hitler's unrelenting onslaught had eliminated the possibility of any allies on the Continent. With the fall of France and the subsequent establishment of Nazi-controlled Vichy as the new capital, the verdict was sealed. Britain stood alone, the last holdout against the insatiable appetite of Hitler's Third Reich. In fact, Hitler was knocking on Britain's door and had no plans to stop until Britain was his. Britain had ordered evacuation of the Channel Islands on June 20, and not everyone had gotten out before Germany overran it ten days later.

Churchill, fully aware of what was ahead, was already preparing for war on more than one front, and it involved a great deal more than deploying the armed forces. At home, it was taking on the trappings of closing up the beach house for the winter. Storms would indeed be raging on the

English Channel, but they wouldn't be waiting until winter. It was a given that whatever you did wouldn't be enough. In a way, this was Round Two, with last year having turned out to be just the dress rehearsal. The most precious of Britain's treasures, the children, had been taken by train from the cities to the hoped-for safety of the countryside. When the bombings began, the children would be far from London and other likely targets.

In late August, during the ten days preceding the declaration of war on September 3, Britain's art treasures worth millions — Rembrandts, da Vincis, Turners, Constables — all were sent from the National Gallery to various places in Wales, where it was hoped they would be safe. Some went to the University of Wales at Bangor, others went to the National Library of Wales in Aberystwth, and the castles scattered about the country — Caernarfon, Trawsgoed, and Penrhyn. From the British Museum, priceless works by Shakespeare and Milton and others, along with two copies of the Magna Carta joined the caravan.

But, the expected attack from Germany didn't come. Parents missed their children, and many were brought back to the cities, only to find that this had just been a brief interlude. It was a hard sell the second time around, but once again, the children were moved out to the countryside. The art treasures, however, were a different story. A better plan was needed, for while most of the art arrived at the intended destinations, not all of it was so fortunate. Some of the most valuable pieces had simply disappeared.

"Hide them in caves and cellars, but not one piece of art shall leave this island," Churchill had roared at Kenneth Clark, the director of the National Gallery. Clark had suggested the art be shipped to Canada to wait out the war, and he suffered Churchill's wrath at the mere thought of the proposal. No, everything would remain in Britain. All that had to be done was find the place. It took some intense work, but that place was found. A slate mine in Manod, Wales, was the perfect location. It just needed some dynamiting, trestle building, acceptable inside temperature and humidity controls, communication system, lighting, and a hundred other alterations. It would take time. It would take months to accomplish all this. In the meanwhile, the art was less than secure.

That was the background to our current situation. Breaking our news to Churchill was going to be as difficult as confessing to your father that you'd wrecked the family automobile. Probably worse. The auto might be fixable. It didn't appear that our situation would be that easily remedied. I had been deadly serious last night when I said I'd be wearing earplugs to protect my hearing against the explosion that I knew would come. As we approached the door, I took the plugs from my jacket pocket, popped them in, and covered my ears with a few stray wisps of hair before we entered the room. The sound was muffled just enough to take the edge off—sort of like a shot of whiskey before surgery after getting hit by a stray bullet on the battlefield. I hoped that wouldn't become my reality.

The earlier briefing on Operation Sea Lion had covered the military campaign against Britain. It had been followed by Operation Lena's briefing that had covered the details of the plan to send German spies to infiltrate Britain, joining up with those already on British soil. Standard stuff. We'd ended the session learning of Hitler's grandiose plans to build his Fuhrer Führermuseum, and now we had some bad news to close that topic.

After a short wait, our request to have a moment with the Prime Minister was granted, and we were escorted to the Map Room, where Churchill was still wrapped in his dressing gown and seated at his customary chair in the center of the long table, a champagne flute filled to the rim at the ready, and his cigar also ready to be called into service.

This was the moment to deliver our news. There are some moments that remain vivid in your mind, regardless of how much time has passed. This was one of them. I knew I would carry it with me forever. I nodded at John and saw him take a deep breath. I would give my life for my husband, but there was no way I was going to share the brunt of Churchill's anger. There are limits to love, and so I stayed back as John approached the table where Churchill was adjusting his cigar's bellybando. His invention was designed to protect his fingers from the hot tobacco, although it seemed that his mouth and lungs needed some cushioning as well. Satisfied with the placement, he inserted the cigar into his mouth and looked up from one of the countless maps he'd been studying.

"Yes?"

"Sir. The situation discussed yesterday concerning the Magna Cartas is more critical than was first believed. We have learned that the fourth copy of Magna Carta on display in America is a forgery. This means that the fourth copy of the original has also gone missing."

I watched, fascinated, as the cigar moved from one side of Churchill's mouth to the other without the man opening his lips a millimeter. When it had completed its short journey, I was expecting it to begin the return trip, but instead, Churchill carefully removed it from his mouth, set it down on the ashtray that was covering Austria—a subliminal attack on the Reich, and inhaled audibly. The silence was more frightening than the imminent explosion would ever be.

"Proof?"

"Sir," John said. "Professor Adam Franta is the one who discovered the substitution and has confirmed that the copy on display is a forgery."

"Franta?"

"Yes."

Churchill scowled. "What's in this for him?"

I watched John's face redden. The color began in his neck and spread upward, as if his blood were indeed beginning to boil. But he said nothing. He just waited. I thought it an excellent tactical move. There can be a great deal of power in silence. Finally, Churchill spoke. As expected, the very walls shook under the outburst.

"Find it." He thundered. "Find them all. The whole bloody lot. Do whatever you must, but find them." His gaze traveled from John to me, back to John, back to me, and finally to his cigar, which he picked up from the ashtray and jammed back in his mouth. "Why are you both still here? You're wasting time. You've got a week. Maybe less. Get busy." And he returned his attention to the map and Operation Sea Lion.

We beat a hasty retreat that would have done Dunkirk proud.

"Well, I think that went about as well as could be expected," I said, but John just shook his head. We were back at the flat, and the coffee from breakfast was still lukewarm. I didn't envy John his assignment. While the rest of us would be operating more or less within defined areas, John had the entire island as his territory. Finding all four missing copies of the Magna Carta was beyond difficult. It would be damn near impossible. However, since I felt I had been included in Churchill's directive to John, having been in the same room when the Prime Minister told John to "find the whole bloody lot," regardless of the particulars of my own mission, I fully intended to keep my hand in his. After all, the copies could be anywhere.

The imminent invasion was priority number one for Churchill, but not too far down the list, there were three areas of concern: the network of Nazi operatives working in Britain, the missing art masterpieces, and the most serious of this lot, of course, being the missing Magna Cartas. It was a grab bag of opportunity.

I had picked up my own folder containing my assignment at Whitehall. I learned I was to uncover and neutralize the network of foreign operatives suspected to be active in and around Port Hope, England. I assumed other agents would have drawn the south coast and Wales as their lots and that Margo Speer would have been granted her home territory as she'd requested. Anything that would increase our chances of success would most likely be considered when dividing up the geography.

I remembered the look Margo Speer and I had exchanged. Curiosity is the hallmark of a good agent, and my curiosity was running wild. I wondered about the assignments of the other agents and if our paths would cross. I'd memorized their faces and builds, but sometimes, an assignment required a change in appearance. Sometimes, a disguise was necessary. Sometimes, you wouldn't even recognize the person who had sat next to you at briefing. Sometimes....and then, everything fell into place, and I knew who was behind this whole operation and the magnitude of what we were up against. I wondered if Margo's determination to talk with her brother indicated her own suspicions. Ronin was always in it for the money. He had a warped sense of ethics, but once committed to an assignment, he'd always followed through. He hadn't been at any of the briefings, and that was all I needed to know about what side he was on now. The last time we'd met he'd been working for Britain. He embraced risk. Was it possible he was behind this whole operation? Lord knew there was money to be made here, and for a man with his talents, it would seem like a gift from heaven.

I put my musings aside and opened my folder. My first question, "Where the hell is Port Hope?" was quickly answered, courtesy of the helpful map of England's east coast, thoughtfully provided for my studies. Port Hope was north of London, about midway between Ipswich and Colchester.

The next question, logically, had to do with my cover. It's one thing for MI6 to tell you what to do; it's another to sort out the logistics of the operation. I'd need a reason for being in Port Hope, but I was getting ahead of myself. The answer was there, in the form of a badge that bore my name, Dr. Katrin Nissen, with a picture of a red rose next to my name. The badge identified me as a representative of the Royal Horticultural Society. It gave me the authority to ask questions, initially of a garden variety, but once you've established a connection, even a rapport with someone, there's a permission to digress, and I had serious intentions of digressing.

According to the document that accompanied the badge, I would be engaged in the task of preserving Britain's heritage roses. This would be accomplished by taking cuttings of roses that might be threatened by bombing or by being uprooted to plant vegetables to feed Britain's population. as goods became scarce. I would transfer these cuttings to vials filled with rooting compound, eventually dropping them back at the Society from which I was to be issued all this equipment tomorrow morning. Quite clever of them, actually. Posing as a professor of botany working with hardy perennials, which was exactly who I was, was the ideal cover. The simpler the setup, the greater the chance of success. And while my cover was a legitimate program, my actual work would be to canvas the countryside, house by house, on the hunt for Nazi spies. To that end, the packet contained all the tips that Whitehall had received by wire or telephone for my assigned area. I rifled through them, pulling out one that had been sent by a Mrs. Colleen Richardson, a concerned subject of the Crown. Mrs. Richardson had sent a list of names of possible German agents operating in and around Port Hope. It would be a good starting point. The last item in the packet was a book of petrol coupons with a stern warning paper-clipped to the cover: *Is This Trip Necessary?* It's an odd feeling, being lectured at by a coupon book.

Interestingly, my guide for the first day would be Mrs. Richardson, who, in addition to being concerned, was also president of the Port Hope Garden Society. This woman was active. No doubt about that. There was a card with her address and an appointment time of 1300 hours tomorrow. From there, it would all be up to me. From the looks of things, I wasn't going to have all that much time to help John with his mission.

· · ·

It was late morning, and I figured this might be my last chance to do some shopping. I hadn't bought anything new to wear in quite some time, and even my favorite garments were beginning to show their age. I'd only been back home in New Haven a matter of days when I'd been summoned back to England. I'd barely had time to wash, iron, and repack everything I'd brought home from my last assignment. It was time to replenish my work clothes and add a new dinner dress to the lot. I may not have great fashion sense, but I do know what looks good on me. It was time for a minor splurge. Clothing wasn't yet rationed, although it would be soon, if it followed along with everything else that required a coupon to purchase. Factories were in full wartime production mode, and dinner frocks and tea dresses would soon be in short supply. It was only reasonable to shop while I still could. And so I did. I thought about the warning on the coupon book and decided to walk to Selfridge's Department Store on Oxford Street. I'd pick up my automobile at the motor pool in the morning.

Feeling thrifty and virtuous regarding the petrol usage, I more than made up for it in the clothes department. New mission: new dress. Or two. And a suit coat. And shoes. If the Land Girls who were going to be digging up the roses were issued an entire wardrobe for their time of service, I reasoned, didn't I deserve as much? I left the department store feeling eminently more feminine and more prepared to tackle whatever Hitler might toss my way.

I returned to the flat to find that Adam had stopped by and that he and were John bent over what seemed to be half a dozen maps of varying sizes and subject matter—railway lines, arterials, geographic features. It was a potpourri of mapdom. Finally, satisfied with whatever they'd been about, John refolded the maps.

"I'd wager that all the stolen art has been copied." Adam said. "If DeMontana is involved,

I'm sure of it. This is about profit, not politics, regardless of what Hitler wants."

"I wonder," I said, depositing my parcels on the hall table. "Hitler will get what he wants. Or will he?" I kicked off my shoes and rubbed my tired ankles. "From what you're saying, perhaps Hitler will only get what DeMontana decides to give him. You mentioned that whoever made the forgery of the Magna Carta was also having a bit of fun with it. I've been mulling this about. What about this scenario? All the copies get shipped to Hitler, who thinks he's getting the originals for his England Room, and the originals are sold to private parties who have no scruples about receiving stolen goods. It would be the ultimate irony. And quite lucrative."

"Provenance," Adam said. "Each piece will have to be authenticated before it leaves the country. Even Hitler knows that."

John took the maps and dropped them into his attaché case. "All right," he said, turning back to Adam. "Authentication. Who is going to risk authenticating all those copies before they're sent to Berlin?"

"Me," Adam said. "It's brilliant, John! All I have to do is find DeMontana and offer my services—for a considerable fee, of course…"

Could it work? I had my doubts, but Adam was already at the door.

"John, Katrin, I bid you adieu. Time is not on our side. I just hope someone else hasn't beaten me to the punch."

And then he was gone. I found myself staring at the closed door. Adam Franta was a breed apart, and there was no way of knowing when or if we would see him again.

.   .   .

That evening, we dressed to the nines, with me in my new frock, a knee-length, three-quarter-sleeved mauve, green, and lilac number with a bias-cut skirt and John in his best grey suit, four in hand tie, and his lightly-starched white shirt with the gold cufflinks. These days, dressing to the nines also included carrying a torch with fully-charged batteries that allowed us to navigate sidewalks without running into obstacles and to cross streets without stumbling off kerbs.

London at night was a city lost in the shadows. Blackout regulations had been in place since the first of September last year, just before war had been declared, and the authorities were deadly serious about compliance. As day gave way to twilight, blackout curtains were closed in every residence and business establishment. Not a sliver of light was allowed to escape to the outside, and the wardens patrolled the streets making sure everyone complied. Traffic lights and automobiles had deflectors to channel the light down to the ground.

Darkness doesn't mean silence, however, and the cacophony of horns bleating as drivers narrowly avoided crashing into one another, indicated their reflexes and reaction times were being severely tested. Not everyone was scoring high marks, and there was the occasional loud crunch of fenders making contact and pedestrians yelling at drivers to pay attention. We hailed a cab that negotiated every obstacle without incident. Finally, turning onto Kings Street, our driver deposited us at the front door of the poshest seafood restaurant in London, Wilton's. If you wanted seafood with a serving of elegance on the side, Wilton's was the place to go.

Our table was waiting for us, and we followed the waiter as he led the way. The white linen tablecloth, the sterling silver, the beautiful china, the crystal goblets, the single red rose in the crystal vase, and the background music of the orchestra all spoke of tradition proudly maintained. And there came with that sense of tradition the realization that whatever Herr Hitler threw at us, we would endure, and God willing, prevail.

"Do you remember the last time we were here?" John asked.

"I certainly do, and I also remember the first."
I lifted my wine glass in a toast to memories. Our
first dinner at Wilton's had been shortly after our
marriage, shortly after we'd been recruited to MI6,
and shortly after we'd come to realize that saying
goodbye would become all too familiar an
occurrence. Tonight, we were saying goodbye
again, but only to London. We'd both be
crisscrossing Britain this time, and the odds of
meeting up during this mission were fairly good,
unless something went awry. No, there would be
no thoughts of that this evening. Our job was
putting things to rights. I looked at John and he
smiled. He'd read my thoughts. He always could.

"We'll meet here again," he said, "when the job
is done."

I returned his smile. It was our ritual. Wilton's
was our place and always would be.

"Tomorrow, I'll start at the scenes of the
crimes," John said, the orchestra rendering our
conversation private. "The British Museum and
then Salisbury and Lincoln Cathedrals. I'm going
to go over the personnel records. Maybe there'll be
something there." He shrugged. "Gotta start
somewhere."

"And I shall be pottering about with the roses,"
I said, "just a hop, skip, and a jump, from London."

"Well, in that case," he said, "I might just have to find a way to slip over to you for a night of wanton passion." He lifted an eyebrow in a poor imitation of Clark Gable.

I raised both of my eyebrows to heaven. "Promises. Promises. Although," I said, dabbing at my lips with the napkin and checking to be sure I hadn't deposited any lipstick on it, "about that night of wanton passion?"

John's expression was difficult to read. "What about it?" he asked.

"I don't think waiting is such a good idea. I mean…"

"I agree." John has this crooked grin, kind of like he's got a secret—it's a good secret—and he's thinking about how to tell you what it is. He reached for my hand. He didn't need to say anything else.

And then the food came. Butter might be rationed, but restaurants were given some leeway, and a veritable feast lay before us. We began with prawn cocktails with cream-laced Marie rose. For our entrees, John chose the *Wild Scottish Smoked Salmon*, and I selected the *Lobster and Caviar Omelette*. Everything was beyond good. It was perfect. Expensive. Really, really expensive, but then perfect doesn't come cheaply. Tonight, no worries. No regrets.

CHAPTER TWELVE

London and Environs

Morning came quickly. Too quickly. The night of wanton passion had gone quite well, and lying next to John, I was thinking that a brief morning replay would be a nice start to the day. I thought he'd agree.

"Do you know what I'm going to miss until we're back here again?" he asked.

Before I could answer, he kissed me on the forehead and vaulted out of bed.

"Coffee!" he called, over his shoulder.

I was barely able to swat him before he disappeared down the hallway en route to the kitchen and the coffee pot. He was right, though. Tea is all well and good. But it's just not coffee, the elixir of life. And like sex, it would have to wait until our missions had been completed. No, I corrected myself, there was still the hotel where I'd be staying. I grinned inwardly.

Breakfast was a clean-out of the fridge. Interesting and marginally nutritious, but coffee made it all good. I tidied up the flat, made the bed, picked my new dress up off the floor where it had landed last night as maneuvers began and hung it in the wardrobe. Shortly, we were off to the motor pool.

John prefers two-wheeled transport and made straight for the Harley that waited last in line near the far wall of the garage. In another time and place, we'd take off on it together, but Professor Katrin Nissen required a more traditional vehicle with room for all the trappings for the horticultural field trip.

John roared away with nary a wave. When the dust had settled, I decided that the 1939 Morris Eight, Series E two-door saloon would do perfectly. According to the information sheet taped to the driver-side window, this 4-speed beauty had a top speed of fifty-eight miles per hour and would go forty-five miles on an Imperial gallon of petrol. I did the mental computations and decided that a lower speed would be necessary if I were to stretch my petrol coupons. Still, it had an electric windscreen and sported a nifty paint job— British racing green, and the interior had enough room to carry a Rembrandt or a Nazi operative, should I be lucky enough to track down one or both or more.

"I'll take this one," I told the mechanic.

"It's a bit tired, ma'am," the mechanic said. "Second is a bit sticky, but if you pop the clutch right into third, you'll be dandy."

All right, then. First to third with just a passing touch at second. Got it. There's a knack to everything.

"If you're in a pinch, reverse is faster than second."

I eyed the Morris with slightly less enthusiasm than at the beginning of this transaction but signed the requisition form and found that the mechanic was a truthful man. I needed to back before I could exit the garage, and it did come as a bit of a surprise that Morris, as I had named him, required the lightest of touches to accomplish the deed. We shot across to the opposite wall with a time that the most dedicated Olympic athlete would envy. I blinked hard, braked, shifted into first, and escaped the garage without further incident. A quick stop at the London Horticultural Society to claim my supplies for the rose work and then, on to Port Hope.

. . .

The drive took slightly over an hour. Being mindful of my speed added several minutes to the trip, but I felt virtuous for being a responsible petrol consumer. Actually, that wasn't true. I was still learning the various quirks of Morris, and we hadn't quite yet established any degree of rapport. If an automobile could have a personality, the kindest thing I could say about Morris was that he was willful and a bit stubborn. He also preferred a cruising speed around forty miles an hour, considerably less than his glowing spec sheet had proclaimed.

Port Hope was a logical starting point for my investigations. Situated at the mouth of the Orwell River that flowed into the North Sea, it was also on a rail line and directly north of London. Logistically, it was a hub for shipping, and my hope was that some of the cargo intended for shipment would be the stolen art and that the shippers of said art would be the Nazi agents I'd been sent to find. In a perfect world, that would be the case. In the world we had, it was somewhere between unlikely and remote. As I closed in on Port Hope, I passed Ipswich, one of England's oldest towns, King John granting its charter back in 1200 A.D., only fifteen years before he'd been forced to sign the Magna Carta. Maybe this was an omen. I just hoped it was a good omen.

With the unholy trinity of tasks ahead — finding the spies, finding the art, and finding one or more of the Magna Cartas, I was beginning at the end and going backwards. Everyone else on assignment had sprinted away from London, bound and determined to retrace the ill-fated routes of the missing transport vehicles. They were welcome to this line of investigation, but it was irrelevant. It didn't matter what had happened. The only thing that did matter now was intercepting the art before it left England for Germany. Accomplishing that required a different approach. My colleagues were wasting valuable time going back over plowed fields. That tack would always have them God knew how many steps behind the thieves, and they'd never be able to catch them up.

My thinking was different. If I were correct, the art was likely already in the possession of the Nazi spies operating in England and they were holding it until….until when? That was the part I hadn't figured out. Yet.

There hadn't been any more thefts. Did that mean the thieves had gotten everything that was on some sort of master shopping list? What else could it mean? The art that was scattered about the countryside would soon be gathered up and moved to the caves at Manod, in Wales. That wouldn't happen until the caves were fully prepared to accept the shipments. It was going to take months to get all the preparatory work done. Only then would the art be on the move again. By then, if all accounts were accurate, Britain would be fully at war and nothing would be safe on the waters or in the air which were the only ways off the island.

So, I'd considered other options. What would be other reasons for not moving the goods now? Hard as I tried, I couldn't come up with a good answer. But there had to be something I wasn't seeing. Were they intended to remain here? That made no sense. I clenched the steering wheel a bit harder and urged Morris to pick up the pace. It all boiled down to the fact that the Evil Mastermind

KAREN K. BREES 135

was waiting for something. What was that something? I shook my head. It was maddening and more of a challenge than I might have time for. And then I hit the brakes and pulled over to the side of the road. *"He always visits their graves on the anniversary of their deaths."* That was July 15. Ronin would certainly leave England either that day or the following one, barring any complications. Today was July 9. That left me only six days.

Morris and I motored up the road with our immediate destination the Rusty Scupper Inn on the waterfront, just south of the town centre at the bend of the River Orwell. The Inn was strategically placed, almost directly across from the marina, and I'd requested a room fronting on the street which would give me a view of the goings on at the wharf. Slightly run-down but moderately reputable, the establishment had been built sometime in the mid-eighteenth century. It didn't appear to have received a great deal of maintenance since then.

The clerk at the front desk, Miss Berthe Baumgartner, barely looked at me as I registered, being more absorbed in her movie magazine than in a paying customer, and I'd matched that with saying as little as possible. Interesting, her name. Obviously German. Granted, there were many Germans in England who weren't affiliated with the current regime, but it bore some checking. Regardless, John and I were set. A week's worth of lodging had been paid for, his key would be waiting for him at the desk, and we could park our vehicles in the dirt lot behind the inn for an added charge. Our rooms were on the ground floor, as requested, with an unobstructed view of the street. The only complications I could foresee were that using the telephone would require going to the telephone on the corner, the walls were thin as a French model, and the mattress on the bed just as thin. No matter, one week. Anything can be endured for one week. I gave the mattress a parting glare as I left the room to scope out the eating establishments down by the docks.

Settling on the Cock and Whistle, I found a small table by the front window, where I sipped my tea and nibbled at my slice of apple pie, checking out the clientele. With a goodly mix of sailors from both the commercial and public docks, the Pub looked promising for hearing whatever scuttlebutt would be discussed over pints at the end of the working day. I settled my bill and claimed Morris to drive to my first official call as a member of the Rose Task Force.

CHAPTER THIRTEEN

London and Environs

Three remarkably similar repositories for the Magna Carta. Three remarkably similar stories concerning the disappearances of the documents. Essentially, when the facilities closed for the day, all was well. When they opened in the morning, the display cases were empty. With no signs of forced entry and no interior damage to the buildings, there was nothing to go on. No leads. No clues. No suspects, and the decision by the higher-ups to keep the whole affair hush-hush so as not to create fear amongst the populace had effectively canceled any efforts to investigate.

Until now. With Churchill's orders to recover the documents still ringing in his ears, and equipped with credentials from the Yard, MI5, and his home agency, MI6, John Breckenridge, now officially Detective Chief Inspector John Ellsworth of Scotland Yard, was determined to rectify over a year's worth of not so benign neglect. The Yard investigated crime, so that was a logical choice, although any of the three could have been justified, with espionage as the explanation. He'd begin with the identity that might elicit the most information. The Yard.

He hated to backtrack. On days when it wasn't turning out all that well, Katrin called it an obsession and termed it a compulsion when she was feeling generous. He couldn't help it. Every investigation was about bringing order to situations where it was absent. That meant he needed to maintain (Katrin would say *inflict*) order onto everything he did in pursuit of the answers. He maintained it was logical. If you began at point X and then moved 360 degrees, you'd end up at the beginning, and hopefully with more knowledge than when you began. Over the years, their differing approaches had often ended up being more compatible than he would have thought. There was no way to factor in her intuitive gifts, and he'd come to respect them, even if he couldn't understand them.

That said, there was no way to accomplish what he needed to do in a smooth circle. With Salisbury nearly ninety miles southwest of London and Lincoln a bit over a hundred and fifty northeast, it was more like spokes of a wheel with London the off-center hub. He'd start at the British Museum and then go to Salisbury, the shorter spoke of the hub. That would allow him to finish up tomorrow at Lincoln and be closer to Port Hope, Ipswich, Colchester, and Katrin.

Today, he had a hunch. Actually, it was not so much a hunch as an educated guess that had taken a while to come together. And while Katrin would have made a case for it being intuition, it had all boiled down to two possible scenarios. The thefts of the two Magna Cartas at the museum had either been an inside job, with an employee or former employee being the thief, or else an employee or someone with access to the Museum had aided the thief. If the latter were true, he reasoned, there would have been some communication between the two conspirators, and logically, that communication would have been made over the telephone. It was a place to begin.

The first step had been obtaining the telephone logs for the Museum, as well as for Salisbury and Lincoln Cathedrals for the two weeks leading up to the reported thefts and for the same period following. Two weeks had been a random choice, but it was as good a starting point as any. If it turned out that he had to broaden his parameters, he'd broaden them until he had something to go on. For now, he had to begin and end somewhere, and two weeks was as good as a year. Once he'd received the logs, he was dumbfounded at how many people called the British Museum or made calls from the Museum on a given day. It would take more time than an evening to sort this out. Frowning, he returned the logs to their folder and stuffed it in his case. Time to deal with the situation at hand.

The Museum had lost both of its copies on the night of August 23, 1939, the day before they had been scheduled to be removed to the National Library of Wales. No alarms had sounded. The Director and Principal Librarian, John Forsdyke, had nothing else to offer. "One copy had been on display, and the other, the copy that had partially burned in a fire back in the 18th century, had been housed in a secure wing. I truly cannot fathom how they were taken. Come along, I'll show you what I mean."

The subsequent tour of the facility confirmed the administrator's account. Everything was at it should be except that the Magna Cartas were missing.

"I'll need a copy of your employee roster for the month of August," John said. "Also, if you will, a list of researchers who were granted access for study."

Forsdyke nodded. "Anything we can do to get to the bottom of this and recover them. The previous investigators didn't seem all that interested, if you don't mind my saying so. I hope you have more luck. If you'll have a seat in my office, I'll get you those records. Also," he added, "we have consultants who come in to assist from time to time. If there were any in residence last August, I'll bring that list as well."

The wait was worth it. When Forsdyke returned with the information, he'd had time to think. "Just on a whim, I also had a copy made of all requisition requests for August and have included contact information for our researchers and consultants." He shrugged. "One never knows. Most of the time, requisitions are for office supplies — paper, typewriter ribbons, carbon paper — that sort of item. Sometimes, however, someone loses a key or needs a lightbulb or a ladder. Perhaps it may prove of help."

With the sheaf of papers tucked into his attaché case, John took his leave and pointed the Harley southwest to Salisbury and the Cathedral that had been the home of the third Magna Carta.

As the Harley roared along, John did some mental comparisons of the structures associated with Magna Carta. The British Museum was a great deal like the Smithsonian in Washington, D.C. It was massive. There was no other word to describe the sheer enormity of the conglomeration of buildings with their collections of everything that could be collected. Salisbury Cathedral, on the other hand, was a house of worship, and if a building could have a soul, a cathedral would probably be first in line to claim one, kicking a museum to the end of the line. Interesting, though, that two cathedrals would have been chosen to display a legal document and especially one of such importance. Why was that? He wondered. Cathedrals aren't noted for their extensive security systems, and the copy that had been on display here was the best-preserved of the four.

"That's an excellent question," the administrator admitted, "but it's got an absurdly simple answer. Elias of Dereham was King John's steward. His task was to distribute the various copies of Magna Carta, and since the king had assigned him to oversee the construction of this new cathedral, Elias dropped off a copy here."

"Where it stayed, until…" John said.

"Yes. Until it was nicked last year. Seems a pity. All those centuries and," the administrator snapped his fingers, "gone like that. Everything is ephemeral," he said, giving John a sorrowful look, "including us."

"That's quite true," John said, impatience creeping into his voice. "Shall we take a look at the scene of the crime?"

"Of course."

They walked to the Chapter House, the scene of the crime. It was a scene without props, and the actors were long gone. Looking around at the emptiness, John asked the obvious question. "Where was Magna Carta displayed?"

The administrator waved his hand at the central portion of the room. "There. It was in a glass case."

"What were the security measures?" John asked.

"I just explained that," the administrator said. "It was in a glass box."

"Fingerprints? Anything? Anything at all?"

The response was a vague head shake.

John stared at the room for a good minute, but there was literally nothing to see there, and nothing else to say.

.   .   .

It was close to sixteen hundred hours, four o'clock civilian time, when John reached the outskirts of London, and he was debating whether to return to the flat and sort things out there, see if Adam might have returned to his hotel and use him as a sounding board, or press on to Lincoln Cathedral, a good three hours away, and then have to find a place to spend the night.

"What the hell!" he said to no one in particular and found a spot to park the Harley outside Adam's lodgings.

Luck had been with him, and now, he was relaxing with a generous portion of Jameson, courtesy of his friend who had decided to return to the hotel after his own tiring day of chasing down dead ends.

"We need ideas," John said.

"We need answers," Adam replied.

"Right. Let's start here." John opened the case and retrieved everything Forsdyke had given him. "We're looking for a name." He dumped the telephone logs from both cathedrals and the museum on the table, and with Adam reading the contact telephone numbers for the consultants and researchers that Forsdyke had provided, he was making slow progress at matching them. The Cathedrals' logs hadn't paid off, but the Museum's logs held promise. Most calls had occurred randomly throughout a four-week period, but one number had received seven calls from various numbers beginning ten days before the thefts with no further calls after the documents had been stolen.

The phone number that had been working overtime before the thefts at the British Museum belonged to Douglas Hyde-Stuart, a retired ornithologist and occasional consultant on matters of an avian nature.

John sat back as best he could in the straight-back wooden chair and studied Hyde-Stuart's curriculum vitae. "Graduate of Oxford."

Adam sniffed.

"What? You have something against Oxford?"

"Another time. Continue."

"Spent his professional career in the Galapagos Islands off the coast of Ecuador in South America, studying," John looked up, "I am not making this up—the mating habits of the Blue-footed booby." He set the paper down to wait out the burst of sputtering as Adam inhaled the mouthful of mineral water he'd been about to swallow.

When the spasms had passed, Adam let out a slow, painful breath. "Let's go get a bite to eat. I'm going to break training and find a lovely Merlot. Blue-footed Booby, my ass."

. . .

Half an hour later, comfortably seated at Romano's, a mid-priced Italian Restaurant down the block, the lovely Merlot in front of Adam and a fresh Jameson by John, the two men picked up their discussion that had been interrupted by Adam's choking attack.

"That 'another time' I mentioned back at the hotel?" Adam said, "it's here." He swirled the wine expertly, inhaling the complex aroma. "Perhaps a tad stale. Still, it's decent."

"Oxford," John said.

"Yes. Well, yes and no. More Stuie than Oxford, and it goes back quite a few years. I'd just arrived in London from Prague. It was a sabbatical year, and I was knee-deep into my research. Stuie and I struck up a conversation at some lecture — don't remember much about it. The lecturer was standard fare, and, as we were seated next to each other in the auditorium and bored out of our minds, Stuie suggested we make our escape and visit the first pub we ran across. It was one of his better ideas, actually. We remained friendly acquaintances for the next year until he compromised the affections of someone I was quite interested in. Never spoke to him again." Adam looked at John with smug satisfaction on his face. "And the point of this little side story, is that shortly afterwards, I heard that he'd plagiarized a term paper and was out on his bum before the ink dried."

John, who'd been half-listening, suddenly was all ears. "What did you just say?"

"I said, he got himself expelled. Kicked out. Whatever you want to call it. But it all boils down to the same thing. He never got a degree from Oxford. So, either one of two things..."

"Yes," John said. "Either he lied to the British Museum about his credentials, or this fellow who is passing himself off as Hyde-Stuart is an imposter. Damn, Adam."

"Damn, indeed. Ah, here comes our repast. I'd forgotten how interesting it is working with you. Which do you suppose it is? And wait until we tell Katrin."

"It might have been enough to turn him against the homeland. Revenge, they say, is a dish best served cold. If that's the case here, though, the dish isn't just cold. It's stale and decayed." John drained his glass. "I'll wrap up this first go-round tomorrow at Lincoln Cathedral, home of the ill-fated World's Fair copy. I need a break. Something. Anything."

CHAPTER FOURTEEN

Port Hope

Even in the best of times, people tend to regard official visits from the government with suspicion. If we weren't living in the worst of times yet, to paraphrase Dickens, we were pretty damn close, and I wasn't sure what kind of welcome I'd be receiving on my visits to document the roses. I pinned on my badge and freshened my lipstick. Morris wasn't all that eager to move this fine late-summer morning, and it took a serious amount of finessing the clutch to wake him up. Slug. Finally, he moaned, gave a half-hearted sputter, and decided resistance was futile. We were Off to the Roses, motoring up the A12 with hopes of protecting more of Britain's horticultural treasures and unearthing whatever Nazi spies had been planted in our path.

Most of my work as a botanist involves the propagation of hardy perennials, and roses fit neatly into this category. Much of the hybridization that's been done from the original stock has created dozens of new varieties, and while these are more disease-resistant than the older stock, there is always a tradeoff. In the quest for bigger blooms and a more expansive color palette, fragrance has been lost. The heirloom roses have a fragrance that has inspired poets, lovers, and other romantics. Today, however, it seems to be all about size and color, forgetting what a rose ought to be. I suspect that even if this endeavor of taking cuttings from the heirlooms to safeguard them from Hitler's bombs weren't my cover for this mission, I would have undertaken it gladly. If these specimens are lost, they are lost forever.

. . .

In slightly under half an hour, I arrived at the home of my tour guide, Mrs. Colleen Richardson, President of the Port Hope Garden Club. She was a bit past middle-age, somewhere in the vicinity of five foot seven, and her blonde hair showed some grey. She had the look of someone who was interested in everything around her. After the introductions were completed and we'd consumed the required cup of tea and the plated biscuits, I was wishing I'd met her twenty years ago. Sometimes, meeting someone for the first time seems more like picking up a friendship where you'd left off a while back. In another time and place we might have become friends. But this was not another time or place, I was the dreaded government representative (on more than one level), and I didn't really know her at all. It's one of the realities of the job. Friends are a luxury none of us can afford. Someday, I plan on doing something to address that—but then again, maybe not. Trust is hard-earned and it doesn't come quickly. It takes a great deal of time, and time is precious and fleeting. So, today was business as usual. Until it wasn't.

It appeared that Colleen had sensed what I was feeling. She was watching me intently, and I waited. There are times in this business when intuition comes into play, and this was shaping up to be one of those times. Finally, she made her decision.

"Would you mind waiting just a bit? I've something I'd like to share with you, and I'd like Denise to be here," she said.

Curious as to what that something would be and hoping it might help me in my quest, I nodded my assent.

"She'll be outside this time of day, so telephoning wouldn't be helpful. Besides, it's not all that private these days. I'll take my bicycle and be back with her in a jiff. Help yourself to more tea, if you like. There's plenty still in the pot." She was gone in a flash, leaving me to speculate on Denise. I didn't have long to wait. In the time it would have taken to have another cup of tea, had I been of a mind to have one, Colleen was back with another woman I assumed was Denise. They were deep in conversation as they parked their bicycles by the front porch and then joined me in the parlor.

Denise Pritchard was an attractive woman in her mid-forties and from the get-go, it was obvious she took no prisoners. Her shoulder-length dark-brown hair was restrained by a kerchief she'd tied around it. She was not a small woman, and there was an energy about her that was contagious. After the brief handshake that concluded our introduction, she dropped into the chair facing mine and regarded me with suspicion. "So, tell me about this new government program that's going to save our roses," she said. "One more pie in the sky idea by someone who sits in an office all day and now has suddenly remembered his grandmother's prized garden."

Suspicious and skeptical. Two qualities that were going to take a little finessing to get around. I'd been expecting it at some point, so best to deal with it from the onset. For the moment, I just nodded, listening.

"Spare me," she continued. "The children are gone. The men are gone. Don't get me wrong. I love flowers, but does anyone care about mushrooms? No." She folded her arms across her chest and leaned back.

"That's enough, Denise," Colleen said, patting her hand. "Dr. Nissen isn't part of the government.

She's just doing her job, but I want you to tell her about the body."

Denise didn't take long to shift gears. "It was the oddest thing, actually," she began, "but it turned out that it was just one more in a string of odd things. It was the body, you see. Well, not to begin with. It began with the hand." She leaned forward. "I'd been out scouting truffles with Cherry—that's my dog—and she disappeared behind a copse of trees. When I called her, she brought me a hand. Not a truffle. A human hand, would you believe. Well, to put it mildly, I had trouble believing it myself, but there it was, big as life. No, that's not right. The hand was quite dead. So, I put a pail over it and bicycled here to tell Colleen and notify Bill."

"Bill Barton," Colleen interjected, "our local constable."

"Do you mind if I make a few notes?" I asked.

"Not at all. Not at all," Colleen said, and Denise nodded vigorously.

"And then, well about two weeks ago," Denise continued, "Dave, the postmaster got himself run down on his way home. Totally wrecked his bicycle, don't you know. And he ended up quite dead. And of course, Alese also."

"Alese?" I asked.

"Alese Farmer was the old lady who lived next door to the abandoned house—the one with the truffle patch," Colleen said.

"Oh. Don't forget the Polish boy," Denise added.

My head was reeling. I'd been listening intently, and it was apparent the two women needed someone to listen to them without judgement. I believe it was in that moment that we forged some unwritten pact. Wherever all this was headed, we'd be working together in some form or other.

"All right. This is what we think." Colleen looked at Denise who nodded her agreement. "We think the Germans are involved." Colleen rose and went over to her desk. She took out a sheet of paper and handed it to me. "Here's our list of potential German agents," she said.

It was the same list I'd received at Whitehall. I felt a slight chill. In the ensuing silence, I could hear my heart beating. Had I let down my guard? Had I divulged too much? But no. Colleen simply wanted to know what to do with it.

"I tried to show Bill," she said, "but he laughed. Granted, Bernice and her husband probably didn't belong on it, but the others most definitely do."

More notes in my pad.

"And then I sent a wire to the Government, but I didn't get a reply. So, when I learned you were coming, I thought perhaps someone at the Horticultural Society would have an idea. It was a sort of desperation move on our part. There's nobody else who will listen to us. We don't want to show our hand here, so to speak." She and Denise exchanged glances.

Now, my heart was racing. "German agents?" I ventured.

"Yes. They're here. Make no mistake about that. You'd have to be a fool to doubt it. And, yes," Colleen leaned forward, confidingly. "I placed a call to the Horticultural Society to be sure you could be trusted." She smiled. "But, what to do about those who concern us is the difficult part, and each of these," she pointed to the list, "have roses on their property. Not all the roses are heritage, but it's an excuse for you to see what we're talking about."

I took the paper with the names from her, although I already knew what it contained. I made a brief show of reading it, then folded it and stuffed it in my notepad. "Well then," I said. "Shall we go?"

"I've a route mapped out for us that will cover the ten stops suggested by the Garden Club," Colleen said, settling herself in the passenger seat. "We'll be heading towards Colchester, then curving around when we're done to see one that's on the list and then the two at the end that I added. Those roses are my favorites," she confided. "They're small cottages up the road a ways, but the roses are quite old." She smoothed a crease in the map and pointed to a section at the upper right quadrant.

"That's fine," I said. "I'd also like to have a look at where Denise found the body. And the locations of the other two deaths, as well." I looked at her and grinned. "You've piqued my interest."

"I'm glad I've piqued someone's interest," Colleen said. "I can't get Bill to even look seriously at my sheet of names. It's all quite strange and unsettling. One can't help but wonder if there will be more."

The three of us taxed the seating in Morris, my horticultural supplies hogging most of the back seat, but we stuffed ourselves in. It seemed as if even Morris was interested and for once was willing to move along at a decent pace. Our first stop, Bellesford House, had been the former residence of the First Lord of the Admiralty a couple of centuries back. It had fallen on hard times and the current owners, industrialist Gerry Taylor of diesel engine fame and his wife, Anne, had spent a king's ransom on repairs and renovations. With Anne's passion being horses, however, there was no great sorrow that the massive flower gardens, hedges, and shrubs were scheduled to be plowed under as part of the Dig for Victory Program. With rationing impacting food supplies, the War Agricultural Executive Committee was encouraging everyone to plant vegetables, and that meant plowing the ground and uprooting whatever was in the way. Unfortunately, that meant the roses.

"Look!" I said, pointing to two tractors already positioned by the peonies and hydrangeas. "We're none too soon."

"They'll probably begin today," Colleen said, her expression dark.

Under the direction of Lady Gertrude Denman, the Women's Land Army would take over the agricultural work left behind as the men joined the armed forces. Some of these Land Girls would soon be arriving at Bellesford House and be billeted in the apartments above the stables.

"That's quite a gesture of patriotism," I said, trying to find a safe answer.

"Hmmm," was Colleen's noncommittal reply. "Priorities. The Taylors aren't having anyone destroying the pastures, I see. The horses will have their grass."

And, indeed, we saw close to a dozen horses grazing peacefully as we proceeded up the drive. "They seem to all be the same breed."

"Yes, she raises Irish Sport Horses. Quite athletic, I understand." She gave a thin smile. "Both her and the horses."

They were warmbloods, as she told me. Well-muscled and tall. Mostly blacks, although a few were lighter. "Not a poor man or woman's sport," I said, as we approached the entryway to the house.

"We'll wait in the car, if that's all right. The less I see of that woman, the happier I am. She will keep you waiting exactly ten minutes in the library. You can set your watch by her." She pointed to her own watch. "Ten minutes."

Denise nodded a vigorous agreement, and so I parked by the front porch and fetched my carrier of supplies. Announcing myself to the maid who answered the doorbell, I was given the once-over before being led into the main hall. The maid waited beside an immense wooden door on the right that opened into the library. "Please wait here," she said. "I shall inform Madame that you have arrived." She took her leave and I took my seat in one of the overstuffed easy chairs alongside the massive fireplace. It wasn't just the fireplace that was huge. Everything was on a grand scale. The bookshelves extended from floor to ceiling along three walls and were filled with books that were dusted more than they'd ever been read. The fourth wall, where I was seated, was occupied by the stone fireplace with a carved wooden mantel, above which hung a portrait of a woman in her prime. She was seated in a chair that appeared to be more throne than standard fare. Her red dress was carefully designed to show off her jewelry. A diamond pendant, diamond earrings, and a bracelet also weighted down with carats. All she lacked was a diamond tiara that would let her pass as royalty. I moved closer to read the artist's name in the lower righthand corner. I'll be damned, was my first thought. The signature was a bit larger than what you usually find, but then when you're *Angelo DeMontana,* it's to be expected. Fancy that. It was something to mention to Adam. How had the lady of the manor come to have DeMontana do her portrait. Interesting, indeed.

"Ten minutes," Colleen had said. I pursed my lips. All right. Ten minutes it would be. Perfect. There might not be another time. Mrs. Taylor's affectation of a busy socialite would give me an opportunity to check out the surroundings. Upon entering this room, my attention had been drawn to the closed door to my left. Closed doors within closed rooms always seem a bit odd. I left my chair and walked to the door, where a brass plate announced that this was *The Red Parlour.* I tried the handle. Locked. Locked doors mean secrets, and secrets intrigue me. I glanced at my watch. With my camera in my jacket pocket and ready to document the roses, all I needed was the right pick lock from my set inside my handbag. Within half a minute, I was inside The Red Parlour. The name must have come with the mansion, because there wasn't anything red to be found inside the room. There was, however, a mess. The room was a jumble. At first, it seemed reasonable to have the door locked to conceal the chaos, but that turned out to be not the case.

With time passing quickly, I started at the left of the door and moved clockwise, snapping pictures of each wall, the furnishings, and the contents on the library desk which I plowed through to get as much of the clutter on film as possible, and that included a calendar next to the telephone. When I'd come full circle, two more quick shots of framed photographs on a pair of side tables with lamps, and I was back in my chair in the library, The Red Parlour door closed, if not locked, and my equipment safely stowed in my bag, with a minute and fifteen seconds to spare.

And then, ten minutes to the dot, the library door opened as I was wiping a bit of perspiration from my brow. Quickly turning the action into a bit of a nose blow, I stuffed the handkerchief into my handbag and rose to greet the lady of the house.

Anne Taylor, as she introduced herself, was a more mature version of the woman in the portrait above the fireplace. "Tea will be along directly," she said.

Oh yes. Tea. Of course, and with nine more stops and as many cups to go, I felt a bit apprehensive, possibly queasy. I smiled.

"Tell me more about the project," she began. "I understand you will be taking samples of our rose bush. It's quite old, you know. The house dates back to the early 17th century and the grounds were fully landscaped at that time. Perhaps this rose is sufficiently historic for your purposes."

The tea plate with the second or third-best china arrived, and Mrs. Taylor poured. With no side table, the balancing of the teacup, saucer, and biscuit was tricky, and eventually, I gave up and ate the biscuit in one chomp. "Yes, thank you," I said, after a fast chew and swallow. "It's most gracious of you. This rose, according to the Society does indeed date from the construction of the house. It's listed as a *Rosa alba* — the White Rose of York." Mrs. Taylor's blank expression prompted a few more details. "The War of the Roses was an important event in British history, and so this rose may give us some insight into the politics of the original occupants." I took a sip of tea.

Mrs. Taylor, her expression still blank, took a final sip of her Earl Grey and wished me success. Interpreting that as my dismissal, I returned my cup to the tray, thanked my hostess, and took my leave.

Once back outside and in the custody of the gardener, I returned to Morris to get my kit from the back seat. Then, accompanying the gardener to the flower bed, clippers at hand, rooting vials prepared, and labels and pen at the ready, I snipped three cuttings and placed them in the containers. The rose had been well-tended and was healthy. Sometimes, these old roses can be a bit leggy if they haven't been pruned well. This was a beauty. It was a shame it would have to make the ultimate sacrifice for the War Effort. But, under the oversight of the Horticultural Society, it would live on. It would just begin again in a new place. Sort of like me. A transplant three times planted — Demark, America, and now England — at least for the foreseeable future. We adapt and we live. "I'll make some sketches, now," I informed the nameless gardener who, once satisfied I seemed to know what I was doing, told me he'd be working around the side yard if I needed anything.

While I had my box camera, the sketches I intended to make were best done by hand. I'm a fairly accurate technical artist. It's a necessary skill for a botanist, and I had a passing thought of my young niece Margarete who was besotted with ferns and who filled my sister's house with her sketches. They were quite well done, too, especially for a fourteen-year-old.

I'd just settled myself on the ground and flipped open the drawing pad when the sound of angry voices caught my attention. It was difficult to make out the conversation from this distance and at ground level with the stables being west of the gardens, but a man was clearly bellowing his displeasure at someone. Shortly, a woman came out the side door, and she was giving as good as she was receiving. As she made her way in my direction, closing the space between us, her voice carried clearly.

"I will visit him and touch him and you cannot stop me. He needs someone who will treat him well. Your training is cruel. You deserve what you got." She disappeared around the side of the main house.

What, I wondered, was that all about? I made my sketches, bid the war casualty goodbye, collected my things, and returned to Morris.

"Well?" Colleen asked, as we putted down the tree-lined, fenced, and graveled drive and turned onto the main road. Denise was leaning forward so as not to miss a word.

Weighing my response, I hesitated.

"Right," Colleen said. "I don't trust her either, and judging from that final scene, there are secrets here."

I glanced at my handbag. I needed to get the film from The Red Parlour developed as soon as possible. "Perhaps some of those secrets will reveal themselves, given a bit of time," I said. "At least, we've saved one rose."

The rest of our morning stops proceeded in a less dramatic fashion, with most folks not being home but with the dutifully signed permission slip provided for them by the Society taped to the front door.

"This last stop I'm taking you to before we stop for a bite," Colleen said, then hesitated. "They do have roses." She paused. "They're not heirlooms, but the residents don't know that. They are devoted to birds. Never without their binoculars, in case some specimen or other flies by. They're a bit gaga. They get on all right, though. They have lists everywhere to remind them what they need to do. And they have a housekeeper to keep tabs on them. You'll see what I mean."

"I'm staying in the car," Denise said. "No way in hell am I setting foot in that house ever again."

My interest ratcheted up a notch.

Douglas Hyde-Stuart and Miranda Hainesworth lived in a charming cottage that looked like something out of a fairy tale. Thatched roof, bird boxes scattered about the garden, a tangle of wildflowers, a white picket fence, and the roses, of course. The elves and fairies from the deep woods probably spent their vacations there.

I was admiring the blue door and the blue wood trim that framed the two upper and ground floor windows. Admiring, that is, with a stooped posture, as the porch roof was a good three inches shorter than my height. The doorknocker was a bronze woodpecker, its beak delivering the rap that announced our presence.

We waited a minute or so and then knocked again. This time, a voice from inside called out, "Come straight in. Don't let Peeps out, if you don't mind. He's having his midday airing," a female voice said.

Sure enough. Peeps was airing his rather large body by striding up and down the parlor floor and regarding us with a baleful stare. Peeps was not a chicken. Peeps was a fully mature Macaw the size of a Christmas goose and possessed of a voice that could outshriek an artillery battalion. He did not look friendly.

"Is he friendly?" I asked, shifting my handbag in front of me as a sort of barrier in case of attack. Whipping out the stiletto or my service pistol would have offered more protection but also would have blown my mission. An inglorious way to end a career. I figured if push came to shove, I could swing the handbag over my head like a lariat and give the bird a resounding whack, stunning it while we ran for cover.

"Friendly? Not especially, no," the voice replied. "He does take a while to warm up to guests if he decides it's worth it. Have a seat. I'll be right there. I'm fixing his elevenses."

I looked at Colleen. "I think I'll stand."

"Good decision. I'm with you on that."

A few minutes later, not ten as with our first stop, a grey-haired woman with a walking stick emerged from what I suspected was the kitchen. She had a plate with an apple that had been cut into wedges, and I assumed we were not the intended consumers. Peeps confirmed that deduction with a series of wing flaps and intensified squawking before hopping over to his elevenses.

"Now, that's done," the woman said, wiping her hands on an apron. "Isn't he just lovely?"

"Yes," I said. "Lovely. I'm Dr. Katrin Nissen. I've been sent by the Horticultural Society to take a cutting of your beautiful rose bush. We'll plant it in safe quarters and make sure that it survives the war with no damage."

"That's lovely," Miranda said. "It's outside."

"Yes. Yes, it is," I said. "I'll just pop outside then and take my cutting and be on my way."

"Are you taking Mrs. Richardson with you?"

"Definitely."

"Good. Peeps doesn't like her overly much. Lovely to meet you." She smiled and returned to the kitchen, leaving us to fend off Peeps who had finished his elevenses and was looking more threatening by the moment.

"Shall we?" I said to Colleen.

"I'm right behind you. Don't slow down."

The cutting took just a moment and we were back in Morris, heading to the pub for fish and chips. I bet Peeps would have killed for our lunch. Killed us, that is. Sometimes, an escape is a victory.

"I told you," Colleen said, sprinkling malt vinegar on her chips.

"You did. Now tell me the real reason we went there."

"All right. Again, it's just a feeling — a sense, if you will." She looked at Denise for affirmation. "You saw the way Miranda greeted us. Or didn't greet us, would be more correct. She's like that always with the locals. I mean those of us who've been here forever. It's different with the newcomers, though, and she and her companion,

Douglas Hyde-Stuart, can be counted among them. People are always coming and going. I'm confident that that vicious Peeps isn't running around as a watchbird at those times." She leaned forward and lowered her voice. "She doesn't want *us* inside, and she uses that bird to be sure we don't stay. Why? That's the question." She sat back and took a sip from her pint, waiting for my answer.

"Do they go out at all, or does everyone come to them?"

"I believe the latter, although Douglas is a consultant for the British Museum and pops over to London from time to time. Why do you ask?"

I'd picked up a chip and was about to take a bite but put it back on my plate. "Why, indeed?" I wondered aloud. "Perhaps they feel isolated and have chosen to socialize with others who haven't been living in Ipswich for so long. Or, perhaps these 'newcomers' have more in common than a move that put them all here by chance. Perhaps," I reclaimed my chip, "they're here by design."

With nothing left on my plate, but a great deal to digest, I returned Colleen and Denise to their homes and Morris and I raced back to the Scupper—petrol coupons be damned—after a brief stop for groceries. It had been a long, tiring day, and having a bite of supper in the hotel room was more appealing than dragging myself to the pub. I didn't expect John to show up tonight, after a full day of investigative work in London. If he

KAREN K. BREES 167

did show, though, the cold cuts, cheese, rolls, and bottle of wine would easily stretch for two.

Traffic was light, and Morris and I drove down the side alley and found a cozy parking spot in the dirt lot close to the rear entrance of the hotel. I pulled into an empty spot next to a delivery truck. Shutting off the ignition, I grabbed my handbag and trudged over to the back door of the hotel.

It was past eight o'clock—20 hundred hours by the official clock. The desk clerk gave a faint look of recognition this time, although it wasn't an overly friendly look. She gave me the once-over before retrieving my mail from the slot. I checked the seal on the envelope. The faint puckering along the edge of the mucilage was all I needed to know. All right, then. I ran my finger along the seal, looking at her all the while. She'd opened my mail. I said nothing, merely tapped the envelope against my hand, and I felt her eyes boring into me as I left. Various scenarios played out in my mind. Was she another "newcomer" to the area, keeping tabs on the comings and goings of traffic at the docks and checking on the business of guests at the Inn? It was possible. And if she were, I needed to encourage her interest in me. It might lead to something. Time would tell.

Back in the relative safety of my room, I dropped the mail on the bed and did a brief washup before settling down to read what "Mama" had sent. The envelope contained a birthday card with a short note, "Happy Birthday, dear Katrin." Nothing unusual, except the note was written in German: *Alles Gute zum Geburtstag, liebe Katrin.* If this worked to flush out a contact, that would help the mission, no end. I took out my notepad and wrote down as detailed description of the desk clerk as I could. I wasn't sure Berthe Baumgartner was her real name, and if it were an alias, a German name was not the best choice. All I knew for sure was that she suspected I was German and was here either to check up on her or was on a mission of my own. I was gambling she'd try to find out which one it was. And that would mean she'd be searching my room first chance she had, and then contacting someone who knew the answer. She was going on the list. Not too shabby for Day Number One. All I could hope for was that it would be a portent of things to come.

Funny thing about portents, however. I could have sworn a portent was a good thing. Now, I'm not so sure. Omen, maybe, would be a better choice of word. I decided to pour myself a glass of wine, and after staring at the table that held my handbag, realized I'd left the damn grocery bag in the car. So, two choices. One, go hungry. Not a good choice. Number two, haul my tired body back out to Morris and retrieve the goods. The only choice there really was.

Mostly, I'm careful. It's a requirement in my line of work. There's an occasional lapse, of course.

I'm only human, and today sort of fell between the cracks. To be blunt, I got lucky. And tonight, being careful probably saved my life. I debated just taking the car keys out of my handbag to lighten the load, but that little voice that sets me on the straight and narrow from time to time let me know this was a bad idea. So, I grabbed the handbag and walked what felt like two kilometers to the lot and Morris. This time Berthe didn't look up as I passed by.

I got the groceries, gave a cursory look around and, not seeing anything untoward, locked the door, tossed the key into my handbag and made for the back door with a purposeful stride. Between the short time I'd gone out to the car and back, Berthe had locked the door. I sighed. And it wasn't one of those theatrical sighs done for effect either. It was as real as a sigh gets. Why is it when you're dog-tired, it seems to take forever to get anything done? No answer from my brain, so I turned and trudged across the lot to the alley and was nearly to the main drag when I heard it.

"Hey, fat-girl!"

Damn. Where the hell had that come from? I in no way looked like a whore. It didn't matter. It was here now. People melt into the shadows on the docks, and it was dusk. Not late, but late enough for shadows. This would have been a good time for a bobby to be making his rounds, but that would be too much to hope for. Shifting my handbag towards my chest, I kept walking. Kept walking, that is, until a rough hand grabbed my shoulder and yanked me around.

"Let go of me," I said, with as much authority as my tired voice could muster. I activated the spring mechanism on my handbag, releasing my stiletto, my weapon of choice for these types of unexpected situations. It's quieter than my service revolver. "I said, let go of me." I really wasn't expecting he would, but it was worth a shot.

Instead, he laughed.

"Last chance," I said. When I finally got a look at him, my heart sank. This was one big bruiser, and he wasn't going to do anything I told him to. In fact, he was probably the type that got his jollies from a bit of resistance.

"Let's go, fat-girl. I'm going to enjoy this." He swung me around and pushed me forward. "Drop the bag. You won't be needing it."

He was right. I dropped the groceries on his foot. It didn't make any impression on him. Not a good sign. He raised his other hand to strike, and that's when I flashed the stiletto. He stepped back, releasing me just long enough to pull a knife from his belt. Final warnings are just that. In the instant that he moved his arm to cut my throat, I was just a second faster. I was quite fond of my throat, actually, and had every intention of keeping it intact. But one second was all I needed.

The problem with slitting someone's throat is the blood. There's so much of it, and it spurts everywhere. It's a mess. So, I opted for the bloodless route. Behind the clavicle and straight down to the heart. He was dead before he hit the ground.

I looked at the inert form lying at my feet. *You didn't even know me.* The thought ran through my mind like some sort of runaway train. *You didn't even know me.* I was an object. I wasn't a woman. And that kind of thinking is what led to the evils we were facing from Hitler. When it's convenient, just decide the person you're facing isn't a person at all, but something inferior. Something not worthy of life. I took a deep breath. Whoever this man had been, he would hurt no one else, but I'd carry the scar with me. This was not the time to ponder deep thoughts, however. *Get the hell out of here and don't look back*, my mind told me. And so, I did just that. Retrieving my slightly rumpled grocery bag and returning my stiletto to its case in the handbag, I briefly studied the man's face. There was no "aha" moment of recognition. He was a stranger to me.

With an abrupt about-face, I returned to the main street and approached the hotel from the front. Schlepping my bags across the foyer, I passed the desk clerk behind the counter and didn't bother with the small talk. I trod down the corridor to my room. This was actually some sort of record for me. I'd been officially on assignment two days and the body count—not mine, thankfully—had begun.

I fell into the threadbare easy chair, leaning my head back and closing my eyes to blot out the memory of killing the man who would have killed me. Just another day at the office.

Murder is a routine occurrence on the waterfront. There wasn't really any reason to expect the police to come door to door, interrogating everyone within a defined perimeter. More likely, the killing wouldn't be considered anything more than a debt repaid or some other business dealing of the underworld either gone wrong or rectified. It made no difference to me, although now, with the adrenaline having subsided, I counted my blessings and hoped the body would have been taken away before Morris and I set out in the morning.

And then, I considered the issue of timing. Pressing my fingers against my throbbing temples, I went back over the whole episode, scene by scene. Everything had been business as usual until

I claimed my mail and noticed that the envelope had been steamed open, the contents obviously read, and the envelope resealed. In the time it took to process that, the desk clerk and I had made eye contact, and I believe she was the first to blink.

The next time I'd tried the back door, it was locked, forcing me to take a short walk in the twilight. With blackout rules and regulations firmly in place, I would have needed my torch had I waited any longer. As it was, the shadows were creeping in, along with the creeps.

The question that I couldn't ignore was one I'd dealt with before. Had the desk clerk decided that the easiest way to deal with me was to be rid of me? It was an interesting premise, and if it were true, the attack was not random. My cover hadn't been blown. I was confident about that, but something else was at work here, and I didn't know what it was. Yet.

And then I poured the wine.

CHAPTER FIFTEEN

Lincoln, England

The trip to Lincoln Cathedral was not a trip John was looking forward to, but making it on the Harley-Davidson WLA took much of the edge off. The bike had blackout head and tail lights, a luggage rack, an ammo box that he didn't expect to need, a Thompson machine gun scabbard, and other embellishments. The other option had been the NortonWD BIG4, Britain's alternative to the Harley, but the additional weight of the sidecar and the altered center of gravity didn't work in its favor.

Motorcycles were his favored mode of transportation. It was the freedom they afforded, and, given a choice, John opted for a bike every time. What most people preferred about automobiles, the security of being enclosed and away from the elements, was the exact reason John didn't fancy them. There is time on a bike. You're apart from the traffic, maneuvering through it but you don't belong to it, and John's thoughts wandered, even as his eyes kept their focus on the road ahead. On a bike, you're free, and enclosed spaces triggered memories he'd worked hard to suppress. When they got back to the States, he and Katrin would take that road trip they'd been talking about. She loved motorcycles almost as much as he did. She was a good rider— "fender fluff" — she called herself, when she rode on the back. He liked the feel of her arms around his waist. He liked it so much, in fact, that he'd proposed to her on their first ride together. He smiled, but that was for another time, and he pushed those thoughts aside.

Today's trip to Lincoln and the cathedral of the same name, or more completely, The Cathedral Church of the Blessed Virgin Mary of Lincoln, would take the better part of three hours and possibly longer. The cathedral dated from the 11th century. Originally Roman Catholic, it was now Church of England. It had once been the tallest building in England, and even today, it had a presence. The structure, with its spires pointing heavenward, seemed to have been intended to pierce the skies. John studied the building, not with any religious interest, but with an eye towards possible sites of breaking and entering. It appeared to be a futile exercise. The cathedral almost seemed like a tomb, sealed against any possible breach. With one last look, he approached the office where he would have to break the news to the administrator, Louis Brattleby. With Dean of the Cathedral, R. A. Mitchell being out of town, Brattleby would be the one to inform that the copy they had sent to the World's Fair was a forgery. How that would play out was anyone's guess, but it wasn't going to be well-received. Of that he was sure.

"So, Detective Chief Inspector," Brattleby began, "what is this matter of extreme importance that brings you to Lincoln Cathedral?"

Sometimes, John thought, in fact most times, when the news is bad, it's best to just lay it out there and get it over with. "It concerns your copy of Magna Carta that was shipped to the United States. It's been stolen and replaced with a forgery." He waited. What happened next was a pale imitation of Churchill's outburst when he'd been given the same news, but then, everything Churchill did was on the grand scale.

Brattleby was a rather oily fellow. John couldn't think of another way to describe him. His pale skin had a sheen to it, and the man seemed intent on removing it with the handkerchief wadded in his left hand. "Are you mad?" Brattleby wiped his forehead. "You're obviously mistaken. That copy is on display at the World's Fair and has been since April of last year." He wiped his left cheek. "What sort of joke is this? Who sent you?" Louis Brattleby was incensed, outraged, in fact.

Answering the last question in Brattleby's list was easy. "The Prime Minister, Winston Churchill, sent me. And I have the documentation for you." John opened his attaché case and removed the folder that held Franta's report and a letter signed by Churchill, confirming the theft. Additionally, the letter instructed the administrator that the news was to remain confidential for national security reasons. "I'll give you a few moments to study this. It's quite a bit to digest."

As the administrator read first the report and then the letter, John watched whatever color remained drain from the man's face. His hands were shaking so badly he had to stuff the handkerchief in his pocket before he set the letter down on the desk and fell into his office chair to finish reading it there.

"Those damned Americans!" He slammed a fist on the desk. "They swore their security was top notch! They swore nothing would happen to Magna Carta on their watch!" His volume was increasing but he had a long way to go before he'd give Churchill any competition.

"Sir, it didn't happen in America," John interrupted. "The Magna Carta was stolen from here, sometime in the two days before it was shipped."

Brattleby had gone speechless. His mouth opened and closed like a fish on the line, but no sound was forthcoming. You learn to read people when they're presented with the details of a crime, and John would bet all three of his official credentials that the man's reaction was genuine. As soon as he'd gotten back some control, they needed to move on with this.

"Sir, if you're finished with those documents, I'll need them back."

Silently, Brattleby handed them over.

"I'll need to see where Magna Carta was displayed prior to being wrapped for shipping."

A weak nod was the first sign that the administrator was coming around. He pulled himself up from his chair more by willpower than by conscious act and retrieved the handkerchief which he used to blot his chin. "Of course. Follow me." His eyes averted from the empty case, the administrator waited at the entrance to the hall while John searched the room.

The hall where Magna Carta once resided was vast and well-lit. The windows were what one would expect in such a setting. The furnishings were absent, save for a large glass case positioned on a wooden table. The case was empty, the area surrounding it housing a display dedicated to the document's history, the cathedral's history, and their historical relationship. A large placard, a recent addition to the display, explained the reason for the document's absence.

While he didn't expect to find anything, but going through the motions nonetheless, John began at the entrance, looking for possible angles of entry or scuff marks on the floor that might have been caused by equipment being dragged along. There was nothing. The theft had occurred over a year ago, and time is the enemy of detection. "Were any keys reported missing? Anything out of place when the exhibit opened the next day?"

"No. Everything was perfectly normal," Brattleby said, as if by denying that something had been as far from normal as possible would somehow negate the fact that Magna Carta had disappeared from under his appointed watch.

Giving one last look around, John had been about ready to call the search a failure, but then, just as he turned to leave, the overhead lights flickered. "Does that happen often?" he asked.

"Does what happen often?"

"The lights flickering. Does that happen often?"

"It didn't use to. It does occasionally now. Why do you ask?"

John ignored the question as he moved back to the wall and walked its length, checking each wall outlet. By the time he'd reached the third wall, he'd found what he'd been hoping to find. He snapped a photo of the wall outlet and then photos of the entire room, from that spot. Returning the camera to the attaché case, he walked back to the entrance. "I'd like to see the security logs for April of last year."

The expression on the administrator's face was a mix of annoyance and puzzlement, but he nodded briefly and led the way to the storeroom where shelves along both walls were filled with cardboard boxes, each labeled by month and year. John pulled the box labeled *April 1939* from the shelf and set it on the work table in the center of the room. He looked around and then at the administrator. "I'll need a chair, if you would be so kind," he said.

Brattleby looked around the room as if one might materialize and save him the trip back to an office. "I'll be back in a moment," he said.

With Franta's estimated dates in mind, and the chair ready for occupancy, John sat at the desk and began his search, starting on the 12th of April. The logs contained entries made by the guards after each security round, done on the hour. There were notations of when the cleaning staff clocked in and out, and finally, listings of maintenance issues.

On April 12th at 1700 hours, the power had gone out in the exhibit hall. The security guard noted that no one was viewing the displays at that time, and so he felt free to leave briefly to report the outage to building maintenance. The problem was determined to be a blown circuit and was quickly repaired. John closed the log and returned it to the box.

"Thank you for your time."

"Anything we can do to assist…"

With a brief handshake and a final reminder, a warning actually, that secrecy was the order of the day, John took his leave. There were definitely further questions, but none the administrator could answer. Who had been in the exhibit hall, unseen, at 1700 hours on April 12th of last year? That person, John would wager any amount, was the one who had stolen the Magna Carta, leaving no trace behind except for a scorched wall plug where he had inserted a device that shorted out the power just long enough to switch the documents and disappear back into the crowd outside the hall. Someone who understood electricity. But who?

. . .

"The thief had to move then or face the possibility of not being able to pull it off in New York City where security would be first priority," John said, as he dropped his attaché case on the floor and his body into the chair next to the small table by the sofa. Adam had returned to his rooms for the night, and the day's debriefing was underway. "Our thief was confident nobody would discover the switch. I think," John said, "that once he knew the forgery had been uneventfully unpacked and exhibited in New York, he'd have enough time to steal the rest at his leisure without being found out."

Adam drummed his fingers on the desk as if each tap were a thought, with each thought leading to the only logical conclusion. "The bomb went off at the World's Fair on July 4th," he said. "The goal was to destroy the entire exhibit. That would have accomplished several things. It would have prevented anyone from discovering the forgery, of course, and it also would have increased the individual value of each of the three surviving copies."

"If these were intended for private auction, that would be a nice bonus," John said. "Or, taking another tack, by using the American Independence Day to destroy a document linked to the foundations of Western law, it might have been designed to demonstrate power and control."

"Hitler," Adam said, "or his toadies, the Bund. But that sounds too subtle for them. They lack finesse."

"Then, someone using Hitler's game plan for his own purposes. Our thief, again? It would have been convenient, to say the least. When was the date the last delivery truck disappeared?" John rubbed his forehead, trying to remember what Churchill's last briefing had told them. "It was July 4th. Somebody's got a macabre sense of humor."

"A game? This is a fucking game?"

"I just don't know," John said. "But we need to find out. It's more than theft. There's more to this plan than we know right now. What does our thief have in mind?"

"You've got me there. I am not a psychologist."

"No," John said. "But if intuition can help, I'll go check in with Katrin tomorrow. See what she's turned up. Sometimes, she can read a situation better than any so-called expert."

CHAPTER SIXTEEN

Port Hope and Colchester

The '35 grey Austin Coupe was nothing fancy. Not too new. Not too old. He'd chosen it for its bland appearance. It would have been a good idea, but rationing petrol had sent people back to bicycles and buses, and any car on the roads was subject to scathing looks from patriotic Brits who had given up driving for the duration. As he turned onto the A1124 and houses became farther apart, vehicles became even more of a rarity.

Checking to see if anyone was behind him, he caught a glimpse of his face in the rearview mirror. The scar that ran from his eye and down his left cheek had faded over time. He had to look hard to even see it. His hair was longer now, and without the frequent application of dyes, the pale blond color with a hint of grey came as something of a surprise. Use enough aliases and enough disguises, and eventually your own name doesn't ring true to your ears and you don't recognize yourself.

The Abwehr had one list they used for him; MI6 had another. This time, he was using the name they'd least expect: Erdmann Speer. Minus the "Reverend" of course. That was a part of his past he'd never reclaim. God was a farce and prayer meant nothing. If Satan had his soul, so be it. God didn't want it, but He'd taken everything else that had ever mattered.

Speer ground the cigarette butt into the ashtray, glancing at the paperwork on the passenger seat. He'd reproduced the diagram of Hitler's Führermuseum from memory and had put a check mark against everything he'd been contracted to get — with one exception, and an important exception it was. Once he had that, every item on the shopping list would be accounted for, and according to Hyde-Stuart, the painting was scheduled to move to another temporary location tomorrow. Speer gripped the steering wheel more tightly. Four more days. It would be the last visit. Given the current circumstances, regular habits could turn on you, but the payout when all this was done would be enough. More than enough. One more painting. One more assignment for the Italian. One more delivery. If today's visit to the Italian went the way it should, everything would be crated up and the lorry would take it to the ship tomorrow and in three days the lot would be in Berlin. With the exception of that one last piece that was playing hard to get. It was another Constable, and the broker in Berlin had negotiated a handsome price for it. The damn Brits and their constant shuffling of the art from one place to another was creating problems. Move a piece here, then there, then back again. It was like a chess match played by drunkards. There was no order. It was sheer mayhem, and it made keeping track of the inventory difficult. Last week's reported location of the Constable was no longer accurate. Hyde-Stuart had proven to be less than reliable, and if this report turned out to be bogus, Hyde-Stuart was finished. Speer stretched his thin lips across his teeth in a caricature of a smile. Yes. He'd enjoy that.

Twenty-nine paintings plus the four Magna Cartas were a damn good haul, nonetheless, and a large part of the satisfaction was knowing that der Führer would be furnishing his England Room in the Führermuseum with a shitload of fakes. Every picture. Every copy of the Magna Carta. Every bloody one of them a reproduction. God, he'd love to be a fly on the wall the day they were proudly installed, dutifully authenticated. Authentication. He slammed on the brakes.

The bloody hell. Fuck. He'd been so caught up in the acquisitions, he'd forgotten the final step. Shit. A horn bleated, and he started up again. Now. Someone had seen him. What else could go wrong? One more expense in this private venture.

A rush job for anything is always expensive. This was going to make a major dent in the profit, *if,* and it was a big *if.* If he could even find someone on short notice. There was just one hope. Perhaps the Italian knew someone who could be bought. He probably did. In his line of work, he needed an authenticator frequently. Everyone had a price, and after the paintings had been authenticated, the expert wouldn't be needed any further, nor would he be needing his fee. The situation was salvageable, after all. Hitler wouldn't have a clue.

Hitler was an artist of sorts in his own right. His work was pedestrian, but he was knowledgeable enough to necessitate the expense of hiring DeMontana to do the copies. The man was a genius, he granted him that, and even if he hadn't, DeMontana reminded him of the fact at every opportunity. Catering to that genius, however, was taxing Speer's wallet. So far, it had all been outlay against a projected windfall of millions. Tens of millions. No matter. One more painting and then he'd be sitting out the War somewhere far from the chaos. He'd done his part for both sides. It was time to let the drama play out from a safe location. He looked at the shopping list once more. He had drawn circle after circle around the painting that still eluded him, pressing so hard he'd broken the pencil point. Turning off onto a side road, Speer allowed the car behind him to pass before making a U-turn and proceeding. The car was probably safe, but it was best not to take chances.

.   .   .

Castel del Mare II, Angelo DeMontana's country estate in Colchester was one of The Master's numerous residences scattered about the world. Speer knew of at least three others. There was one in Italy, one in France, and one somewhere on an island in the South Pacific. DeMontana flitted from one to the next as the mood took him, and his preferred mode of transportation was his sailing vessel, a seventy-foot beauty he'd christened *Carpe Ventum*. His all-female crew lived aboard when they weren't under sail, although there were frequent day excursions to the estate when that mood took DeMontana's fancy. He was a man of various moods and possessed the extreme wealth that gave him the freedom to indulge all of them.

This estate's formal gardens were divided into various "rooms", as DeMontana referred to them. Meandering paths roamed the flower beds, orchards, an orangery, and expansive lawns—all with stone walls defining their borders. Everything was a testimony to symmetry, gentility, and refinement. DeMontana was not enamored of either gentility or refinement, but he did tend towards an appreciation of symmetry in his art. His life was a testimony to the benefits of random breeding. He was a bear of a man with appetites that he enjoyed satisfying whenever the opportunity presented, with wine and women predominant among those pleasures, and when Speer was welcomed into the house by a young scantily uniformed maid, he found DeMontana so engaged. A naked woman was standing by the window, holding the curtain aside with her right hand and stretching as if hoping to see something just outside her view. Her long, dark hair fell in a braid down her back. The Master was absorbed in sketching her.

"Lovely, my sweet. Lean forward just a little. No! Too much! Just enough so that your breasts catch the light from the window. Ah! Yes. Much better. Turn just slightly to your left. No, love. The other way. Yes. Yes. Bellissima!"

"I see you're hard at work on what I'm paying you for!" Speer said.

"Life is about balance, signore," DeMontana said, his eyes still fixed on his model. He gave a dramatic sigh and set his brush down. "Cover up, dearest. I'll be upstairs soon!"

The girl released the curtain and donned a robe draped across the chair. As she passed DeMontana, he slapped her on the bum. She giggled.

"You are supposed to be finishing up," Speer said.

"Inspiration comes unexpectedly, signore, and in many guises." DeMontana sighed, his expression one of pure or perhaps impure satisfaction. "However, I am finished, as I said I would be."

"Who is she?" Speer gestured towards the staircase.

DeMontana shrugged. "A woman. There is nothing more of any importance to concern you."

"Some women have brains."

"I try to stay from those. Do not worry, signore. Worry makes for a short, unhappy life."

.   .   .

"Absolutely not. I forbid it." Angelo DeMontana was incensed, which usually meant some object or another would find itself being hurled across the room. In this case it was a minor assault on the far wall with a wine glass that shattered into enough pieces to inspire the creation of a mosaic at some future date. He regarded the shards with some interest, before returning his attention to Speer and the reason for the outburst.

"You cannot wrap these. You will destroy them. The oils must set for two weeks, minimum. They are soft. You will end up with mush—like English porridge. No. It cannot be done."

"Do your best. Wrap them as you must. The fools who get them will never know the difference."

"But I will, signore. I have few scruples and no inhibitions, but this I cannot—will not— allow. You must wait. I will let you know when they are ready. Do not fear. I have no desire to do anything beyond what you see here. I have no intentions of crossing you. You must trust me. I am only doing this for the art. This, and only this, is my concern. You deal with your schedules as you must, but the art—that is for me to decide."

Angelo DeMontana was a large man. Not muscular, but big of frame. He met Speer's gaze straight on. "How much art does der Führer need? I have been creating for the past three months. Ten each month as was our arrangement—minus the one you couldn't locate but for which I expect payment, nonetheless. I am quite satisfied with your patronage, but I am wondering where all this," his arm swept expansively about the room where paintings were on easels, leaning against the walls, and generally strewn about much as the glass shards, "is really going." He raised a quizzical eyebrow at his patron.

"It's none of your concern. Does it really matter? Who really cares, anyhow? Once the flak settles, it's all going to boil down to how to make a buck or a pound. We just need to wait out the war someplace far from it. And it's not the first collection to be sold under the table."

"I have the Magna Cartas prepared for the auction. They will be delivered by courier on the date you have specified. Frankly, signore," DeMontana said, "I will be most relieved to have them out of here. I have never overly enjoyed being in the presence of any vestige of legality, regardless of its age."

Speer, finally resigned to DeMontana's position, dropped into the easy chair to the right of the easel. DeMontana removed the canvas of the woman and set it aside. He walked to the dining room table and retrieved a small Rembrandt, taking it to the easel where he positioned and admired it.

Speer studied the copy. "Is it accurate enough?" His tone was dubious.

"I am wounded." DeMontana grasped his chest with both hands. "How can you say such things? Besides," he winked, his mood taking an abrupt swing, "I know how this works and how much you can believe in things if you want to. The ones who have ordered these paintings, believe. Belief, and of course, greed, are an unbeatable combination. The brush strokes, the artistry, the essence of the thing." He pointed at a section of the canvas.

"I make them slightly more intense to convey power." DeMontana traced a section of the canvas with an index finger. "I improve on the original. Do you see these cracks in the oils? It can take half a century for these cracks to appear, and they add evidence of authenticity. My mixture of oils and water-based liquids artificially ages these works. Poof! They are now cracked! Genius! I am a genius! Then," he continued, "I fill the cracks with umber. Age means dirt. I wipe everything down and finish with a coat of varnish. Is anyone going to question my work? My talent? I am The Master!" DeMontana laughed, decanted a bottle of wine he'd set on the floor, looked around for the glass, then realized it was now in pieces by the fireplace. "An excellent Bordeaux. My own label." He raised the bottle.

"Authentication?" Speer said.

DeMontana waved a dismissive hand. "My work will be authenticated without difficulty. The experts don't want to be exposed as fools, or suffer a worse fate in regards to Germany." He took a healthy swig and wiped his mouth with the stained sleeve of his smock. "And the originals? Where do they go?"

Speer rose from his chair, ignoring the last question. "Speaking of authentication, get me someone to do the work. Get them ready as quickly as you can. There is not much time."

"This is the first I have heard of this, Signore," de Montana said. "Oh, do not worry. These are minor details but they also will take time. Yes, but now perhaps the wait is more than a week." He threw his hands in the air.

Frustrated, Speer tossed a final look around the room, just as a black cat entered and made for its accustomed bed by the fireplace, ignoring the glass as if it were nothing unusual at all.

"Angelo?" a voice called from the top of the stairs. "I'm lonesome."

"Coming, my sweet." He turned to Speer. "You can find your way out? Good." He left without waiting for an answer.

How the hell was he going to find one more week? Or longer? God. Who had the bigger ego, Hitler or DeMontana? It was a tossup. The whole thing was getting out of control. One problem just led to another. Now, there was the problem of telling the Schneider woman about the delay and listening to her hysterics. He'd telephone her. Less chance of her going on forever with her histrionics. He could always break the connection. It was safe to telephone now. The new operator could be trusted. Then, the shipping arrangements would have to be altered. He ran his fingers through his hair. There was nothing else for it but to start over and hope to hell he had another week. And he still had to find the goddamn Constable.

· · ·

The call to Anna Schneider went as he'd expected, and now he held the receiver at arm's length while she threw her tantrum.

"What the hell do you mean I have to hang on to these another week? Are you insane? Every day those things are here, the danger increases. The Land Girls arrive in three days, and they'll be all over the place. Nothing will be secure." Her voice grew desperate. "And the cocktail party can't be postponed. The cleaning staff is working today. Do you have any idea what's involved in getting MPs to attend? It's a nightmare. Their schedules are made up months in advance. It can't be postponed. Suppose someone stumbles across them while the artwork is here?"

Speer returned the telephone receiver to his ear. "That's enough. You'll do what you're told and you'll make sure that nobody finds them." He slammed the receiver back in the cradle and drummed his fingers on the desk. Too many details to clean up.

The ship was sailing tomorrow. The captain had made it clear there would be no allowances for changes in plans. So now, in addition to everything else, he needed a ship, a crew, and favorable winds. It was too much to hope for. The crew he could get at any of the pubs on the docks if he paid them enough. The ship was another matter. He needed a sailboat with an auxiliary engine in case the winds didn't cooperate. He slammed his hands on the desk and set off to the docks to see what he could rent or steal. Then he'd have to meet with Hyde-Stuart and Hainesworth. More details. More chances for things to go wrong.

CHAPTER SEVENTEEN

Ipswich and Port Hope

It must have been after midnight when exhaustion finally overcame my restlessness, my thoughts finally settled, and I drifted off to a dreamless sleep. Shortly before seven the next morning, I awoke to the sounds of traffic on the street. I stretched and lay abed for a few minutes, feeling every muscle in my body rebel at the physical exertion. I ached all over and I was hungry. Last night's slim rations hadn't been enough, and I was craving a cup of coffee and a donut. What were my chances?

As it turned out, my chances were excellent, and that was good because I wasn't moving all that quickly this morning. My shoulder where I'd been grabbed was throbbing like a broken castanet, and the rest of me was sore from being twisted and wrenched. I dressed with effort, but before breakfast, I walked to the telephone on the corner and placed a call to Whitehall, requesting a courier. No questions were asked of me, a necessary precaution given that public telephones were not secure. With an estimated wait time of two hours, I rang off and then set out on the quest for food.

Two shops down the street was Frankie's American Diner, and the large window streetside was awash in decorative art consisting of a hamburger with all the trimmings on a bun the size of Manhattan and accompanied by a chocolate milkshake. That wasn't morning fare, but it augured well for breakfast.

Frankie's offered decent fare for homesick Americans and Brits wishing to expand their culinary horizons, but its essential purpose was as a front for MI6. It was a place for agents to check in, report any intelligence they'd gathered, and get backup or other assistance as needed. This morning, all I wanted was breakfast. Grabbing a copy of *The Daily Mirror* to get caught up with the news, I settled into the first available booth. The cup and saucer, napkin and spoon were waiting for coffee to make them complete, and the coffee came immediately, the waitress, Billie, already having the pot in her hand.

The coffee was a thin liquid that may have met the acquaintance of a coffee bean sometime in its life, but they hadn't gotten along, and the relationship never took off. Regardless, necessity rules, and I took a healthy swallow and nearly choked when I saw the headline: *Convicted*

Murderer Found Dead on the Waterfront. The details were sketchy, but a man named Ollie Wilson, convicted of the rape and murder of seven women had escaped from custody while being transported to HMP Shepton Mallet, a maximum security prison. The body had been discovered behind the Rusty Scupper Hotel by a guest returning from a night on the town. Authorities were investigating.

"You think they're investigating?" the waitress commented, leaning over my shoulder to read. She straightened and topped off my coffee. "They're celebrating. That bloke killed a Copper's wife. Investigating, my aunty Rose!"

I watched my waitress return to the counter to impart the good news to the customers. I felt somehow vindicated, not that I'd needed vindication. I'd fought for my life. But now, as I waited for my donut to arrive, I took a more leisurely sip from my cup, and thought how, in a way, I'd avenged those other women who had died and saved the law-abiding citizenry the expense of feeding and housing a killer. Fate is strange and it's fickle. Some days, it all works out.

The donut was chocolate and chewy and balanced out the mediocre coffee. One more day with the roses, and I'd have everyone on the list scoped out. That was on tomorrow's agenda. Today, it was the marinas and the docks along the waterfront, checking the status of moored vessels, new arrivals, and imminent departures. Captain

Brunner's information had indeed proved accurate, and last night, the Luftwaffe had engaged the Royal Air Force over the English Channel for the first of God alone knew how many nights to come. The Battle of Britain had begun, and no ships with valuable cargo would venture out unless they were confident they'd either be across the Channel or out to sea before dusk, when the bombs would fall and the planes would begin a macabre dance of death in the skies above London.

I lingered over breakfast, not because the donut was so great, but because I had an unobstructed view of the street and the sidewalks. There wasn't much going on. People knew what was coming, and while there was no way to prevent damage, there were some precautions that could be made. Many of the dinghies had been hauled away to safer locations, and dock carts, loaded to the gills with personal belongings and anything that could be offloaded from the private vessels, were also abandoning ship and the marina, seeking safety, as well. The larger, commercial vessels — the tankers and cargo ships had no choice but to hope they'd be spared. There were no guarantees.

Taking a final sip of coffee, I decided it was worth a walk down the length of the main dock and a check of the side docks to get an idea of what might be the intended carrier for the stolen art and Magna Cartas. Stopping just long enough to drop the newspaper on the counter for someone else to read, I was just about to the door when I caught a glimpse of a man apparently engaged in the same activity I had planned for myself. A tall man was standing on the main walkway in front of a large sailboat. He could have been a banker or a barrister judging by his attire. He wasn't dressed like any of the workmen, and he didn't have the sense of ownership of someone checking on his boat. He moved towards the side dock and continued his examination of the craft. By the third step he had taken, I noted that he had a slight limp, and my heart began to thump loudly enough that I wondered if anyone else could hear it. There was nowhere to go to escape recognition, should he decide to enter the diner or look through the window as he passed by. Once again, however, Fate had other plans. A burly fellow wearing a striped jersey and workpants and a grimy neckerchief tied around his throat, called out from the next dock down, and Ronin left the sailboat and walked over to meet him.

· · ·

The grace period might not last long, but when Fate hands you a gift, it's best to take it.

As soon as their backs were turned, I slipped out the front door and put some distance between us as quickly as I could without looking as if I was trying to put some distance between us as quickly as I could.

Back in my room at the Scupper, I took my chair by the window, waiting for Ronin's return. It didn't take long. Within minutes, he came striding back down the sidewalk, the limp a bit more noticeable now, and from what I could see of the expression on his face, things hadn't gone well. I drew back from the window as a matter of reflex, but he had no interest in surveilling this morning. I wondered what was on his mind, but I think I knew. Time was growing short. Had arrangements to ship the art to Germany taken a bad turn? I could only hope.

It's about a hundred and thirty kilometers — eighty miles, give or take, — from headquarters in London to the hotel, and by all rights, it would be at least half an hour, maybe longer before my courier arrived. I was wrong. There came a knock on the door. "Courier," a male voice announced. It was a familiar, most welcome male voice, and I wasted no time opening the door. There stood my husband, courier envelope in hand and one of those little-boy grins on his handsome face. "Courier, ma'am."

"All right," I said. "I give. How did you manage this?"

In lieu of an answer, he stepped inside and tossed the envelope on the counter that held the hot plate and the water pitcher, the hotel's frugal attempt at providing food services for guests. The kiss was brief, the conversation even briefer. "I need this developed ASAP, John," I said. "And how on earth did you get here so fast and why, come to think of it, are you even here at all?"

"I happened to be more or less in the neighborhood, and when I checked in, they told me you'd requested a courier. Simple as that."

I handed him the film and he slipped it in the envelope. "I'll be back tonight," he said, giving me a brief hug before reaching for the doorknob. And that's when he saw me wince. Damn. That meant an explanation I was hoping I could have avoided.

"Katrin."

When he says my name in that tone of voice, I have come to realize he isn't going to let whatever precipitated it, slide. "It's all right," I said. "Everything's fine. Really."

"Let me see."

"No, really, John. I'm fine. We need to get the film developed. That's more important." He didn't budge. And he calls *me* stubborn. "All right." I unbuttoned my blouse and let it fall back so my right shoulder was visible. My seriously bruised right shoulder that actually hurt like hell. I looked up at him with one of those, '*Are you satisfied now?*' stares.

He touched my shoulder lightly and brushed his lips across the bruise. "This is fresh. Last night? Yes? The press was all over Scotland Yard this morning," he said, releasing me and giving me one of those appraising looks I have come to dread. "Interest is running high, along with speculation, I might add, about the circumstances surrounding the discovery of a body in this hotel's parking lot. Isn't that interesting?" he said.

"Interesting."

"The Yard, however, has determined that Oliver Wilson died of a heart attack as he was fleeing the police."

John was enjoying this little game. Heart attack. Well, that would be about right. My stiletto has a twelve-inch blade. Heart attack most definitely. I'd go with that. So, the Yard was indeed celebrating and not investigating. All's well that ends. "Well," I said, "that's interesting. About that film…"

"I'll be back tonight," John said. "We'll have supper. And."

"And."

"And."

Shortly, I heard the roar of the Harley as he peeled out of the lot. *And.* I smiled. That was the second conversation we'd had just now without saying anything. Anything at all.

·   ·   ·

While I waited, I walked to the grocer's and did a better version of last night's attempt at dinner. It would still be cold fare, as I didn't trust the hot plate with its frayed cord overly much, and the conversation we would have wasn't for prying ears at a restaurant. The green grocer had a decent head of lettuce and I pounced on the only apple in the case. It was in fair shape with just a small bruise on the side that I could cut out. I bought it.

I put together some sandwiches with cold cuts, cheese, and the noble lettuce leaves. With the cheese, crackers, and apple plate for an appetizer, and the bottle of red wine of dubious vintage for our beverage, the feast awaited John's return.

True to his word, an hour and a half after he'd left, I heard the distant roar of the Harley. When the Yard commits to a rush job, they hop to it. I poured the wine. My courier had arrived. The radio was on for atmosphere, and more importantly, to keep our conversation from being overheard, although I'd booked the adjoining room for John and mine was by the outside wall, leaving this one sort of the filling in a sandwich. The only danger would be someone on the floor above with a listening device aimed at the ceiling of our apartment or someone on the floor below with the same setup. It wasn't likely. I was counting on Glen Miller to help out the war effort, by giving us the freedom to talk, and he was doing a commendable job, beating out "Pennsylvania Six-Five Thousand". England's own Big Bands had disbanded, as the men enlisted in the armed forces to fight Hitler. Glen Miller was a touch of home, and rumor had it he was one of us.

"You never told me you could cook," John said, taking in the lavish banquet I had prepared and arranged by the offensive hotplate.

"Another secret in a profession of secrets," I said, eyeing the courier envelope with something akin to a child watching out the window for Father Christmas to arrive. "Shall we?" I had the two chairs pulled up to the small table, and we settled in to eat and drink and discover the secrets the photographs would reveal.

There were a dozen photographs. Two were blurry. I must have moved the camera at the wrong time. Damn. Regardless, the rest were decent, although they wouldn't win any photography awards.

"What are you looking for?" John asked, barely rescuing a slice of cheese that was doing its best to slide off the cracker and onto the floor.

"Not sure. Something. Anything." I was bent over the picture I'd taken of the photos on the table in The Red Parlour at the Taylor's home. It reminded me of going to one of those hall of mirrors where you look into a glass that looks into a glass and goes on forever or until you're so dizzy you give up. Sort of like that. I picked up the photo, wishing I had a magnifier. My rose kit had one, but it was in the car. Not anxious to get up to fetch it, I tried the squint method but finally gave up. I needed the glass and started to get up to fetch it.

"Where are you going?" John asked.

"To Morris," I said. My husband looked at me as if I had lost the last functional marble in my brain. "Morris," I repeated. "My car."

"You named your car."

"Of course. It fits him," I said. "I'll be right back." I didn't even get as far as the door before I found myself being turned around and plunked back in the chair.

"Give me the key. One body is enough. What am I looking for?"

Honestly. Last night wasn't a normal occurrence. Sometimes, these things just happened. Still, discretion was probably advised. "The magnifier in the tray in my rose kit," I said.

"I'll be right back. Stay put."

I did and he was. Now, with the extra help of the magnifying glass, the picture was clear, and there was no doubt about who was in it and where and when it had been taken. The venue was the 1936 Olympics that had been held in Berlin. The swastikas in the background attested to that. And the woman on the podium receiving her gold medal for the equestrian dressage event was Anna Schneider. The English translation of Schneider being Taylor. We were looking at Anne Taylor before she'd transferred to England to spy for her homeland. I traded my magnifying glass for my wine glass and sat back in my chair.

"Well, then," was the most eloquent thing I could manage to say.

"Where did you take this?" John asked. "When did you take this?"

"At her estate in Colchester, just above Ipswich, It's a ritzy area, and she and her husband, Gerry — who I would hazard a guess is actually Gerhardt — are among the ritziest residents." I took a sip of wine and returned the glass to the table so I could start on my sandwich. "And yesterday. That's our first pair of Nazis. What can you find out about Gerry Taylor/Gerhardt Schneider?" I asked.

"I'll see what I can dig up tomorrow. Anybody else?"

"Possibly. Colleen is suspicious." John's puzzled expression reminded me he needed some getting up to date. "I'll explain, but there are two more names for your search. Miranda Hainesworth and Douglas Hyde-Stuart. I don't know anything about Hainesworth, but Hyde-Stuart is retired from the British Museum and still consults for them." I jotted down their names on my notepad and handed the sheet to him.

"This Hyde-Stuart chap gets around," John said. "He and Adam have a history. It's not a good one, and Hyde-Stuart's name and telephone number are suspiciously present in the phone logs at the British Museum just before the Magna Carta was taken."

"So, how was your day, dear?" I asked and ducked as John flicked a cracker at me.

"Actually, not all that great. All I know now is what I knew yesterday, and that's not much help. Except," he added, "that I'm pretty sure all four copies of Magna Carta are being held in the same place. If they're headed to the Führermuseum, that is. All I have to do is find that place." He snapped his fingers. "Piece of cake."

"When do you think they're going to move all this stuff to Germany?" I asked. "And why are they waiting? The dogfight's going on over the Channel and there's no letup in sight. Hitler is moving forward with his plans. What's keeping the art and the Magna Cartas still here?"

"Honey, if we knew that, we'd be home free. But you're right. They're waiting for something. Damned if I know what it is, though. The British Museum." I could almost see the wheels turning in John's brain. "Stuie. That's convenient. Coincidence? Probably not," he answered himself. "Now, you were saying something about a Colleen?"

"Back up a bit, dear. The British Museum? Stuie? You first. Then, I'll tell you what I've learned."

With a brief recap of what Adam had told him about Hyde-Stuart being a former friend until the betrayal and the flunking out of Oxford, John finished with the two possible scenarios now present: Hyde-Stuart was either dead and being impersonated, or he was acting in concert with German agents to steal England's art and possibly the Magna Cartas. Adam tended towards the latter, and so did John.

"Interesting," I said. "And what you've learned may fit in nicely. Before I tell you the Tale of Port Hope, guess who I saw today?" I took a sip of wine. It was a nice color, reminded me of garnets. "Ronin," I said without waiting for a reply. I set the glass down and waited.

John raised an eyebrow. "Where?"

"On the docks. He met up with a rough-looking character, possibly a sailor, hard to tell. But the meeting didn't go well, judging from the way he stormed back down the docks a few minutes later. And no," I said, answering the question before it was asked. "He didn't see me. I'm positive. I'd left the Diner and was back here when I saw him go past."

John reached for the wine and poured himself another glass and refilled mine. It gave him time to think. "Interesting," he said.

It was our word of the evening. And events were indeed interesting to say the least.

"Wonder why he was here?" John said, swirling the wine in his glass while he spoke.

I went to get a napkin. He doesn't swirl all that well, and a disaster was looming. I gave him the napkin, although a bit late, as he used it to mop up the puddle on the table.

"I think he's looking for a way to move the art and the Magna Cartas away from here and, if that's true, he wouldn't have waited until now. My guess is that something happened to put a monkey wrench into his plans and he's desperate now, knowing what's coming. No transport is safe, and it's going to get more and more difficult to find someone willing to risk taking a shipment across the channel, regardless of how well he's paid. Ronin's missed his window of opportunity, and now he's scrambling."

"Bad for him. Potentially good for us," John said.

I agreed.

"Your turn," he said.

"Right." We were now back to my day. By the time I had given him the pared-down version of the body found in the field by the abandoned house, the parachuting Polish teenager who survived the crash of one of Hitler's airplanes, and the murky details of the deaths of both the postmaster found by the roadside, his bicycle a mangled mess, and the grandmother, found by her prized rosebush, a spade lying by her head and probably the cause of her death, we had eaten our way through most of dinner.

John is an excellent listener. He doesn't interrupt, but he keeps a running account of questions that occur to him while he listens. Judging by the number of notes he was taking, he had quite a few questions. And so, as my story drew to a close, our discussion began.

"The locals are suspicious of new arrivals to the community, especially given the political situation. And I'm not sure what's considered new. The Taylor/Schneiders have been here since '37, and the Hainesworth/Hyde-Stuarts go back over ten years. I don't know what the normal murder rate is in Port Hope and vicinity, if there is such a thing. But they're having an uptick and that could definitely be related to the spy situation and it's something to look into. I have one more newcomer to scope out tomorrow. It's the new postmaster who arrived on the heels of the death of Dave. Tomorrow is shaping up to be a busy day."

"One more thing," John said. "One of our agents hasn't checked in since we received our assignments. The attrition is beginning, it appears."

Attrition. That was a way to sugarcoat it. We all knew the risks, but when it happened, it drove the point home. I sighed. "Who?" I asked.

John set his fork down on the plate. "Margo Speer."

"No." I shook my head. "No. Not her. She's always watched her back. She's just involved and can't get away. She's working the sector that includes her home, down in Canvey. She knows that area well."

We all check in on schedule, unless we can't for whatever reason. We report what we've learned and share what intelligence we have gathered that may assist other agents in completing their own assignments. We also have to account for any damage to property or persons that we have inflicted. Usually, it's a somber accounting of death. Sometimes, rarely, there's a comedic aspect to this. John's last motorcycle had ended up in the shrubbery outside Bletchley Park when he'd swerved to avoid a mathematician riding a Penny Farthing—one of those oversized three-wheeled bicycles. The Harley hadn't looked badly damaged, but by the time he got it back to the motor pool, the engine was toast. Something about no oil. Engines don't like that.

I gathered up the dishes to take to the little sink in our shoebox-sized kitchen area, shoving the hotplate out of the way again with more force than necessary. It was always in the way. "That's Ronin's home, too, remember," I said. "She said she was going to find out what side he's working on this time. But he's her brother. She's fine." But I had one of those feelings that she wasn't fine. If I told John, he'd dismiss it out of hand and remind me to focus on my own assignment. He'd be right, of course, so I let it go. "There's no dessert," I said, instead, looking disparagingly at the empty counter. "I forgot to get something for dessert."

John refilled our wine glasses. "This will do just fine," he said. "And…"

I smiled at him. "And."

.   .   .

Later that night, after John had fallen asleep, I lay awake. My mind had a death grip on one thought and kept worrying at it like a hungry dog with a bone. I wondered. Had Ronin slipped so far that he'd harm his own sister? I knew the answer, but it was tough to accept. He'd kill whoever got in his way, and I'd said before, that it would be without remorse or regret. Whoever he had once been was no longer who he was, and if Margo had challenged him, it most likely hadn't ended well. Tomorrow, I'd go looking for her. And if what I feared were true, I would find him before this assignment had run its course. I would find him, and he would not kill again.

CHAPTER EIGHTEEN

Port Hope

"You're up with the roosters, Bill," Colleen said.

"I have news. It took them bloody long enough to get back to me, but here it is." Bill tossed a folder onto the kitchen table and bestowed a peck on Colleen's cheek. "They were able to collect some prints from that grocery list and, assuming the corpse wrote it, our corpse is Brian Fitch. Name mean anything to you?"

Colleen shook her head. "You want to move that folder over a bit and I'll set our places. If you're happy with porridge and toast, you're all set."

"That's fine." He poured himself a cup of tea and reclaimed his folder. "I've got the coroner's report, as well. But first things first. Fitch is, or rather was, the driver of a van transporting art pieces from somewhere in Wales to somewhere safer in Wales."

Colleen paused. "Port Hope is not in Wales if I recall my geography. Last I heard we were firmly in England. Regardless, safe is a relative term these days."

"True. The details of Fitch's route are classified, but since Port Hope isn't all that much safer than London, being a port town with a railroad, I'd hazard a guess this wasn't where he was originally going. So, how he ended up here ..." Bill shrugged.

"When are they going to get those art pieces settled? I thought they did all that last year. It's the worst-kept secret in England. Every time anyone sees a Cadbury delivery van or some other truck, it's 'Oh, look! There go the Renoirs!' or 'Here come the Constables!' Really. People just aren't that stupid." She rummaged in the fridge for the pitcher of cream which was hiding out of reach. "I am so grateful for Denise's milk cow. If we had to get by on coupons for our tea, I'd attack Hitler myself." She took the sugar bowl off the counter by the bread tin and frowned at the scant supply inside. "Sugar, on the other hand...". She sighed.

Absorbed in his reading, Bill hadn't heard a word she'd said, but the silence when she stopped chattering made him look up, and he continued as something she'd said finally registered. "They've got a final place now. The art. Wales, if you can believe it."

"Bill, the art is in Wales."

"No, I mean they've finally found the final, final, final place in Wales. There's a slate mine in Manod that they've decided is the proper place for the entire lot. They're doing renovations so the big pieces can fit into the cave, or whatever the entrance to the place is called. It's enormous, apparently. Has railroad tracks, hydraulic lifts, and all. I read that they're going to install temperature controls. Should be quite something to see." He splashed a bit of cream in his tea but returned the sugar bowl to Colleen. "We'll keep this for something more memorable, right?"

Colleen looked dubious. "I suppose they know what they're doing." She replaced the sugar bowl in the cupboard. "Right. I'll save up enough and make us something decadent for your birthday, Bill." She laughed. "Not sure which birthday, but one day."

"That's the ticket. Looking ahead. We could all use a bit more of that. Anyhow, on a less pleasant but more relevant note, the coroner's report is just in, and I thought it would make cheerful breakfast reading, so I brought it along."

Colleen gave a tsk sound and shook her head. "Poor fellow is probably our first casualty of war here." She took one of the season's last tomatoes she'd picked yesterday and set about slicing it for the breakfast plates. It would be a traditional English country breakfast, rationing be damned. Then, an idea crossed her mind, and she set the knife down. "Bill?"

"Hmm?" Bill was immersed in the coroner's report.

"What if Mr. Fitch hadn't been an innocent driver?" Wiping her hands on her apron, Colleen sat down at the table. "I mean, why was he here if Port Hope or any of the towns close by weren't on his route? We know they're not hiding the art here..." She settled herself more comfortably. "Perhaps he was kidnapped. That would be interesting. Or, what if he'd been involved somehow, and something went wrong? Well, obviously something went wrong, him ending up dead and all, but I mean the something that made him dead?" She rearranged the toast on the serving plate to make room for a few dollops of jam. "What about this scenario? Let's assume Mr. Fitch is a thief. Somebody has contacted him somehow." She waved a hand in the air. "They know what he is supposed to do, and they think they can make some money off it. They don't have to be German agents or art dealers or smugglers. They could be local opportunists who have learned about the movement of the art. I don't know. Those are minor details to work out. Anyhow, they take a gamble and see if Mr. Fitch is interested in making some extra money. Perhaps a great deal of extra money. He accepts the deal and agrees to be paid when he delivers the paintings to the person who is paying him to steal them, but then when he gets to the place he's supposed to go, he decides he wants more money." Colleen had to stop to take a breath. "This isn't received well by the one in charge, and there's an argument. Whoever he's arguing with picks up—what did you say he was killed with?"

Bill didn't look up from his plate as he spread the jam on his toast. "A blunt object."

"A blunt object. Really? Is that the best you can do? What exactly is a blunt object? I mean, I know it's not a sharp object, but do you have any ideas as to what that blunt object was?"

"Nope. None." Bill took a respectable bite of toast.

Colleen waited, but with no further help from Bill, she plowed on. "All right. This is what I think. Are you listening to me?"

"I definitely am."

"All right. Whoever he was dealing with obviously had a temper."

"Obviously."

"You said before there was just one blow to his head."

"That's what the coroner's report says."

"On the left side."

"Yes."

"Well. There you have it then." Colleen stood and returned to the stove, where the porridge was simmering.

"Have what, for God's sake? Colleen, sometimes you can be the most infuriating woman."

Colleen reached for the handle of the cookpot and lifted it from the stove, testing its weight as she moved it to the table. "You're looking for a woman, about his height, maybe a tad shorter. Stout or athletic. Either one would work. A personality type that doesn't react well to any challenge to her authority. And whether she has any authority in reality, she believes she does. Impulsive." Colleen smiled, warming to her subject. "Lacking in self-control. He wasn't expecting the blow. He thought she was storming off, an interlude in their argument, but she turned away from him, picked up the first serious object she saw. I'm thinking something with a handle that would be easy to grip, and she let him have it. Doesn't fit a masculine profile. Most men would be more direct with maybe a punch to the face or whatever, but direct physical contact would be more like a man. Anyway, that's my theory." She set the porridge on the table and smiled. "*Cherchez la femme*. Prove me wrong, Bill."

Filling his bowl, Bill took a small portion of the cream and added a spoonful of the jam. "You've been reading too much Agatha Christie again, Colleen. It's always the woman. Is this some sort of modification of the old 'woman scorned' scenario?"

"I don't think so. I think this was a straightforward business deal that went sour. Do you have any leads?"

"You know as much as I do, and with everything else that's about to happen with the Germans at the doorstep, it's almost a certainty that this case is going to go quietly into the open morgue along with the victim. I've got to call the Yard this morning to look more into the Fitch affair. I'll see you tonight." He paused by the door. "Promise me you won't do anything foolish. Leave the investigating to the police. I mean it, Colleen." He hesitated. "You're going to get involved. I know you. You're not going to listen to me, are you?"

Colleen cleared the dishes and set them in the sink for a wash later on. She turned to Bill and cocked her head. "I always listen to you, Bill."

He groaned the way he always did when he knew he'd lost the battle.

Standing at the sink, she smiled. It was good to be loved. She glanced at the clock and realized she'd lingered overly long at breakfast. There was much work to be done.

. . .

This morning, when I was about ready to leave for some investigatory work into Margo Speer's disappearance and a reconnaissance visit to the post office in Port Hope to take stock of the new postmaster, I'd checked my remaining petrol coupons and frowned. The situation was not favorable, and all being fair in love and war, I took the path of least resistance. I stole a sheet from my husband's ration book while he was shaving. I knew it was wrong, but it wasn't wrong enough to cause major marital problems. At least, I hoped not. If it did, I'd think of something. Maybe a new frock a bit more daring than my current dress. It had been a romantic evening, and John's mood was light. I wasn't foolish enough to believe it was light enough to forgive petty theft, however, and I was now a common thief. Maybe an uncommon one. That sounded better. Anyhow, operating on the belief that it's easier to get forgiveness than permission, I left a note in his pocket for him to find later in the day.

"I'm sorry. I stole a few of your petrol coupons. I'll pay you back. It's urgent. I love you."

The daring frock was also a good idea, though.

. . .

First stop this morning was a short one. I'd already learned from Colleen that the new postmaster's name was Leavesly Pendergast. His family had been in the area since Cromwell was a baby, so there was no way he was one of the "newcomers", but, as we'd come to learn, not all our adversaries came from across the Channel. Everyone had their reasons for what they did, and Pendergast might be a loyal Brit. Then again, maybe not. So, I wrote myself a short note and stopped by the Port Hope post office to purchase a stamp and mail the card. I wanted to get a good look at him and do a sketch before I made my next stop.

Pendergast was a rotund man, about fifty, on the short side, balding, and with a thin nose that seemed out of place on his fleshy face. His eyelids drooped so low, it was a miracle he could see anything at all. He was a character Dickens would have conjured up, and I could picture him threatening David Copperfield with a soup ladle. He wasn't one for small talk and sold me my stamp without anything more than a brief "Good Day".

Back in Morris, I made my sketch, added what little I had learned about Pendergast in my notes, and set it aside for delivery to Whitehall later that afternoon after I'd returned to the hotel.

I next motored down to Canvey. The day was already heating up, and I had the windows fully open to let in as much air as there was. It did cool off slightly as I got closer to the water, and the tang of the salt air was fresh. I turned onto a gravel driveway, passing several homes that had been boarded up as their occupants had undoubtedly fled the coast, seeking safety farther inland. Margo's home was the last house on the drive and closest to the shore. I pulled up to the garage and parked. The garage door was open, and inside was an older model blue Riley 9 Monaco Saloon. I walked up to it and tested the door. It was unlocked, so I took the liberty of opening it and checking the interior. Nothing. Not even a cigarette butt in the ashtray or a tissue on the floor. I shut the car door and walked around to the front of the house.

Somehow, given Margo's worldliness, I'd gotten the impression her home would reflect that. Instead, it was a modest structure, a two-story clapboard house, the wood weathered to grey. There was no front porch, just two stone steps up to the door. Simple in design, the home was a bit of an eyeopener. Margo was just one of those women whose manner projected wealth. Her speech, poise, mannerisms, clothing, confidence. The whole shebang was...I couldn't come up with the right word. It wasn't an act. It was as if she were the real deal and somehow it was the house that came up short.

No one answered my knock on the door, so I continued on around the side to the back where a spacious back porch with two rocking chairs moved at the whim of the wind. Everything was quiet with no sign of life. Truer words were never spoken. Just behind the house, there was a fenced area, not terribly big, but then, it didn't need to be. Inside the fence, two headstones had been planted side by side in the sandy soil. There were no inscriptions. No names. No dates. It was a cold, bleak, barren place, and I hoped the souls of the two people buried there had found something better on the other side. These had to be the graves of Ronin's wife and child. I tried to remember if Margo had said whether the child was a girl or a boy. I think she said a little girl. I couldn't remember for sure. I picked a bouquet of wildflowers and set it between the stones.

The only other place that might yield any information before I used my pick locks to gain entry to the house was a wooden stairway that appeared to lead down to the shore. The wood, as with the house, had weathered to grey in the harsh salt air, and I moved cautiously, not quite trusting its sturdiness. With my eyes on my feet, making sure I didn't trip, I counted fourteen steps to the sand. I took off my shoes and walked along the shore, with its small bits of shells, green and brown strands of kelp, and driftwood, worn smooth over time. The waves were gentle today, not a whitecap to be seen, and the salt air filled my lungs, bringing back memories of the coast of Sankt Peder, my Danish birthplace. I had a pang of homesickness. They came less frequently these days, but when they did, I felt a longing I couldn't explain for something that was a part of me that had been lost.

Melancholy has no place in espionage work. A deep breath, and I banished the moment to memory—its proper place. I exhaled, looked seaward, and then saw what, in my heart, I knew I'd find but had hoped against hope that I wouldn't. The tide was going out, but I knew that with each tide, the body would be carried farther and farther out to sea. Each fifth wave was the biggest, and I marked how far the body was retreating with each wave. It should have been gone and beneath the surface by now, but then I saw the reason why it remained, fixed in place. The body was held secure, entrapped in a field of kelp, anchored on the rocks about 50 meters out, the blonde hair floating on the water, resting, waiting. Waiting for what? Margo's time on earth was done.

I am a strong swimmer, but this recovery was more than I would attempt. The distance alone would be a challenge, considering I'd need to get there and back, but freeing a body from a kelp bed and then towing it back to shore is the stuff of movies, not real life. No. I had seen enough. I'd call the sighting in at the next opportunity and let the professional recovery teams bring Margo home.

CHAPTER NINETEEN

Colchester and Port Hope

Maid Marian's Merry Maids Housekeeping Service Ltd. had been dispatched to Bellesford House, where they were working en masse to get everything ready for Mrs. Taylor's evening affair on Saturday. At least they were attempting to, in between tongue lashings by Mrs. Taylor about their slipshod efforts. A dust mote still hanging from the chandelier was all she could find, but she was harping on it as if the women had thrown a tub of grease against the wall and danced in the puddles it had made. Their efforts to explain that they were waiting for the handyman to bring the ladder they had requested fell on deaf ears. Mrs. Taylor was not in a mood to listen, and she warned the women they must vacate the premises before afternoon tea or she would simply not pay for their services.

The three women had been dispatched from the main office on short notice and advised not to initiate any conversations with the lady of the estate. They were to be part of the furnishings, as it were, a throwback to earlier times, and this rankled Bobbie Aldercroft no end. Money was money, however, and she held her tongue as the tirade ran its course. It happened. It came with the territory. There was a time when being "in service" was an honourable profession and much respected by both society at large and the employer, in particular. Those times had disappeared into the past, but the need for services was still there. Small businesses had stepped in to fill that need and provide the services required, but the adjustment on both sides had been painful—even more so when dealing with the newly rich who hadn't learned their place and that there were rules that governed their behavior as much as they governed their social inferiors.

Bobbie huffed. She was no social inferior to anyone. She worked for a living and made a good wage. Good enough that, when combined with her husband's salary on the police force, they were able to buy a home with a nice yard that would hold their garden and, she smiled inwardly, a play area for their child. So, in spite of the curses hurled at her, Bobbie Aldercroft was on top of the world and counting the hours until she could tell Jim the news.

Maggie had been dispatched to the upper floor to work on the master suite and the guest bedrooms that some of the guests would be using.

Bridgit had been assigned the kitchen. Ordinarily a plum job, but in this household, the number of cooks that had come and gone over the past few years would have been enough to fill a battalion of soldiers. Essentially, the kitchen and the larder were a jumbled mess, each cook having done her best to sabotage the area as revenge for the ill treatment Mrs. Taylor had dished out. Maggie didn't have to deal with that, but she did have to work around the new cook, who was attempting to establish some order before the onslaught of guests began.

Bobbie had the ground floor, and while it entailed a considerable amount of dusting and vacuuming, and the occasional dust mote — she glowered at the offending strand of filament that wafted unconcernedly above her head — it was the easiest job to have. And she was grateful. She was tired, and no amount of sleep helped. *It's going to be like this for quite some time, I fear. Little ones do wear you out.* She sat on the sofa, a definite breach of allowed behavior, and her thoughts wandered. After a moment or so, she dragged herself back to her feet and picked up her basket that contained her dusting cloths and polish. She moved the dustmop and the Hoover over to the far corner of the room. She'd begin there and work her way around the room, out into the hall, and down to the next room, where she'd begin all over again until she was done or it was time to leave. Her schedule rotated. Next week, she'd begin where she left off. The work was never done, and she was only contracted by the hour. The one blessing today was that she'd been told not to clean the office, and it meant that she might actually finish the floor, which would be a first. The office was off the library, and she was eyeing the massive number of books she needed to dust and align edges. *"I swear. That woman deliberately pushes books in until they hit the back wall, just to be sure I've done my job,"* was her thought. *"What makes a person act like that? What is her problem?"*

Pushing the Hoover over to the electrical outlet to the left of the office, and plugging it in, she bent over to pick up a scrap of paper from the floor. She stuffed it in her pocket, adding it to the rest of the trash she'd collected and was about to fetch her basket, but the insistent ringing of the telephone in the office caused her to stop. She chuckled. Finally, there was something that Mrs. Taylor had to answer to. It was oddly satisfying that an object could have that much power.

It was impossible to ignore the noise coming from the office. Mrs. Taylor had finally picked up and was screaming at the top of her lungs. It was one of the more unpleasant sounds Bobbie had ever encountered. The woman sounded like a banshee. Bobbie dusted her way over to the door, giving a token touch to the mouldings and baseboards, although she could have remained where she was. The sound carried clear across the room. Curiosity, though, triumphed over discretion, and she was hoping to pick up something of the conversation apart from the noise.

Kunst and then again and again came the same word — *Kunst.* The rest of the conversation was impossible to make out. Then, Bobbie stopped cold. The woman was speaking in German. *What is Kunst?* She shook her head. The word had no meaning to her, but it obviously held great meaning for Mrs. Taylor.

The screaming stopped abruptly as if the person on the other end of the call had had enough and had hung up. Bobbie made a quick retreat back to the Hoover and revved up the motor just as the door to the office swung open and Mrs. Taylor stormed out and strode across the room and out the door which she slammed loud enough to wake the dead. She slammed it with such force that it flew back without latching, and she was moving so fast she didn't notice.

Intent on her vacuuming, Bobbie never looked up as Mrs. Taylor left, but she heard a car motor start up. Pulling the draperies aside, she saw Mrs. Taylor's automobile speed down the driveway, spewing gravel and dust in its path. Bobbie dropped the draperies and gave the room a final look to be sure she hadn't forgotten anything. The dust mote was gone, and the ladder was ready for the handyman to return it to the barn.

Bobbie hooked the basket handle over her arm and gave one more look at the office. Normally, she'd respect a client's privacy, but these were not normal times, and she was a police officer's wife. Jim might be able to use whatever information she could find. And, besides, the door was open. She pursed her lips and set the basket down by the sofa, a dusting cloth positioned over the wooden arm, just in case she needed to look busy in a hurry. What was in this room that she was not supposed to see? Any other time, she would have let it go, but not now. Not when Mrs. Taylor was speaking German to someone on the phone who was obviously speaking German, as well. Bobbie waited another moment, then, decision made, entered the office. Hands on hips, duster at the ready, just in case someone should find her where she didn't belong, she looked around.

The only thing that caught her attention was the desk calendar with July 12 circled in red. That was today. Before she could continue her search, a sound in the dining room alerted her, and she began flicking the duster around the lamps and the shelves by the desk.

"We're not supposed to be in here," Bridgit said. "If I have to listen to that harridan scream at us one more time, I'm not going to be responsible for my actions. I'm done. You don't need to clean here. It's time to leave."

"Oh. You're right. I forgot," Bobbie said. "Fine by me. One less room to Hoover, but I'd best take care of the dining room rug. If you can help with the dusting, we can be out of here on time."

"At least it's not as bad as the kitchen. Do they throw food on the floor on purpose? It was worse than I would have believed. How cook can work in that pig sty is beyond me." She picked up the duster. "Let's finish. I don't like this place."

Bobbie nodded. "I don't either. Some places just seem to take on the personality of their owners. No fault of their own, of course, but it's true."

"I suppose. When do we get paid?" Bridgit asked. "Mrs. Taylor left. I heard her tearing up the driveway."

Bobbie shrugged. "Not our problem. I guess Marian will send her the bill. Let's go. It's time to go home."

Shortly, the three women piled into the company automobile and thankfully left the memory of the obnoxious Mrs. Taylor and her screaming tantrums behind.

. . .

Supper at the Aldercroft home was generally a simple affair, especially since rationing had determined the ingredients of whatever one wanted to prepare. Tonight, however, reaped the rewards of Bobbie's planning. She'd saved the sugar coupons along with the milk and flour and had gotten some eggs from Denise, whose chickens were totally unconcerned with rationing and were just going about the business of being chickens and doing what chickens did.

Because of that resourcefulness, tonight Bobbie had been able to prepare a feast worthy of Christmas at the Aldercroft home, and it was Christmas of a sort, in July. There was leg of lamb, courtesy of Mildred. The potatoes had come from the cupboard, but the gravy that had required flour had come as a loan from Jeanne that she'd repay next time the ration books were issued.

The planning for the meal had taken almost as long as the actual preparation, but tonight was like no other night before and like no other night would ever be again. She brought the bowls and plates of food to the table and smiled at the befuddled expression on her husband's face.

Finally, there was trifle, and that was enough to cause Jim to break his silence. "Bobbie," he said, "what the hell is going on?"

Bobbie lifted her tea cup and then set it down carefully, adjusting its place on the saucer. Finally, with nothing else to serve as a buffer, she took a breath and sat back in her chair, her eyes meeting Jim's. Her cheeks were flushed and her heart was racing. "I went to see the doctor today."

"What's wrong, honey?" Jim set his fork down, concern on his face.

Bobbie smiled, and the joy on her face came through in her words. "Nothing's wrong. I'm pregnant, Jim! We're going to have a baby!" The silence only lasted a moment, but seemed an eternity. Jim's expression went from blank to puzzled to comprehension.

"A baby."

"Yes, honey. A baby. In the spring."

He shoved his chair back and stood, then took her in his arms. "Honey. I…" he held her close. "A baby."

"We're going to be a family, Jim. A real family."

. . .

Lying in bed that night, her hands cradling her belly, she felt as if everything she'd ever wanted had come true. She couldn't sleep. She climbed out of bed, being careful not to wake Jim, and went to the kitchen to make a cup of tea. She'd wanted to tell Jim about what she'd overheard at work, but in the excitement, she'd forgotten. It didn't matter. The world and all its troubles would keep until morning. Today belonged to them. She returned to bed and this time sleep came easily.

. . .

"Good morning, Papa," Bobbie said as Jim entered the kitchen.

"That's going to take a bit of getting used to, honey." His face grew serious. "I think you should give your notice to Marian. All the lifting and climbing is too much. We'll have enough with my salary."

"Jim, it's going to be tight without it. Police officers don't make that much. You know that as well as I do. When you become Detective Chief Inspector like Bill, then I'll become a lady of leisure. Right now, however, we need my income." She brought the basket of muffins to the table. "I can ask Marian if there's an opening in the office. I'm good with maths. And after yesterday, I don't fancy going back to Bellesford House ever again."

Jim looked up from his plate. "What happened yesterday?"

"With all the excitement," she smiled at him, "I forgot to tell you what happened at work. It was most odd. Something is going on at Bellesford House, Jim." She poured their tea and passed him his cup. "Mrs. Taylor was on the telephone in her office, and she was speaking German. Actually, she was screaming in German at whoever was on the other end of the line."

Jim paused with his muffin halfway to his mouth. "What?"

"Yes. I know it was German. I couldn't understand what she was saying, but she was angry, and you could hear her in the next room even with her door closed. She was that loud." Bobbie chewed on her lip, trying to remember.

"*Kunst.* She said *Kunst.* More than once. What does that mean?"

Jim shrugged. "Not the foggiest idea, but I'll ask the Chief this morning. He may know. Bobbie, I don't want you going back there. Whatever this is about, it's not good."

"I know, Jim. I don't want to go back there, either. She's not a nice woman." Bobbie paused. "When she'd finished her call, she burst out of her office and blew past me like a windstorm. I was plugging in the Hoover and I don't know if she saw me, but what if she did? What if she realizes that I heard her? When she slammed the door to her office, she did it so hard it bounced back instead of closing. What if she thinks I went in?" Bobbie looked at her husband. "And I did. All I saw was her calendar before Bridgit came to get me. It had yesterday's date circled." She shrugged. "Maybe that means something. I just don't know." Bobbie stared into her teacup as if it might hold the answers. The teacup didn't, but her husband did.

"Pack a bag. We're not going to chance this. When the Germans attack, nobody will be safe, but in the meantime, you are not going to be hurt." He paused. "You or the baby. I'll wait while you get your things together. We'll go to the station first. You can talk to the Chief. Tell him everything you remember, and then I'm taking you to my folks' home. You'll be safe there until we sort this out."

CHAPTER TWENTY

Colchester

Morning at Castel del Mare arrived shortly after noon. At least it did for Angelo DeMontana who had slept so soundly he hadn't heard his young female companion rise in the pre-dawn, dress, and steal away from his bedroom. He hadn't heard her return, either, with her male companion and the lorry that had killed its motor and coasted to a halt outside. Nor had he heard the carefully muted sounds of the art being moved from his studio to the lorry, the lorry's engine starting up again, and the soft putting of the vehicle as it made its way back down the driveway and onto the main road, after which it picked up speed on its way to the docks and the waiting vessel.

When DeMontana did finally regain his senses, the dire condition of his circumstances was slow to sink in. First, there was the incessant pounding in his head. Too much wine. But, no. He'd had only one glass, having had other matters on his mind.

Where was the girl? What was her name? He couldn't remember.

"Where are you, love?" he called out but did not receive an answer. He finally stood, but the room was spinning out of control and he was forced to reclaim his bed and once more fell unconscious on the bed covers.

The sun sped on its course through the heavens, and with its mid-afternoon rays reaching through the window glass and warming his bed, DeMontana finally awoke to a universe that was considerably calmer than the one that had greeted him earlier. The girl was gone. That much was evident. No matter. They came and went. What happened in the hours between was all that mattered. Still feeling a bit odd, he dressed and went downstairs for coffee, stopping by his study on the way.

Instantly, he was awake, as his eyes took in the nothingness that greeted him. Everything he'd done over the past three months was gone — even the sketch of the girl he'd started last night. For some reason, that bothered him more than all the rest, although he couldn't fathom why it should. Betrayal. The unkindest cut of all. He stumbled into the kitchen, his muddled thoughts desperately needing coffee but knowing it wouldn't be enough to begin to undo the damage that had been done.

Two cups of the hot, black liquid later, and DeMontana's thoughts shifted into how to turn the situation around. He'd never dwelt on the past, but turning events of the past into something that would benefit him was a talent he possessed. Time. Time was the crucial element, but there wasn't enough of it to start over. In the week that he'd insisted he have, the most — the very most he could do would be the Rembrandt. For the rest, he's need another two months, and that would mean working a full day and into the night — something he hadn't done since he'd apprenticed. That did not appeal to him in the least. It didn't matter. His employer wouldn't give him that much time no matter how convincing a case he set forth. There had to be something else he could do to salvage this and turn it to his benefit.

It had all started, unfortunately, down at the docks where he'd met the girl. Perhaps there was a chance she was still there. How long had she been gone? Sometime after midnight was the best he could do. She'd been gone maybe ten hours. That was a long time to hope she was still within reach. If he could find her....

Within the hour, he was at the wharf, checking every boat tied up at the marina for some sign of activity, but in his mind he knew it was a fool's errand. There were three empty slips, but how long had they been empty? Out of ideas, he sought refuge aboard *Carpe Ventum*, and while today, he had no interest in the charms of his female crew, he hoped they might have seen something that would turn this thing around. It was all he had before he would have to call his employer with the news. That was not going to happen, regardless of what transpired today.

The women were all on board. Three were below decks and two were topside working on their tans. His girls were first class sailors, but he still checked the lines before boarding. He knew his craft, he knew sailing, and in this area of his life, he took no chances. As Captain, he was responsible, one of the few responsibilities he willingly accepted. At least on *Carpe Ventum,* all was well, and he took a modicum of pleasure from that. Surveying his maritime domain, he wondered if perhaps he should just cast off now and leave the whole mess behind. By the time the war was over, his employer might be dead, playing the dangerous games he did. That would be an immense relief, but it was too far in the future to help now. Rejecting the idea almost as soon as it came, he called his crew together.

"This is important, my lovelies," he began. "Think carefully. Did you see or hear any boats leave the docks today? Any at all?" The girls who had been below decks hadn't, but Gina, who'd spent the day topside, washing down the teak decks in the morning and lounging with a movie magazine in the early afternoon had. The nearly derelict vessel — that 20-footer three slips down — was loading cargo and there had been a great deal of yelling and cursing, which was what had gotten her attention. They had cast off shortly after 1300 hours. The sailors didn't seem to be in sync, almost as if they'd never sailed together before.

"Gina, my love, you are a treasure," he said and dismissed the girls to do whatever it was they did when they weren't sailing. It wasn't important; he didn't care. They were always available, they were loyal, and there was no bickering about favoritism. He shared the wealth equally on all levels.

Crews who spend time together develop a rhythm. Each member of the crew has a job to do and with everyone working together, the result is a seamless tapestry. He had selected the women for their ability as sailors, and Glenna, his favorite, had been an Olympic athlete. He trusted her instincts and her knowledge. In matters pertaining to sailing, he never questioned her. And, as an added bonus, she was a tigress in bed. What man could ask for more?

Glenna told him that this two-man crew, or rather one man and one woman who had absconded with his art, didn't seem to know what the hell they were doing. They rammed the dock twice before they managed to pull out of the slip, then slammed into the dock across the lane before they got their boat going in the right direction. Glenna watched them finally succeed in getting out of the marina and wouldn't be surprised if they were now at the bottom of the Channel.

DeMontana winced at the thought of the art undergoing such trauma. Dear God, no, please not. "What did the woman look like?"

Glenna shrugged. "I don't know, Angelo. She was a woman. Young, long black hair. Thin. Not strong enough to do anything from the looks of her." She shook her head in disgust. "Nobody that would interest you."

Hope. The faintest, slimmest glimmer of hope took hold. "Prepare to cast off in ten minutes. We're going after them."

A sailboat loves the wind, and a crew that knows how to sail her is pure poetry. Today, the wind was a light but constant seven knots; the sea a light chop. Perfect conditions for the *Carpe Ventum* and its experienced crew, but a nightmare for an inept one aboard a poorly maintained craft. Two and a half, maybe a three-hour head start. At a speed of seven knots, the most distance between the vessels would be less than twenty miles and most likely considerably less, given the inexperienced crew aboard the smaller boat.

The distance to the horizon is a given eleven or twelve miles, that being as far as the human eye can see. So, DeMontana reasoned, estimating that the boat was around fifteen miles out, that would mean *Carpe Ventum* needed to gain around three miles, give or take, before there was a chance of being able to see them on the water.

The next question. Where would they go? There were three options. They could go across, north, or south. Across meant entering waters controlled by Germany. Nobody could be that stupid. At least, he hoped that were true. That just left north or south. DeMontana weighed his limited options. *Carpe Ventum's* size and faster hull speed would ensure they would overtake their quarry, but only if he made the correct guess as to direction. North meant a headwind and slow going. It also meant fewer ports of call. South meant a following sea and numerous ports of call. He moved the rudder forty-five degrees to starboard and *Carpe Ventum* carved an arc in the water and sailed effortlessly southward.

Apart from a few fishing boats brave or reckless enough to chance the waters as the fight for the skies continued on a daily, or rather nightly basis, the Channel that would normally be teeming with activity was eerily vacant. It was one of the few things operating in *Carpe Ventum's* favor.

•   •   •

Aboard the craft with the stolen art, things weren't going as smoothly as they were aboard the *Carpe Ventum*. "What the hell are you doing?" the man screamed. "Are you trying to capsize us? You told me you knew how to drive this piece of shit!"

"It's not my fault. The boat's crooked. It keeps wanting to tip over."

"Stop your constant whining! Just pay attention and keep on course, and for the love of God, try to go straight. It's not that difficult. There's no wind, no current, and the tide is with us. At this rate, we'll never get there before dark and then we'll be screwed."

The woman muttered something under her breath but gripped the wheel harder.

.   .   .

"Captain!" Arianna called from her position off the starboard bow. "Ahead twenty degrees to starboard!"

DeMontana peered through the binoculars. The mast of a sailing vessel was now visible at a point just before the horizon swallowed the sea. He made the course adjustment and returned the binoculars to their case. From here on, it was just a matter of time. They were in full pursuit.

With each minute, the distance between the two vessels lessened. The other boat was having little success making forward progress, and finally, *Carpe Ventum* came alongside to port of the other vessel. Victoria and Glenna tossed lines onto the cleats along the boat's railing, securing the boat to *Carpe Ventum.*

Arianna had traded her binoculars for a shotgun and now stood balanced in the gangway, the gun leveled at the occupants. "Get down. Flat down on the deck. There's nowhere to go."

The girl couldn't obey the order fast enough, but the man let out a final curse and dove over the side, disappearing under the boat. The minutes ticked by, but he didn't resurface. A search of the water around the two vessels was fruitless, and the girl, now alone, sobbed.

Victoria boarded the smaller vessel and brought the girl aboard *Carpe Ventum* where she collapsed in a heap. "Captain, you want me to tie her up and toss her in the cabin?"

DeMontana nodded. "We need to transfer the art before this tub sinks. What's our depth here?"

"We're good, Captain," Elisabetta said. "Plenty of room and some to spare."

Over the next twenty minutes, the five-woman crew and DeMontana formed a relay line, working silently as they passed piece after piece of the art along and secured the lot below decks of the *Carpe Ventum.* After one more search of the derelict, Glenna took the helm.

"I'll beach this wreck and you can come get me in the dinghy," DeMontana said.

"Aye, Captain," Elisabetta said.

. . .

An abandoned vessel afloat is a threat to navigation. Sailors understand this and accept the moral responsibility for doing whatever they can to either mark the vessel so it is easily seen and a collision can be avoided, or tow it to shore and secure it there. This derelict nameless vessel had reached the end of her days, and now salvage crews would piece her out, leaving the hulk to rust away, leaving nothing behind but a bad memory.

Carpe Ventum's homeward cruise under a moonlit sky was markedly more relaxed than her outbound one had been, even accounting for a few close calls as planes roared overhead hellbent on destruction. DeMontana stood alongside Glenna at the helm, marveling at the smoothness of her skin. She was loyal and forgiving of his little transgressions.

"Angelo?" she said, her eyes fixed on the water ahead.

"Yes, my love?"

"Stay away from skinny women. You can't trust them."

DeMontana shook his head. "Sad, my love, but true. Turn her loose when we tie up at the dock. She won't bother us again."

"No, Angelo, she's still skinny, and she's learned what didn't work. Her type is always looking for the next big score. She's an addict and she'll blab to anyone who will give her a fix. You can't trust her to keep her mouth shut about what she's seen. Even if she's given up, there'll be somebody else coming along soon to finish what she and that slimeball started."

"So, what are you suggesting we do with her? Kill her? That's out of the question."

"It would solve the problem."

"No."

"You have too soft a heart. One of these days, you're going to regret it. All right. We'll keep her on ice here until this is done. The only other option is to move the art to somewhere safe." She gave him a hard look. "And we can't waste any time doing it. Whoever comes for it needs to find the cupboard bare and you safely out of their reach."

"There will have to be some minor repairs to a few of the pieces before that can happen. The treatment hadn't completely set, and our friends weren't overly careful." The concern in his voice reinforced her fears.

"Then I'm coming with you and bringing Elisabetta with me. The other girls can handle *Carpe Ventum* and the girl. We'll take care of any intruders that show up."

DeMontana studied the face that had been the inspiration for so many of his female portraits. Her eyes dark as night, her lips, full and sensuous. "Glenna, my love, shall we marry?"

"No. We most certainly shall not. Things are fine just the way they are." She scanned the docks as they made their approach. "At least they were fine." She pointed to two male figures standing by their slip, watching them make their approach. "Should I do a hard about and head back out to sea?"

DeMontana took the binoculars and then set them back down with uncharacteristic force. "No, love. I'm expecting a visit from Professor Franta." His brow furrowed. "I don't know who the other one is, though.

. . .

"Overblown and uninspired, with flashes of mediocrity," DeMontana stood at the primary easel in his workroom, facing Adam Franta, while he completed a pencil sketch. "I believe that was your last critique of my art."

"And I noticed you took it to heart. Your later work was much improved, although you've been noticeably absent from the public eye since you decided to flee *Il Duce*."

DeMontana paused in his sketching. He pursed his lips, considering, then shrugged. "Perhaps. Just biding my time." He turned to John. "I don't believe I've had the pleasure." He glanced at Adam. "I've certainly had the displeasure."

Adam answered the implied question. "My associate."

"Bodyguard, you mean. I've had experience running from irate husbands, but it appears your reviewing has also led to a need for increased measures of security. Tell me, Professor, how many death threats have you received over the years as a result of your acid pen?"

Bodyguard. If that was what DeMontana believed, Franta had no intention of disabusing him of the idea. It was actually better than he would have come up with. It also meant John wasn't expected to speak, and that was an added benefit. He winked at John while DeMontana left the easel and walked to his desk where he went through the deliberate motions of lighting a cigarette.

Ignoring the jibe, Franta gave a thin smile. "You wanted to see me. It would seem that a civil attitude would work more in your favor than your current line of approach. Shall we stop the dance and get down to business? Your sort is eminently predictable. You fancy yourself a bohemian." He sniffed. "You're a hedonist. And you need to fund your vices."

DeMontana waved the cigarette in the air, the tendrils of smoke forming a pattern that in another time he would have sketched. "Passions, if your will. Vices are so common."

"And your 'passions' as you call them, require funding."

"Occasionally." He nodded. "I try not to disturb my retirement funds, so I take the occasional commission."

"Like now," Adam said.

"Like now." The expression on DeMontana's face was hard to read.

"Enough of this chit chat. I know, and you know as well, that what you've got ready for sale won't fetch a bloody farthing without provenance and authentication. And while I've no doubt you'll create a provenance worthy of noble lineage, you need me for the authentication."

"Unfortunately, that is true." DeMontana's eyes narrowed.

"You are no doubt aware of the thefts of the art masterpieces from the National Gallery," Adam said.

"I've heard of them."

"Perhaps you've wondered where the pieces went."

With no response from DeMontana save for a shrug and hands thrown in the air, Adam continued. "What if, and this is just a supposition, of course. What if whoever stole these paintings intended to sell them to private parties?"

Warming to this game, DeMontana countered. "That would show great foresight."

Franta nodded. "But shortsighted foresight, wouldn't you agree?" Without waiting for a response, he forged ahead. "What if, and of course this is just speculation again," he said as their eyes met, "What if copies could be made that could also be sold? The profits have increased dramatically, wouldn't you agree?"

DeMontana gave a throaty chuckle, his eyes dancing. "Yes, I agree."

"And that brings us to the reason we're here. Each piece would need to be authenticated before the sale could be transacted. Hypothetically speaking."

"Hypothetically speaking, that is true."

This time Adam's smile was broad. "Here is my offer. For 20% of each sale, I will provide authentication of whatever you show me. No questions asked."

DeMontana returned the remains of the cigarette to the ashtray. He turned, "No questions asked?"

"None."

"Obviously, there will be no written contract."

"Obviously. If you cross me, DeMontana, you'll never paint again. Broken fingers. They don't heal all that well." Adam gave a pointed look in John's direction, then returned to DeMontana. "I know what you were thinking. You'd show me a few paintings, I'd verify them, and you'd pay me now from your own finances against the future sale. But that would just be the cost of doing business. Once you had one sheet of authentication with my signature, you wouldn't need me any longer, would you?"

The flash of pain in DeMontana's eyes was all Adam needed to verify his silence and compliance.

"Well played, Professor," he said. "I underestimated you." He motioned to a door along the far wall. "Follow me, if you will. There's a desk in there for your writing. There are twenty-nine for you to authenticate. My patron will be here tomorrow to claim them."

CHAPTER TWENTY-ONE

Port Hope and Environs

Again this morning, on her way to her bookkeeping office behind the barn, Jeanne Feltham put three pieces of carrot on the ledge of the Dutch door of Onyx's stall. In the beginning, Onyx had viewed her in the same light as everyone else. But Jeanne was not everyone else. She was patient. She was also careful to be absent whenever the trainer or Mrs. Taylor was there, not wanting the stallion to associate her in any way with his tormentors.

The stallion used to turn his head away from her and ignore the carrots. With barely repressed rage at what had caused him to so distrust humans, Jeanne acknowledged what he had said. Averting her gaze from him, she would turn sideways and lean against the half-door, forcing herself to relax and pretending to watch with interest the hay bales stacked close to the barn entrance.

Each evening, after she'd finished the bookwork, she'd take another carrot that she'd cut into pieces from her handbag and set them on the stall railing. She'd take a step back and wait quietly to see if he'd come for his treat. And each night, he turned his head away, unwilling to engage with one more human who would most likely hurt him. She could see the pain in his eyes. It was a pain that ran deep, and his only defense was to withdraw from everything around him and go inward. Jeanne knew that kind of pain. She respected it, but she was determined to banish it. Each night she tried again, but while his body was forced to occupy the stall, his mind had retreated to some distant place where nothing could hurt him. There was no pain there, and coaxing him away from his safe place was the most difficult thing she'd ever done.

She'd begun this training, for training it was, about a month ago. There's really only one way to work with a horse, slowly building a connection until the horse is ready to work with you, but so few trainers understood that. A horse isn't a tool, although history would tend to make you think otherwise. "Someday, Onyx," she said, "if we live long enough, perhaps things will change for the better. I don't know. We're not all like Fitzgibbon and that witch that owns you." She hadn't expected a response, but there was the briefest nicker. She was sure of it. It was a start, and then, she felt a push against her shoulder. Turning slowly, so as not to startle him, she watched as he first sniffed at the carrots and then began to eat.

"Good boy," she said. "Good boy." She reached out and rubbed his neck, just behind the ears. Onyx stood, accepting her touch. Then she leaned towards him, resting her forehead on his cheek. "What I do know, is that there's not much time left." She straightened, took a piece of the carrot and held it in her outstretched palm for the horse to take. "If I could just get you to understand that, you'd have a chance. I'll see you in the morning."

Jeanne was nearly to the barn door when the trainer, Duncan Fitzgibbon, shoved them open and strode towards the stalls, whip in hand.

"Get out of my way, if you please," Fitzgibbon said. "We've work to do, and I won't have you breaking his training trying to turn him into a lap dog."

Jeanne drew herself up to her full height, which was a good two inches more than Fitzgibbon could claim, and the set of her shoulders matched the tone of her voice. "I'll say it again. You watch yourself, Fitzgibbon. If I see you lay into him with that whip once more, it will be the last time you ever do anything with it."

"That horse is a killer, and you'd be best advised to stay from him. He's got no manners and a mean streak that will take you down if you're not on top of him every minute. Don't tell me my business. I know horses, and this one is good for nothing. He needs a firm hand."

"You watch yourself, Fitzgibbon. I've been around horses since before I could walk, and there's not one I can't ride." Her eyes were fire. "Your wife may stand for that kind of treatment, but Onyx won't and, as God as my witness, I won't either. Remember what I said. If I see one mark on that horse in the morning, you'll live to regret it."

As Jeanne stood her ground, refusing to leave, Fitzgibbon slapped the whip against the stall. Onyx, sensing anger from the trainer, reared and then struck with his front legs. Fitzgibbon jumped back, hesitated, and then lashed out. "I'll be back when he's calmed down. There's no working with him when he's like this. You'd best leave too."

Standing her ground, Jeanne watched the defiant trainer storm out of the barn and then turned back to Onyx, now trembling, his eyes anxious and worried.

"I won't let them hurt you," she said, watching Fitzgibbon stumble down the path that led to his small cottage at the bottom of the drive. "You're drunk again. God help me. I'd kill you if I could," she said, watching his uneven progress. A rustle from Onyx's stall brought her mind back to the problem at hand and she went back and stood by her friend. "I'll think of something, and I'm not leaving you until you've calmed down." Her voice was soft, gentle, and strong. "Do you understand what I've said? They will not harm you again."

There was really no way of knowing if the horse understood, but now another problem was at hand. Noises from the junction where the road separated — one branch leading to the house and the other to the stables — had effectively set up a roadblock, and Jeanne was trapped. Both of the Taylors were coming towards the barn and there was no way out until they left. There was no logical explanation for Jeanne being in the stables, and try as hard as she could, she couldn't come up with even an illogical reason. Her bookkeeping office was in the adjacent building, and Mrs. Taylor had made it clear that Jeanne had no access to any other building on the premises. Unless, Jeanne thought, Mrs. Taylor was hiding something, there was no reason for it.

All that meant for Jeanne, in reality, was that her twice daily visits to Onyx had to be done secretly. It had worked up to now, but the unexpected appearance of both of the Taylors put her in a sticky situation. The only place of safety was the place deemed the least safe of all. And so, talking softly to Onyx, she slid open the bar and pushed the stall door open.

Used to her gentle presence, the stallion watched her close the door behind her and make a place to sit in the shavings as close to the wall as she could so as not to be seen from the aisle.

Curious to see what this was all about, Onyx moved towards her and nuzzled her head. She reached up and rubbed his neck, but as the Taylors entered the barn, he stiffened and retreated to the far wall. If the Taylors were to open the stall door, Jeanne knew it would take less than a second for the stallion to charge them. There was no way they would chance it. All she could do was wait until they had done whatever it was they had come to do and left.

· · ·

"Do you think it's wise to close up this operation so soon?" Jerry asked, watching his footfalls with care and side-stepping a few piles of manure that the groom had neglected to pick up.

"There's no reason to stay. We've gotten everything on the list, with the exception of the documents that Speer claims to have and the one last piece he's picking up today. I don't want any of it on the premises any longer. As soon as they're gone, I am too. Having stolen goods on the property was never what I agreed to. That was all your doing. So, stay if you wish. There's nothing here for me. Home is where I want to be, and England is not it. We can list the property and deposit the check in Berlin, when it's sold. I hate this godforsaken place. It does nothing but drip and fog and mist and whatever else water does. I want to go home." She shoved one of the barn doors open with enough force that it slammed against the brace and nearly came off the roller.

"You're never happy anywhere. You won't even give this place a chance. The Brits are hard-working folk, and, if you remember what der Führer has said, they are of the same stock as we are." He stomped his feet on the rubber mat.

"Stock." She sniffed. "Cattle are stock. These people are..." she was brought up short by the sudden appearance of Fitzgibbon who had overheard some of their conversation as he was relieving himself against a tree set back from the driveway. His interest piqued and the possibility of turning what he'd heard to his advantage, he'd circled around and was waiting for them just inside the door.

"If you're here to ask for more time, don't waste what you've got," Anne said, pushing past him. "I don't want excuses. I want this horse ready for the hunt, and you've got three days to get him to run the course without a refusal at any jump. Three days, or you're gone. The both of you! I've no time to waste on a worthless animal, regardless of the species." Anne Taylor glared at the trainer. "You tell me he's dangerous. That may be. So am I."

Fitzgibbon grabbed her arm. "Not so fast, dearie. Nobody talks like that to Fitz. And that goes for you too, mister," he said, nodding at Jerry.

"Just in case you got any fancy ideas. No sir. I have a proposition for you, and you'd be well advised to consider it." His words, faintly slurred, didn't carry the threat he'd intended. He grabbed the railing of the nearest stall for support but misjudged the distance and pitched forward, landing face down in a pile of muck he'd neglected to clean.

"What the bloody hell is going on?" Jerry stepped around the inert form and threw his hands in the air. "Who is this clown?"

"He's my trainer. Was my trainer. He came highly recommended by the best people. But, again, there you have it. What the hell do the bloody Brits know about anything. He's done nothing. Nothing. Now, look at him. Trainer? He can't even keep the bloody aisle clean. Serves him right." She gave the body a vicious kick that didn't even cause a flinch in the unconscious Fitzgibbon, then looked up, her eyes wide. "He heard us."

Jerry consulted his watch. "I've got to transmit in twenty minutes. Bring the horse box around and park it by the garage. We'll move the art into it and padlock it. Out of sight, out of mind. When Speer shows up, it will be his problem." Jerry looked at the drunken trainer sprawled in the manure. "That thing," he said, "is your problem. And if he did hear us, it's a problem that needs to be taken care of now. Get rid of him."

Frustration, now mixed with desperation, was making it difficult for her to think, and Anne Taylor's head spun as she searched the barn for something to solve the problem. "Here," she said. "I'll open the stall door and you drag him in. We'll let the horse do the job. Onyx hates him. Shouldn't take long for him to trample Fitzgibbon into a pulp. We'll leave him there until the morning. After the party, there won't be anyone else around, and I'll discover him in the morning and call the police." She rubbed her hands together. "It's perfect. I'll be rid of both of them."

Inside the stall, Jeanne tensed and it took all her willpower to remain still as stone.

"Are you out of your mind?" Jerry said. "There's no way in hell I'm going in to that stall for one blasted second, let alone long enough to drag a body past that horse! You want the body in there, you do it." And he was gone.

Anne stared at the trainer, still out for the count, then at Onyx, and made the only rational decision. She left them both and took off after Gerry, screaming as she ran out of the barn and down the drive.

As the noise faded in the distance, Jeanne scrambled to her feet. Onyx, still standing against the back wall of his stall, seemed to sense that the danger had passed. His trembling ceased, and the fear in his eyes melted away. One blessing about the whole horrible situation was that horses live in the moment. It's a survival instinct. An animal worried about the past can't assess present danger. "Soon, Onyx," she said. She let herself out of the stall and brought the horse an armful of hay. Scratching his ears and rubbing his shoulder, she watched him eat. "You'll need energy," she said. "As soon as I can make arrangements. You're going to like it where you're going. All the food you need and you'll have a herd to make you feel secure. And you'll never be hurt again. I promise."

．　．　．

"I've just come by to let you know I'm closing out the books on the Sport Horses." Anne Taylor reached for her pack of Gauloises and her lighter. "My plans have changed." She crumpled the now-empty pack and tossed it on the floor by Jeanne's desk. Lighting the cigarette, she inhaled and then blew the smoke in her bookkeeper's face. "I expect you'll need a day to draw up the paperwork for the fillies and the mares. Let's arrange for your termination to take effect at close of business tomorrow. That should be sufficient notice."

And just like that, Jeanne learned she'd been sacked. With barely a pause as she made entries in the ledger, she merely said, "I see." Damned if she'd let the bitch have the satisfaction of seeing her distress. "Will there also be a bill of sale for the stallion?"

"No. I've made other arrangements. Write him off. He'll be gone Monday unless some sort of miracle occurs." She ground out the barely started cigarette in the ashtray. "And I don't believe in miracles."

"I'll need some sort of paperwork to close out his entry for tax purposes."

Anne gave a theatrical sigh. "Oh, very well. I'll have the knacker man scribble something on a scrap of paper. Will that suffice?"

Jeanne's fingers moving across the columns in the ledger did not betray the terror that had sliced through her like a knife. "That will suffice."

"Good. I'll expect all of your personal items removed from the office by tomorrow evening."

. . .

Bicycling home, Jeanne's thoughts had only one focus. She had less than twenty-four hours left of access to Onyx. Less than twenty-four hours to save his life. With each push of the pedal, each rotation of the wheels, her mind kept pace, plans forming and then being discarded. There had to be some way to get him safely to Sir Thomas's stables and freedom. Turning into her yard, she leaned the bicycle against the fence, but instead of walking up the path to the front door, she crossed the street and walked the short distance to Millie's cottage. Her rap at the front door brought a "Come on in" from the kitchen where Millie was making soup. The aroma of bread baking in the oven filled the kitchen and spilled over into the parlor, where Jeanne dropped heavily into the parlor chair closest to the old stone fireplace.

Paring knife in hand, Millie peered from the kitchen doorway at Jeanne's worried face. She set the knife on the table and took two glasses and a bottle of elderberry wine from the cupboard. She poured a bit in each glass and took them into the parlor, setting Jeanne's down on the side table by the chair. "Feels good to sit for a bit," she said, stretching her back and flexing her shoulders."

"Smells wonderful, Mill."

"Stay for supper. There's plenty. I always make too much. Old habits die hard."

Jeanne hesitated, then nodded. Taking the glass, she cradled it in both hands, then the tears started to fall. She sighed heavily and wiped them away with the back of her hand. "Sorry. It's been one hell of a day." She took a sip of her wine, letting the warm liquid rest on her tongue a moment before swallowing. "Nice. A bit tarter than last year's batch, I think." She took another sip. "I like it."

"You're not here to discuss my wine-making prowess, dear. And judging by the expression on your face and the bit of waterworks, something is obviously troubling you. What's wrong?"

Jeanne set her glass back on the table and pressed her fists against her eyes to hold back the tears that were ignoring her determination to keep them at bay. "In a nutshell, everything. Everything that could possibly be wrong is wrong, and I need your help if I'm going to set the worst of it to rights."

"That's more like it, dear. Action. That's the ticket. So, start at the beginning, and we'll see what needs to be done." She picked up her glass of wine and held it to the light, admiring the rich color. "I think it's a bit darker, as well. So, on to the problems at hand. How many are there?"

"Hmmm. Well, I guess there are two."

"Excellent," Mildred said. "Not that the problems are excellent, but two is a manageable number. Let's begin with the lesser of the two evils."

"I've been sacked. No notice. The witch."

Millie raised an inquisitive eyebrow.

"No, I did nothing wrong." Jeanne waved her hand in the air, a gesture of helplessness. "She's selling the horses. The whole lot of them. Said her plans have changed. But, that brings me to the big problem. She's not selling Onyx. She's sending him to slaughter."

Millie paused with her glass of wine nearly to her lips. "She's what??"

"Yes. She says he's a killer. Rears and strikes. Refuses the jump. Apparently he's tossed her more than once. But Mill, he's not. They beat him. And he's afraid. They punish him by not feeding him enough. I'm at my wits' end. I've got less than one day to save him. What can I do?" The pain in her voice matched the pain in her eyes. "I've only one choice. One chance. And I know it will work, but they'll find him. They'll find me. What to do?" She sank back in her chair, defeated.

For a few moments that seemed an eternity to Jeanne, her friend sat without speaking. She took a few sips of her wine as she considered the problem, and finally she'd worked it out. "Have you ridden him?"

"Twice. When they were away. He was a gentleman, Mill."

"Yes. They know people. If you're confident, you can handle him, and I'll deal with the coverup, as it were." She grinned. "We'll give him a nice white blaze and perhaps some white on two or three legs. Even if she sees him, she won't recognize him. Getting that woman will be a pure joy. Just trust me to take care of everything, dear. And, as for your employment, I happen to know there will soon be an opening for a bookkeeper at the bank, if something else doesn't materialize. You'll just need to be frugal for the next month. So, finish your wine, don't ask me any questions, and let's have a nice supper." She reached over and patted Jeanne's hand. "When do you ride?"

"Dusk, tomorrow. After the party has had a chance to get going and the Taylors are occupied with their guests."

"Excellent." Millie said. "She's about to reap what she's sown. I do believe this is the beginning of the end for them."

"I hope you're right."

CHAPTER TWENTY-TWO

Port Hope

Yesterday, after I'd reported finding Margo's body to the local police and shown them my credentials so I wouldn't be tied up with questioning, I'd returned to Morris, bowed my head, and said a prayer for her soul. That was my goodbye to her. There's no time for grieving in this business. It's why we try not to get attached to anyone. It hurts too much when you lose someone you care about. If I lost John, I don't know what I'd do. And so, I push that thought so far back in my mind that it only surfaces when we lose someone we've worked with. *"Don't get involved. Do the job and get out,"* John always reminds me. He's right, but it's easier said than done. Fortunately, in this case, doing the job meant also avenging Margo, and I had every intention of succeeding.

Two days with the roses and I'd acquired a list of possible—no, make that probable agents, courtesy of Colleen and Denise. It's a myth that agents work alone. Hollywood loves the idea of a solitary operative doing impossible feats. That's the problem. It's impossible. We're all connected, and a good agent knows when to listen to those who have information and are acting on it. The local women had begun surveillance on the activities of the suspected spies, and I was scheduled to put in an appearance this afternoon at Colleen's home at 1400 hours to listen to what they'd learned. That gave me the morning to deal with the desk clerk and also see what I could turn up at the Schneider place.

Running in the background were the murders. The odds said everything was connected. My intuition agreed. All I had to find was the nexus — the hub around which all this revolved, and I was leaning strongly in the direction of Anne Taylor/Schneider and Gerry/Gerhardt. They had the money. He had the contacts. It was too much to overlook. Breakfast at Frankie's American Diner this morning was a reminder that life goes on.

"Coffee, luv?"

My waitress, Veronica, according to her name badge, hovered over me like a hen with a chick that needed mothering. Her auburn hair was tucked into a hairnet that, on a woman with less striking features, would have made her look frumpy. Veronica was about the farthest from frumpy I could imagine. She was a looker and had overdone the makeup in an attempt to tone it down. It worked fairly well, until she spoke. Her voice had that throaty Lauren Bacall "come hither" timbre and there was nothing short of sign language that could eliminate the aura of sex.

"Yes, please," I said, then gave her a serious look. "Is it any good this morning?" Hope springs eternal.

"You've got to be kidding. We Brits couldn't make a decent cup of coffee if we tried. And we don't," she said, giving me a wink as she filled my cup. "I don't drink the swill they brew here."

"We Danes love our coffee," I said, eyeing the brownish liquid in my cup and deciding to pass. I pushed the cup aside.

Veronica looked around the restaurant. With only two customers at the moment, she gave herself permission to take a break. She slipped into the seat opposite me in the booth, set down the carafe, and leaned across the table. "My feet are killing me," she said. "We heard the news."

I pulled the coffee back and sniffed. It didn't smell too bad. I took a swallow, grimaced, and pushed it back again. She'd been right. It was swill. "She was good."

Veronica nodded. "Not good enough, in the end." She shook her head. "What do you need?"

"Two things," I said. I took the sketch of the postmaster from my handbag and passed it to her. "See what you can find out about him. And I've got a low-level operative to check out. She's the desk clerk at the Rusty Scupper. Name is Berthe

Baumgartner." I gave Veronica the sketch of Baumgartner, as well. "Wasn't any way to snap her photo, so this is a fair approximation of her."

Veronica raised an eyebrow. "She kept her own name?"

"I told you she was low level. Probably part of the advance guard for Operation Lena. They're not sending their best and brightest. I sent myself a birthday card with a message written in German, and our friend Berthe steamed open the envelope and made a mess of resealing it. If she's been sent to check out the guests at the hotel, she's going to pass on what she's learned. I'm going to keep an eye on her and find out who her handler is. Then, we can get the two of them. He's most likely been here for a while and isn't one of the new crew. And also the new postmaster in Port Hope. The previous one got run over when he was cycling home. He had a reputation for eavesdropping on conversations when he worked the switchboard. If he overheard something, it would explain it. His replacement showed up literally the next day."

"Will do. We picked up a bloke at the pub yesterday morning. He tried to order a pint of beer an hour before opening time and spread out his money on the bar, totally confused about how much to pay. Also, he had a strong German accent. It was pathetic." She snorted. "I almost wonder if it's not deliberate, and if our ally in Hitler's staff isn't behind it."

It made sense. Canaris was doing everything he could. Why not this, as well? "If you could have MI6 hold off a bit on mine until I find that third agent, I'd appreciate it." I cast a final, longing glance at the coffee and swallowed hard. "Would you bring me a cup of tea, please? I need caffeine. And a donut. Chocolate."

The tea was good. The donut, better. Fortified for what the day would bring, I nodded to Veronica and headed back to the hotel, figuring that Berthe might have taken advantage of my absence. I was not disappointed. The magazines on the table had been rifled through and restacked in a different order, and the dresser drawers had also been given the once-over. She'd refolded my underwear a different way. I made a mental note to wash all of it before I wore anything she'd pawed through. Putting on my game face, I marched down the corridor to the lobby and positioned myself by the front desk.

There were two ways to play this. I could be the latest agent dropped off who needed help finding my contact. That would put the clerk in the power position. Or, I could go in guns blazing. I chose that. Operating from a position of strength is always the better choice.

The lobby was empty and Berthe was at the switchboard, leafing through a movie magazine. She looked up, and her eyes widened in either surprise or fear. Maybe a combination of both.

"Sie sind eine tollpatschige Idiotin!" I screamed in her face. "Or, we can speak English if you need the practice," I added. "Did you not learn anything from your training before you came here? Or are you, as I just said, a clumsy idiot?"

She jumped to her feet, the magazine slipping from her lap onto the floor. "Who are you? What do you mean? Nobody told me you were coming!"

I gave an exasperated sigh. "The mail, to begin with. Steaming an envelope open is not difficult. Closing it again so the seal is smooth instead of a puckered, uneven mess takes a bit of care."

She screwed up her face, her brow furrowed. She blinked rapidly. Her eyes traveled from me to the mail slots behind her and when she looked back, I saw the dawn of understanding.

"Then, the room. What were you expecting to find?"

She shrugged.

"What did you find?" I pressed on.

"Nothing." She shrugged again.

"Then it should look that way when you leave it. There are three steps to a search," I said, ticking off the points on my fingers as I spoke. "The entry, the search, the clean-up. Each has further steps that must be followed. They are there for good reasons."

She was frowning, probably trying to remember what she'd done.

"Entry was simple. *Einfach!* You had the key. All you had to do was open the door. *Ja?*"

"*Ja.*"

"That's the only thing you did correctly. Your search was a disaster. Then, you put nothing back the way you found it. Did you think I was so stupid I wouldn't notice someone had been in my room and searched it?"

A head shake.

"If you have any hope of being successful, you must begin paying attention to everything you do. Every detail. Every time. There is no margin for error. You had two simple tasks and you botched both of them." I shook my head in disapproval. "Those were your tests and you failed. This will be reported."

"But," she began.

I waved my hand. "The matter is beyond my control. Why did you lock the back door the other night?"

"I was afraid," she said. "The police came in to the hotel and warned us to take precautions. An escaped killer was thought to be somewhere on the docks. Why do you ask?"

I ignored the question. All right, then. My suspicions that the clerk was merely a low-level operative confirmed, I shook my head disapprovingly and left her staring at her feet. I went to my room to wash up and give Berthe time to place a telephone call to her handler. I took my camera, pulled up a chair to the window, and sat down to watch the street. It was a good hour and a half later that Berthe left the Scupper. She crossed the street to a marine supply store, lit a cigarette, and waited by the display window. We were both playing the waiting game. Ten minutes later, I began snapping photos as a heavy-set man, middle-aged or a tad beyond, strolled up to her and they set off down the street towards the industrial docks.

There were two levels of German agents operating in Britain. Those sent by Canaris as part of Operation Lena were the unskilled, the untrained, the inept, and the easily intimidated. The desk clerk, Berthe Baumgartner, was one of these. The ones already here before Lena were the true danger. And that is why the mystery man was a person of interest.

There was no need to follow them. Berthe would return to the hotel, and her contact would return the way he had come. I pocketed the camera. Grabbing my handbag, I went downstairs and exited the hotel by the rear door. For once, Morris was cooperative and gave me no trouble. I exchanged my parking spot in the back lot for one on the side road, close to the street and waited.

I didn't have to wait long. When they returned, his pace was considerably quicker than it had been when he'd arrived, and Berthe was struggling to keep up. It would have been interesting to have heard what she'd told him, but judging by the iron grip he had on her arm, she'd told him everything, and he had no intention of letting her out of his sight. What his plans were for her were anyone's guess, but I would wager her lifespan was going to be cut short and fairly soon. That wasn't what I wanted. Whatever else she knew, we needed to learn, and that meant Morris and I were going to keep them in range until they got where they were going. After that, I'd play it by ear.

Their destination was half a block to the south on the left, where an automobile, an older version of Morris, waited. The engine started up as they approached, indicating there was now a third person, the driver. There were few automobiles on the road, thanks, once again, to petrol rationing, and I had to keep farther back than I would have liked. Ideally, as we were taught in spy school, we would have two cars involved in the tail, alternating leads, but Morris seemed to understand what was required of him and he settled into a steady, if slow, pace.

Too slow, as it turned out. We hadn't gone more than ten kilometers when a lorry closed rapidly and, horn blaring, passed us and settled in at the driver's chosen pace which was faster, granted, but not all that much faster. The upshot was that I lost the auto I was tailing. Slamming my fist on the steering wheel didn't bring any satisfaction and only resulted in bruising my hand.

My plan to learn the identity of her handler and then rescue the hapless Berthe and transport her into custody on espionage charges had evaporated in the black exhaust of the lorry.

One plan aborted or at least on hold, but with more to be done, I debated how to scope out the Schneider estate. Entering by the main drive was out of the question, so the only other option was revisiting the scene of two murders and checking out the abandoned house and its outbuildings. With my tray of rose equipment at hand and my official badge, I drove to the cottage across the street from where Alese Farmer had been murdered and the corpse of Brian Fitch had been unearthed. I found Mildred Botherwell sitting on her front porch, a cup of tea on the armrest of her garden chair, and several rose clippings by her feet.

"I was wondering if you might stop by again," Mildred said, motioning for me to have a seat next to her. "I made a few cuttings for you."

Setting down my tray, I picked up the clippings. They had been sharply cut at an angle, and each had four nodes. "These are perfect. Thank you." I opened the vials of root hormone and placed a cutting in each one.

"They're all labeled, so you shouldn't have any difficulty when it comes time to catalogue them," she said. "I watched while you worked with Alese's rose." She sighed and shook her head.

Then, she brightened. "Of course, I watch." This time she grinned. "I'm just not obvious about it. Alese…well, she was always ready to erupt. Didn't matter what it was. Never took the time to gather all the facts before she came to a conclusion. A judgement, actually."

"Do you think that had something to do with her death?"

She sipped her tea. Her expression thoughtful. "I believe it had everything to do with it. She was all in a dither about the Land Girls coming to tear up her yard, and I suspect she tore into someone who turned out not to be a Land Girl but something far more dangerous and sinister, if you catch my drift." Mildred's expression grew dark. "And her mistake cost her her life."

I set the tray with the new rose samples aside. "Can you show me where they found her?"

"Yes, but there's really nothing to see there, now." She turned and smiled at me. "Alese would be happy to know someone else valued her rose. Come along." She pointed to the left of the cottage across the street. "Over there and off a ways. I think she was running after someone and had her garden spade with her." Mildred nodded in the direction of a stone wall that had been collapsed for quite some time, judging by the vegetation that had grown up around and inside it. "The police didn't spend much time here. Just enough to decide she'd been clunked in the head by her spade and left where she'd fallen. I think," Mildred kicked at a loose stone, "she caught her foot on one of these, went down and dropped the spade, and whoever she was following saw the opportunity to grab the handle and hit her while she was struggling to get up."

It made sense. A crime of opportunity. Still, it would have taken some strength to wield a tool of such awkward proportions. The handle alone was a good four feet in length. "Where does this path lead?"

"I'm not sure exactly where on the estate it goes, but there are a number of outbuildings. Any one of them. Perhaps more than one." She squinted, trying to get a better view. "If I had to wager a guess, I would say the storage building for the stables. It's in the vicinity. I don't know for sure."

"Is there any way to get there from here?" I asked.

Mildred tilted her head, as if trying to capture an idea that was working its way loose. "There is a road. Well, there used to be a road. Just around the bend over there. It's horribly overgrown now. Hasn't been used since the caretaker retired and moved away. That was," she paused to think, "eight or nine years ago. It's still there, though. If you look hard, you'll see the tracks. Takes years for nature to reclaim her property, but give her enough time, and she will."

It looked to me as if Nature was making excellent headway, and that meant my own headway down that road, if I could find it, would be slow going. "Does anyone come down here?'

"No. After the caretaker retired, the Taylors redid the access roads. Now everything comes off the main driveway. Nobody's been down here in years."

"So," I said, "I guess the question is, 'Why now?'"

Mildred made a sound of affirmation. "That's a good question, dear. If you don't mind, I'd like to take my own cutting of her rose. For all her oddness, she was a good person. I miss her."

"Were there any children?"

Mildred looked at the empty house and the ancient rose bush. "No. Just the rose. Now, it's an orphan of a sort."

We returned to the porch, and I stowed everything back in their proper compartments. "You live alone," I said.

"Yes. Yes, I do."

"Do you get lonesome?" I asked, hoisting the handle of the tray over my arm.

"Oh, from time to time I miss having someone to chat with about day to day things. But, I learned a long time ago that you will be far lonelier living with someone who doesn't respect you than you will ever be living on your own." She patted my shoulder. "We were raised to believe we weren't complete unless we were married, but for me, it didn't work out that way. I was complete before I married. I just didn't know it at the time, and I spent most of my life trying to fit whatever mold I was supposed to fit into." She gave a rueful smile. "Don't get me wrong. It wasn't Steven's fault. That was my husband. He didn't know any other way. And one day, I decided to leave. It was the right decision. So, no. I'm not lonely any longer."

There wasn't any comment that seemed to fit, so I nodded and said my goodbye. All I needed now was a place to park Morris out of the way, a bit of luck locating the old road, and enough time to find out why Alese Farmer and possibly Brian Fitch had been killed. Then I had a thought. "Where was the postmaster killed?" I asked.

Mildred paused, the teacup and saucer in her hand. "Strange you should ask that. I'd just been thinking about it. Dave was run over where this road intersects with the main thoroughfare. There's never any traffic here." She looked thoughtful. "Too much death for such a peaceful place."

•   •   •

Every occupation has a uniform. Granted, some are more identifying than others, but overall, our work clothes are designed to accommodate the work we do, with some noticeable exceptions—my line of work, for instance, being one of those exceptions. My uniform was whatever I happened to be wearing, and sometimes this didn't work out terribly well. This fact was painfully evident a few meters into my investigative foray at the back acreage of the Schneider estate. The first point of pain was my right had that had picked up a thistle spike. The second was something else sharp that had worked into my shoe and was threatening to lodge in my instep. A field gone to weeds is a painful, prickly place.

The unexpected boon of this discomfort, however, was that in stooping to deal with the problems, I gained an entirely new perspective on my surroundings. In fact, as I sat down in a reasonably clear patch and worked on my foot, I looked up and around, and that's when I saw the antennae.

Sometimes, the best hiding place is right out in the open, and this fit that advice perfectly. Forgetting my foot, I took my binoculars and settled in to get the lay of this interesting new land. About fifty meters away to my right was the rear of the main house, and off to its right were the stables. The ground then sloped for a considerable distance before once again leveling out, and this is where the outbuildings had been constructed. There were four of them. Two were obviously used as garages for storing farm equipment, although there was only one tractor visible. The third building, whatever its purpose may have been at one time, was mostly collapsed back onto itself, and was more a den for foxes now than anything else. The fourth building, however, was the mother lode. Judging its dimensions was difficult from this distance, but it looked to be about the size of a large workshop. The roof was peaked, there was a stone chimney on the side closest to the house, and an array of antennae protruded from the other peak. There had been an effort to camouflage them by installing an oversized weathervane in their midst. The large horse that constituted the base of the weathervane currently had his head pointing to the west.

"Look for the odd thing." This was my mantra, drummed into my head at spy school, and as far as odd things went, this was a doozy. I gave my foot a final brush and reclaimed my shoe. It didn't take a lot of brainpower to understand what this setup was all about. Antennae had only one function—well two, if you broke it down. They received and transmitted radio waves. And that meant there would be wireless radios in that building. Given Anne Taylor's facility with German, the logical conclusion was that this station was transmitting information to Berlin. And that meant, I would have to do something about it. I didn't need to see any more. It was time to gather the reinforcements.

CHAPTER TWENTY-THREE

Port Hope and the Schneider Estate

By mid-afternoon, the Port Hope Hunt Club was saddled and ready for an impromptu training session, called by Master of Hounds, Mildred Botherwell. Beginning at the stone wall that marked the terminus of the Taylor Estate and fanning out in an untraditional pattern of crisscrossing, doubling back, and then forging ahead, the riders honed their skills while creating one hell of a mess in the fields for miles in every direction. As the horses' hooves churned up the sod, sending clods everywhere, it was, to all appearances, a free for all. In reality, it was deliberate, well-planned, and perfectly executed. Conceived by Mildred and designed to prevent Jeanne and Onyx from being tracked on their ride to freedom, it was a resounding success.

"Isn't this lovely?" Millie said to Bill, who had pulled up alongside to view the damage.

"Splendid. I believe this should do the trick."

"I also believe the horses enjoyed themselves immensely. Perhaps they understand."

Bill shrugged. "Perhaps."

. . .

"Why wasn't I notified?" Anne stood at the entrance to the driveway, fuming at the slight as she watched the riders streaking across the distant fields. "I am a member of the Hunt Club. How dare they? Who scheduled this? They'll pay for this."

"Yes. Yes, they will in time. It's not important, at the moment," Jerry said. "We've got other matters of more urgency to attend do. It's the perfect opportunity to move the art from the storage room into the horse box. And tomorrow, after Speer takes it off our hands, der Führer will be most generous in his appreciation of our efforts. By the way, what did you do with the trainer?"

Anne, still scowling at the last of the riders disappearing over the far stone wall, shrugged. "He's out in the back field. I dragged him there with the tractor and dumped a few loads of manure on top of him to mask the odor. After running over him, of course."

"I hope you did a better job than you did with the driver of the delivery van, Fitch." Jerry looked at her pointedly. "They found him. You didn't have to kill him. You could have paid him off."

"Why should I have paid him off? We didn't need him anymore. Besides, he would have talked. Those sort can't be trusted. And as for the burial, I didn't have the proper equipment. All I had was a shovel. I had to improvise. What's the big fuss about, anyhow? I took his wallet. They have no idea who he is, and they'll never find out. Stop worrying about it."

"What did you do with the delivery van? That's something that can be traced." Jerry slapped her across the face, his frustration finally at the boiling point. "You are a stupid bitch with a temper you can't control, and when they come for you, I'm not going to be anywhere around."

His wife lifted her hand to her cheek and shot daggers at him with her eyes. There was a level of hatred in them that caused him to take a step back. "Stupid bitch? I just killed two birds with one stone. I had Fitzgibbon drive it back to London and park it in front of the British Museum. Let Hyde-Stuart explain it. He loves to hear himself talk." She laughed, but there was no mirth in it. "Fitzgibbon isn't going to be telling anyone about the delivery van, unless he has a conversation with the devil." She turned abruptly, still holding her cheek. "I'm going to get dressed. And Gerhardt, if you ever lay a hand on me again, I'll kill you too."

The welcome silence that followed Jerry's and Anne's departures from the barn was short-lived, lasting only long enough for Anne to reach the kitchen where she promptly tore into the staff. The words were indistinguishable, but the tone and the volume were unmistakable, as were the sobs of one young girl who ran crying from the house.

Her arms around the stallion's neck, Jeanne whispered, "Soon."

. . .

After struggling to use the barrow to help him move the art on his own, Jerry finally accepted defeat and carried each piece, one at a time, from the storage room to the horse box. His thoughts, however, were on his wife. Regardless of the war, police still investigated crime. It was a concept she couldn't seem to grasp. The war was just beginning in Britain, and until Germany had successfully overcome Britain, they all had to answer to British law. His shirt, now sticking to his chest and back, along with the chaff that irritated his skin, his anger continued unabated against her. Placing the last picture in the horse box, he paused to wipe the sweat from his forehead with his shirtsleeve like a common laborer. He tossed the ignition key on the front seat. When Speer came by in the morning, he'd have everything he needed.

The mission was accomplished, and he was ready to move on, but he'd do so without his wife. He was done with Anne. She was in the house acting as if she were the Queen of Berchtesgaden.

He shook his head. She was a fool. He padlocked the horse box in case she decided to pull some sort of stunt. Then, after a quick washup and change of clothes, he packed a small bag. In the morning, he'd put as much distance between him and her as he could as quickly as he could. He'd completed his assignment, but the danger remained high and he knew it. By morning he'd be beyond her reach and Britain's, too.

· · ·

At 2000 hours Bellesford House was fully lit in a flagrant disregard of blackout regulations. If it wouldn't have meant death and injury to the innocent, I would not have minded in the least had a stray bomb taken the place out. But I didn't have to worry very long. The Taylor/Schneiders might not have thought the blackout was worthy of note, but the members of Parliament most certainly did, and after they reminded the Taylors of that fact, the blackout draperies were drawn and the exterior lights extinguished. This elicited another outburst from the lady of the house, but even her insistence that she would decide on matters pertaining to her domain, had no effect. Once again, she stormed off to her quarters.

· · ·

John and I, attired in our best evening dress, hadn't bothered with the formalities of entering by the front door and being announced. No. We were party crashers of a sort, although we didn't technically attend the party at all. Our interests were strictly *au plein air.*

Snooping about is always a risky activity, and even riskier if one is acting alone. That's why having a companion of the opposite sex comes in handy. It's perfectly natural for a man and woman to take a stroll about during the evening, and should they stumble across something that bodes ill, an embrace and a passionate kiss are often all that's needed to safely extricate oneself from the situation. It had been a while since the last passionate kiss and embrace, however, and any port in the storm, as they say.

The distant sounds of battle carried far on the night air. We began our clandestine activities with the necessary embrace and passionate kiss. Practice is important. "Thank you," John said.

"You're welcome."

That was a strange thing to say, I thought.

He laughed. "Not for the kiss, although thank you for that, as well. No. Thank you for not being her." He tossed his head in the direction of the upstairs where the not so dulcet tones of Frau Schneider couldn't be drowned out even by the efforts of the string quartet downstairs, valiantly doing their best, regardless.

"No worries, dear. Shall we?"

Normally, that would have been an invitation to dance, but as I'd said before, these were not normal times. I took his arm and we began our stroll across the lawns and around the side of the house to the outbuildings where we split up. What were we looking for? I wasn't sure, but I'd know when we found it.

The first item of interest I found was a horse box parked in front of the barn. Nothing out of the ordinary there, as it was a necessary vehicle for transporting horses to events. What was out of the ordinary, however, was the padlock on the back, securing the double doors. I wondered. Even if the latch were broken, the padlock was not necessary. The bar would have been strong enough, and besides, horse owners would never padlock their animals inside a conveyance. When I'd come full circle in my search of the barn, I intended to use my pick locks and find out what was inside.

Next, I moved to the barn itself. Sliding open one of the massive doors, I found the second item of interest. A young woman, dressed in riding habit, was standing by one of the stalls, a bridle and reins in hand. She froze when she saw me.

"Good evening," I said. "I just came by to have a look around. It's a lovely evening for a ride. There's enough light. It's a waxing moon on the way to full in a few days." She didn't answer but seemed to be studying me. She seemed most interested in my face. After a bit, she nodded.

"They're starving him," she said, "as punishment. He's just been trying to protect himself from the beatings."

I could see the tears threatening to spill over, and my heart reached out to her.

"I've been sneaking hay to him. She whips him. I saw her. When she left, I found him covered in sweat, trembling. Who would do that to a horse?"

It was my turn to nod. "Someone without a soul or a conscience."

"She's going to send him to slaughter." Her voice became defiant. "I won't let her. I told him tonight that he'd be free. I promised him." She lifted the bridle and the reins. "These are mine. I'm not taking anything of hers if you're concerned about that."

We hadn't introduced ourselves, and we wouldn't. I understood what she was about to do. "Where will you take him?" I asked.

She shook her head. "No. I can't tell you. Nobody must find him. And if anyone asks you, you won't have to lie. I read your aura. It has kindness in it." She opened the stall door, and a large black horse nickered and approached her.

I watched the two of them. There was something in the way she talked to the stallion that he understood, for the stallion began to prance, anticipating. At her voice, he settled down and waited patiently while she bridled him.

"You have no saddle," I said.

She smiled, rubbing his ears and tickling his whiskers. "I don't need one."

I watched her mount in one graceful motion. Once astride, she stroked the horse's neck and whispered to him. His ears pricked forward and he whinnied. She walked him to the barn door and let him sniff the night air, his energy barely contained.

"Do you want me to do anything for you?" I asked.

"Close the door behind me, if you will, and spit on her grave if we're lucky enough she dies soon. Oh, if you're here looking for something, anything at all, you might want to see what's in the storage room." She tossed her head in the direction of a door at the other end of the barn.

She and the stallion stood one more moment, the scent of the sea and the ripening pastures filling his nostrils, and I sensed he knew what was about to happen. On her cue, he moved forward, and they walked past the horse box and across the driveway to the field where they picked up the trot, finally breaking into a full gallop, effortlessly clearing the stone wall that marked the boundary line of the estate. For a short while after they vanished from my sight, I could hear the sound of galloping hooves as the rider and her mount raced towards freedom.

That piece of information the young woman had imparted left me once again with two items of interest to pursue, and just as I was about to rummage for my pick locks, John returned, a bit out of breath.

"How's it going?" I asked.

"Pretty good. You?"

"Fine." I started in on the lock.

"Just need a few hand tools," he said. "A bit of demolition to accomplish."

"Ah. You've been down at the antennae. Hand me that smaller pick, please."

"Here you go. Back in a while."

There is something satisfying about working with one's hands, regardless of the occupation, and the rewarding *click* as the lock released its grip on the door was one of those satisfying moments. Less satisfying, however, was the fact that the storeroom was completely empty. Odd. Yet I believed the young woman. Something had been in this storeroom the last time she'd been in the barn, but it had been moved somewhere else. I was about to return my pick locks to their case, when realization hit. Of course. I'd wait for John to return and we'd tackle the next phase of this together.

. . .

"All done?" I asked. My husband had returned, this time both out of breath and rather sweaty.

"My attire is not all that well suited to the job at hand," he said. "I left the sledge down there. No point in lugging it back up the hill. They're not going to be needing it." He wiped the perspiration from his brow with the sleeve of his rather wrinkled tuxedo. "It was quite an operation. There were half a dozen wireless sets there, along with a mimeograph machine." He rotated his shoulder and winced. "I need to get in shape. That took more energy than I had. Age is creeping up."

"Nonsense," I said. "It's just a warm evening and you were overdressed for the occasion. But I've got one more lock to pick, and I figured after all you'd done for the cause, you should witness the grand opening, as it were."

"I'm not going back for the sledge if that's what you mean."

"Don't be a baby. This lock is not that hefty. I can manage just fine without the big guns." And I did. There was a bit of suspense as we removed the lock and then opened the doors. This time the cupboard wasn't bare. In fact, it was full to nearly overflowing with what we'd been charged to find. It was, for want of a better word, overwhelming.

"Do you think it's all here?" I asked.

John made a quick scan of the contents. "No." He shook his head. "There are at least a hundred and fifty pieces of art gone missing. I'd wager there's a bit shy of a hundred here, but it's a good haul, nonetheless. Damn good." John took his camera from his jacket pocket and documented both the location and the contents of the horse box. "We need to thank Bill for this."

I agreed. Bill's call to London regarding what Bobbie Aldercroft had heard had put us on the right track. He'd asked why Anne Taylor would be arguing about *Kunst,* the German word for art. It was just a hunch, he'd said, but he'd felt it deserved further investigation. And he was right. The evidence lay before us, or rather was stacked before us, in the horse box all ready to go somewhere, and while we didn't know where that would have been, we were going to make sure the destination would be one of our own choosing.

I walked to the driver's side door, hoping that by some miracle the key was still in the truck. It was the evening for miracles big and small. I took the key and presented it to John with a flourish. "Shall we?" I asked. Again, it wasn't an invitation to dance but rather an invitation to hit the road and not slow down until we'd arrived at Whitehall. We closed the rear doors of the horse box that had no need of a padlock, although we brought it along for evidence.

The party inside the house continued, and I wondered if Anne Taylor/Anna Schneider had recovered from her snit and had rejoined the festivities. I didn't care. By morning, the authorities would have her and her husband under arrest for grand theft and espionage. The first would mean prison, but it was wartime, and the second charge would mean their execution. No amount of tantrums, screams, or threats would save either of them. And, the icing on the cake, her stallion had escaped his prison and was free. The roles had been reversed and poetic justice had been served.

. . .

Sometimes, it seems that you solve one problem only to find you've created two more. And that was the current situation. We'd saved the art. Well, we'd saved a great deal of the art, and moreover, it was in our possession. That was the problem. What the hell were we going to do with it? The whole purpose of moving it out of London was to spare it from Hitler's bombs, so returning everything back to London where the Luftwaffe and the RAF were duking it out every night over the Channel with the occasional bomb causing damage on land sort of nullified the whole undertaking and put us back on square one. Actually, minus square one, since some of the art was still unaccounted for.

It seemed that John and I came to that realization at the same time, for we'd no longer left the Taylor/Schneider estate and turned on to the main road to London that John pulled over and parked the horse box. I did the same with Morris. Once again, England's art was on the move. Again. Destination unknown. I left Morris to have a conversation with John. No way was I going to have him walk over to Morris and have somebody jump out of a hedgerow and make off with the horsebox. Morris would never manage as a pursuit vehicle.

"Where should we go?" I asked.

John did that tuneless whistle he does when he's thinking. He looked at me. "That's a good question." A few notes later, he looked at me again. "A really good question."

I agreed. But it was a question we needed an answer to and pronto. Then, I brightened. The horsebox wouldn't fit in a small garage, but it would do just fine and be right at home in a barn. And I had just the right one in mind. "Follow me," I said. "We won't have to go far. Don't worry, it's perfect."

. . .

I'm fairly certain that the last thing Colleen expected to see on her doorstep this evening was the couple in rumpled, dirt-stained evening dress who had arrived with a stolen horse box and the fairly reliable Morris. "Good evening, Colleen," I said, tilting my head towards John. "My associate, DCI Ellsworth of Scotland Yard."

John gave a slight bow.

"May we ask a favor?" I continued.

Colleen looked first at me, then at John, and finally at the motor vehicles in her driveway. The confusion on her face almost immediately transformed into comprehension, and a smile spread across her face. "You've done it!" she said.

"May we park the horsebox in your barn until the slate mines in Wales open?"

"Of course, my dear. At the south end past the tractor. Will you be staying for dinner?"

"Thank you on both accounts, but no. Colleen, is Bill here?"

At that moment, Colleen moved to the side to give Bill a better view, and nodding at me, he extended his hand to John.

"DCI   William   Barton,   Port   Hope Constabulary."

The handshake completed, John asked, "May we come in for a moment as soon as I've taken care of our cargo? We could use some reinforcements. Things are quickly coming to a head here, and we must seize the moment before it's lost."

. . .

It wasn't difficult to locate the barn, of course, and John parked the horsebox where Colleen had said. I waited until he'd locked everything up and was glad we'd taken the padlock. We didn't have a key, but I figured the folks at the slate mine who were dynamiting tunnels out of sheer rock wouldn't have a problem opening our little lock. And when the Schneiders were out of the picture, the contents should be safe.

. . .

"When Colleen first showed me her list, I was skeptical. It appears I should have taken it more seriously," Bill said, "although, she was overly suspicious of one woman who had come by the station."

"I should have known," Colleen said. "Although, to be fair, I'd only seen Opal Fitzgibbon once before. Her husband had beaten her. Again." Colleen shook her head. "The man is bad news."

The four of us had gone to the kitchen and were now seated at the table. "We don't have the luxury of time for planning this operation," John said. "In fact, we must move tonight."

"What do you need?" Bill asked.

"How much manpower do you have?"

"Half a dozen men at the station. One will need to remain on duty there, so five," Bill said.

"All right. Five it is," John said. "Take the postmaster into custody and keep him isolated. We need him away from the switchboard."

The atmosphere was tense and the tension, while controlled, was building. We now had just four men to wrap this up, and everything had to happen simultaneously to prevent anyone from escaping the net. "I'll take the post office," I said. "I can operate the switchboard. As soon as your man has taken the postmaster into custody, I'll place the call to London for transport vehicles, should there be anyone left to transport." I looked first at John and then at Bill and Colleen. "Orders are to capture if possible, neutralize if necessary."

Colleen reached for Bill's hand. He squeezed it briefly. "The Battle of Port Hope has begun," she said.

"Two of your men will take Miranda Hainsworth and Douglas Hyde-Stuart into custody. They also must be isolated," John said, and Bill nodded.

"You and I and your last man are to the Taylor estate. The real name is Schneider. Anna and Gerhardt Schneider. Their wireless transmission station has been taken down."

There was a sharp intake of breath from Colleen. "I knew it," she muttered. "I knew it."

. . .

For our first effort at a synchronized multi-front attack, it all went rather well, from our point of view, that is. Traditionally, and quite differently from the way it is in my adopted homeland, America, the British Police Force has been unarmed. You can argue the pros and cons of the topic forever, but that's the way it's been. They police by consent rather than through force, with respect for authority the factor that allows this system to function. But with the coming of Hitler and his lack of respect for tradition, human life, and anything else that stands in his way, some adaptations to this time-honored structure were deemed necessary, and certain officers trained in the use of firearms are now stationed at various posts throughout the kingdom, just in case.

Port Hope was not one of those posts with an armed police unit, and it was clear that Leavesley Pendergast, the postmaster, held no respect for the officer charged with apprehending him and taking him to the station. A baton and a uniform don't stand a prayer against a pistol aimed at the heart, which was the postmaster's response to being notified of his arrest. Standing alongside the officer, I drew my service pistol and dropped Pendergast where he stood. His transport vehicle would be a hearse. He didn't even have the good graces to die outside and bleed into the dirt, and I was forced to step around the blood splots on the floor as I took over the switchboard. With no one to warn the others, our team could move in with the advantage of surprise. I gave Pendergast nothing more than a passing thought, but that one thought was that Germany had sympathizers among us, and, for whatever reason, Pendergast had been one of them. His reasons for betraying his homeland died with him.

The second casualty occurred at the Hainesworth home, as I later learned. Miranda Hainesworth was not in possession of a firearm, but she did have Peeps. Hainesworth had answered the knock on the door with the bird perched on her left arm, and when informed of her arrest, she launched her attack bird at the officers. The bird, however, apparently sensing that its moment of freedom, vengeance, or even, perhaps glory was at hand, paid no attention to the representatives of the Crown and turned on the hand that fed it, going straight for Hainesworth's eyes, blinding her on the spot. The bird's next action was its flight to freedom, and it wasted no time gaining altitude and distance.

"Obviously a Brit," Constable Stonewell said to his partner, Constable Bookings.

"Obviously."

In a desperate denial of reality, Miranda launched herself, screaming obscenities, in the direction of the voices, but was cuffed and taken outside to the police vehicle before she could make contact.

Hyde-Stuart was found cowering in the pantry, his arms locked around his head, offering no resistance as he was taken into custody, insisting repeatedly, "She killed her. She killed her. I had nothing to do with it. I told her not to. But she killed her anyway. The *she* and *her* revealed themselves to be Miranda Hainesworth and Berthe Baumgartner, respectively. This did nothing to help Hyde-Stuart's case, as accessory to murder would now be tacked on to the charges against him of espionage and grand theft.

. . .

I made the call to London, requesting assistance, and received confirmation that help would be on the way immediately. Shutting down the switchboard, I closed up the post office and Morris and I then set off for Bellesford, where the last scene of this act would play out.

Arriving at the estate was like *déjà vu*. We'd secured the perimeter, in a manner of speaking, and now needed to tackle the interior. The party showed no signs of abatement. The music continued, with the string quartet having moved on to a rather subdued piece by Handel. If the revelers weren't tiring, it seemed the musicians were conserving their energy. Slower music requires fewer arm movements than do livelier selections.

John, Bill, and the other constable, Jim Aldercroft, were to split up once they reached the mansion, with Aldercroft stationing himself at the rear door that opened onto the drive to the stables and Bill taking the front door and the grounds that led to the road. John was to join the party and locate Gerhardt. Upon my arrival, I would track down the harridan of the household, Anna. I stopped Morris on the main road to smooth my hair and freshen my lipstick. Unfortunately, I'd need to hoof it back to the ball. According to the scenario we'd concocted, John and I had had a lovers' tryst that would explain our absence from the festivities. But our lovers' tryst hadn't ended well, and after rejoining the party which we'd actually never joined in the first place, we'd separate and pointedly ignore each other. The benefit of this, of course, was that I could operate alone, as could John, since we'd be ignoring each other after the quarrel. It was brilliant. I'd need to look emotionally shattered and weep a while. I fished a handkerchief from my handbag to dab at my eyes as I entered.

I spied John moving about the guests, on the hunt for Gerhardt. Briefly, we locked eyes, but John's were concerned, and that left me with an uneasy feeling. I began my own search for Anna Schneider, and after a few moments, understood John's concern. They weren't moving about the ballroom, visiting with their guests. So, I reasoned, if they weren't here, they were somewhere else. Paused at the foot of the stairs, long enough for John to see where I was going, I moved my search to the next floor.

Architecturally, Bellesford House was a symmetrical structure. The Grand Staircase arose from the central ground floor and arrived at the midpoint of the first floor that contained the bedrooms, baths, and parlours that were all distributed evenly on each side. While an interesting structural feature, it made locating Anna's quarters a heads or tails situation. My first guess, to the right, was incorrect, although I could view it as a dress rehearsal that allowed me to learn the location of her bedroom and its layout. It also gave me a couple of minutes to work on my strategy for the encounter to come.

As with Berthe Baumgartner, the desk clerk at the Rusty Scupper, I had two possible approaches. I could either storm the bedroom, announce she was under arrest for espionage, and then wrestle her to the ground prior to dragging her out of the room, down the stairs, out the door, and to DCI Barton, waiting at the front doorstep. With her histrionics and tendencies towards violence, it just seemed like too much work, held the opportunity for escape on her part, although I'd do my best to prevent it, and carried the risk of firing at her while she tore down the stairs and through the crowd of guests, taking out one or more MPs in the process. No. That was not going to work. Option number two, then. I'd said to myself earlier that this would be the closing scene in Act One of this drama. I hadn't realized what that would mean. I took a relaxing breath and slipped into character.

I walked to her door and knocked softly. *"Frau Schneider,"* I called in a stage whisper. There was no response. Not unusual, I thought. *"Frau Schneider,"* I whispered again. This time I heard movement in the bedroom. I didn't expect an answer. She'd wait to see who was on the other side of her door, fearing a trap. When she opened it, I'd need to give a quick explanation and do a few rapid head movements, as if checking the hall for anyone who might overhear us.

Curiosity won over caution, and a moment later she opened the door just enough to see who was foolhardy enough to breach her chambers. I kept to my script and made a big deal of checking the hall, before delivering my lines.

Sie sind in Gefahr! Wir müssen jetzt gehen!"

Granted, there were only two lines, but my delivery was perfect. Anna didn't respond immediately to my warning of danger and the need to flee, but I could see the wheels turning.

"Speak English, you fool! Who are you? I've seen you before."

I shook my head hard enough to make my eyeballs hurt. "I have been sent to protect you. They know who you are and will be here soon to arrest you. Please! I will explain later. We must go now while there is still time." The appeal to her vanity was the clincher. She was so important that Hitler himself must have sent another agent to warn her. "There is no time to pack. Clothes will be provided for you." *They certainly would be, in prison*. "We must go now! Leave everything to me."

She stood, her tongue clicking against her teeth, and her eyes scanning the hall and stairs. Finally, she nodded.

We walked at a leisurely pace down the hall, down the stairs, across the ballroom, and out the front door, chatting like old friends. No one was interested in engaging her in conversation, and we made good forward progress until she bumped into the doorman, Detective Chief Inspector, William Barton. "Here you go, Bill," I said. One down, one more to go."

The chain of expletives she unleashed was enough to make a sailor cringe, but at least her volume faded with distance as Bill marched her down the walk to the waiting police van.

Returning to the ballroom and John, where we did a credible job of lovers reconciling, we were able to share notes. My note was good. His wasn't. Gerhardt Schneider had flown the coop. His automobile was gone, and a thorough search confirmed the reality. It was the only sour note in the operation. All in all, though, not a bad haul. It seemed likely that Gerhardt was on the move now, and our chances of intercepting him were decreasing by the moment.

Leaving John and the officers to make one last sweep of the mansion and grounds, I returned to the switchboard to report. Gerhardt was the one that got away, at least for now. We didn't know what time he'd fled, but I suspected he was already halfway to Berlin. I also had a hunch our paths would cross again.

. . .

With the bodies of the hotel clerk, Berthe Baumgartner, and the postmaster, Leavesly Pendergast, in the morgue, and Miranda Hainesworth, Douglas Hyde-Stuart, and Anna Schneider in the lockup, and most of the stolen art waiting in Colleen Richardson's barn for their next foster home in Manod, my time in Port Hope was drawing to a close.

It was close to midnight. Bill's officers had returned to their homes, Jim Aldercroft with good news for his wife. Bobbie was out of danger. Anna Schneider would never lay a finger on her or anyone else ever again.

John and I were about to head back to the Scupper in Morris, but Colleen had been busy while we were fumigating the Nazi spy nest. She'd laid out a proper supper. Bangers and mash along with fresh green beans from the garden and crusty rolls fresh from the oven.

"There's no butter," she said, and we all laughed. We were back to life's normal tragedies. It was nearly three in the morning by the time we were back at the Scupper where we fell into bed. Three hours later, the alarm jolted us awake. I could swear I'd only been asleep for three minutes. I dragged myself out of bed and said the word that meant the world. "Coffee!"

CHAPTER TWENTY-FOUR

Rhyl, Wales; Canvey Island, England; and points in between

Every man has his price, and Erdmann Speer was hoping the innkeeper's price would be a reasonable one. He would come away with the painting, regardless. Hyde-Stuart had finally located the last piece of art on the list, the Constable, hanging above the bar at the Ox and Boar in Rhyl. The driver transporting a vanload of art had taken a fancy to this particular painting, and, after learning its value, sold it to the first bidder.

Negotiations might take a while, but the public house offered rooms for the night and a place to eat, which fit Speer's plans. It had taken the entire day to drive the nearly five hundred kilometers from his home on Canvey, and the trip had used more petrol coupons than he'd anticipated. Speer had traversed the entire width of England, crossed the border into Wales, and then driven down the coast. He'd traded the English Channel for the Irish Sea, although it all looked the same.

The painting in question was *The White Horse*. It was one of Constable's largest and its massive size would require removing it from its frame and rolling up the canvas, something that would not please the buyer and would reduce the amount he'd be willing to pay, but it was unavoidable. Framed, Speer might as well have paraded it across the countryside with a marching band and a banner emblazoned with a swastika.

.   .   .

"I'm prepared to offer 5,000£," Speer began the negotiations from a table close to the side door that led onto the alley. It was more than likely he'd need to use it. There were a handful of customers. Two were standing at the bar, two were engaged in a heated game of darts, and one was seated at a table by the stone fireplace across the room. Muscular and middle-aged, he had been reading the same page of the newspaper since Speer had entered.

The proprietor, a short, thin man in his mid-sixties with a few strands of black hair clinging to what remained of life on his scalp, wiped his hands on a dirty rag and came from behind the bar after giving the item in question a long, loving look as if it were a family heirloom dating from the birth of

Christ and only being offered for sale to pay for a tombstone on his poor mother's grave. The only prop lacking was a handkerchief to dab the tears from his eyes.

Speer's eyes revealed nothing. He'd already determined a price, but the drama must play out. Ignoring the outstretched hand, he used it instead to pull the chipped ashtray towards him and lit a cigarette.

"I am Alwyn Beddoe," the proprietor began, taking his seat opposite Speer. "5,000£, you say." He shook his head in disgust. "That amount is out of the question." He shook his head in regret but made no move to leave. "I know its worth. The price is 50,000£. He folded his hands on the table and leaned forward, waiting.

Speer merely crushed out his cigarette in the ashtray, pushed his chair back and stood. He'd only taken a few steps towards the front door when Beddoe, panicked, called out, "15,000£. I meant 15,000£." The handkerchief came out again, and Beddoe wiped his forehead.

Hesitating, then shrugging, Speer returned to his chair. This time he extended his hand which Beddoe grasped and shook until Speer wrenched it away. "I'll need a room for the night," Speer said. "Before opening hours tomorrow, if you'd have the painting taken down and set in front of the bar, I'll pay the amount agreed upon."

"I'll be here at 9 o'clock," Beddoe said.

"I'll be here at 8. Now, I'd like to make arrangements about the room."

Beddoe stood and motioned for Speer to join him at the bar which also served as the hotel desk. He produced the ledger and a pen. "The room is 25 shillings."

Speer made an X in the ledger, then took an envelope stuffed with pound notes from his jacket, examined the bills inside, and shook his head. He set the envelope on the counter while he located a second, thinner envelope from which he extracted the funds in coin for the room. Returning both envelopes to his jacket, he accepted the key from Beddoe and climbed the stairs to room 15. The furnishings were what he'd expected, but the only item he needed was the wooden chair which he positioned facing the door, at a distance of six meters. Service pistol in hand, he sat down to wait in the gathering darkness.

The clock on the scarred, wooden dresser ticked away the minutes and the hours until midnight, when the waiting ended. The door handle turned, there was a brief exchange of low voices in the hall, and then the door opened with an audible creak, the bare light bulb hanging from the hall ceiling illuminating the outlines of two men. Speer lifted the pistol and fired twice. The two shots did their work, and the men fell backwards into the hall. Rising from his chair, he walked to the door and stepped over the bodies of

Beddoe and the man who had died, still clutching his newspaper.

Working with just the overhead light by the bar, it took an hour to free the canvas from the frame. The buyer's specific instructions not to cut the canvas from the frame was understandable but added time to the process, and twice, Speer paused at the sound of voices coming from the street. Finally, the frame gave up its hold on the canvas so he could roll it up. He let himself out of the pub by the alley door and walked to the waiting Austin.

. . .

Reaching Canvey took hours more than it should have, but since all the road signs had been removed in case the Germans invaded, he'd had to backtrack several times. Driving on adrenaline and by his mostly reliable sense of direction, it was late afternoon when he arrived back to Canvey. He hadn't slept in twenty-four hours, and he knew as soon as he stopped, he'd have to deal with the fatigue. The extra days waiting for the Constable had been worth it. From this point, it all boiled down to collecting everything waiting for him in Colchester and moving it to the docks at Ipswich. The search for a boat hadn't yielded any results, but there was a possibility of stealing one of the Dunkirk boats there, and there was always

DeMontana's sailboat to fall back on. Finding a crew wouldn't be difficult, and he'd be on the vessel with them to make sure they didn't become a problem.

All that was for the morning. Now, he needed sleep. He'd have to listen to Margo demanding an apology for slapping her, and she wouldn't quit until he had. Dammit, it had just been a reflex. Why did women always think it was all right to let loose on a man, but if he fought back, he was a demon? He hadn't hit her that hard. Christ. But it was her fault. He hadn't even looked back. Maybe falling into the water had cooled her down. He could only hope, and he was too tired for another fight. It was none of her goddamn business if he made a fortune off the war, and she wasn't going to lecture him on morality. How many had she killed? What gave her the right to be judge and jury? She had her own accounting to do.

By the time he'd gotten home, exhaustion was not far away. He parked the car in the garage, brought the painting into the house, and collapsed onto his bed. No sign of Margo. If his luck continued, he'd be gone before she returned from wherever she'd gone.

CHAPTER TWENTY-FIVE

Colchester, Castel del Mare II

"Have you ever been to Tahiti, Angelo?" Glenna was standing by the work table, laying out the four metal cases she'd fabricated. She sighed. "It seems so romantic. A South Sea Island filled with tropical plants and exotic birds." She felt his eyes on her. Of course, she did. She'd caught his interest with the magic word — *romantic* — and more than his eyes, she could feel the heat from his body.

"Oh yes, love. Do you want to sail there? We could, when we're done with this. You will wear flowers in your hair." He raised his arms and moved them about, creating a frame for her body. "I shall paint you against the backdrop of the ocean. You will be the queen of an island kingdom. I will make you famous. Men will desire you, but you will always be mine."

Their romantic exchange was interrupted by the arrival of Arianna. "We've got company, Angelo. I'll stall them. Clean this shit up."

"Every operation requires a manager," DeMontana said, with a heavy sigh. "You finish up, love. I'll see who our guests are."

With a nod, Glenna returned to her task of lining the lid and base of each case with a thin sheet of cardboard, placing a parchment in each, and replacing the lid. For the next step, she took each of the four paintings Angelo had done for this project. *The Four Seasons* was the name he'd given the series that depicted a woman in the four stages of her life—childhood, youth, motherhood, and, finally, old age. To each, he'd imparted his talent, and the beauty of each phase spoke of his undying appreciation for the greatest passion of his life—women.

Glenna smiled. Laying each portrait face down on the table, she slipped a case into the slots she'd prepared in the back side of the frame, added the cardboard backing, glued the paper cover in place, and affixed the authentication stamp. When she'd finished, she moved the paintings to the hidden storeroom, closed and locked the door, and wheeled the massive floor to ceiling cart loaded with framing wood and equipment in front of the door. By the time Angelo returned, the buckets of rags and solvents were in place, concealing the wheels of the cart, and she was cleaning brushes at the sink.

"It's Franta with his muscle, and this time he's brought a woman along. Possibly someone interested in a purchase." He smiled broadly, but his eyes flicked over to the corner where the shotgun was propped against the wall by the drying rack. Glenna nodded and took the brushes to the rack to dry. She wiped her hands on her slacks, then picked up the shotgun, leaned against the wall, and waited, the shotgun resting in her arms. DeMontana moved his smaller easel from the center of the room and repositioned it by the far wall across from her where he resumed work on the sketch he had begun that morning.

.   .   .

John and I had waited for Adam to arrive before beginning our mission today. We expected to increase our art holdings by twenty-nine, bringing the grand total of our acquisitions considerably closer to the goal of one hundred and fifty that had been stolen by German agents who'd planned on shipping them to Hitler for his Führermuseum. Tracking down what remained missing would fall to others. Realistically, those pieces might never resurface, and it was likely they had been lifted by private parties for their own enjoyment.

For us, only one problem loomed large. And it was an extremely big problem. *Where the hell were the Magna Cartas?* It was most vexing, and I knew it was eating at John. He wouldn't quit until he'd found them. I had visions of us in our old age, hobbling about Britain with our canes or in our wheelchairs, still seeking our counterparts to The Ark of the Covenant. It wasn't a pleasant thought or a welcome sight. Neither was the shotgun pointed at us as we entered Angelo DeMontana's workshop.

Some might argue that a shotgun is inferior to a pistol or a revolver or any other form of handgun. In some ways, this is true, but while a shotgun may lack finesse, it has the ability to cover a wide area with lethal results. And, from a psychological aspect, anyone who has ever heard the unmistakable sound of a shotgun being cocked, knows it means business and deserves respect.

"If this is another shakedown, the game is over. I refuse to play," DeMontana said, with a pointed look at his assistant who cocked the shotgun in answer.

"It isn't a shakedown," I said, "but if I fire this," I looked down at my jacket pocket and moved my hand, "and she fires that," I made a pointed look at the firearm, intruding into our personal space, "all we've accomplished is creating a mess for your staff to clean up. No one is any richer, or poorer either for that matter, but one or more of us will most assuredly be dead."

The corners of DeMontana's mouth turned upwards and he slapped his hand against his leg before letting out a roar of laughter. "The women, gentlemen," he said. "Never trust the women! Glenna, my love, return the shotgun to its place."

I wasn't too sure about the woman he called Glenna, but she complied and stepped away from the corner. I nodded at my pocket and slowly removed my hand. For the moment, a truce had been declared.

"All right. What is this about?" DeMontana asked.

John was the next to join the conversation. "I am Detective Chief Inspector Ellsworth of the Yard. My credentials are in my pocket, if I may?"

"You may if you wish, of course," DeMontana said. "But they would mean nothing. I have produced many for any agency you could think of, yours included, and some you could not. Let us get down to business. I have a client coming this afternoon to pick up a shipment and it wouldn't be wise to have an audience for the transaction."

"Who?" John asked.

"Ah! A man of few words, you are, Detective Ellsworth. I do not know his name. It's not something necessary to the contract. He contacts me. And he pays well, so why should I ask questions? I have made a sketch of his face, however. He has a distinctive set to his jaw, and I found it possibly worthy of a study."

The sketch meant nothing to Adam or to John, but when I saw it, I froze. "You are playing with fire, Mr. DeMontana. If your business with this man concludes today, and he has no further need of you, he will kill you." I turned to John. "It's Ronin," I said, "and if we had any doubts before, there are none now. He's been behind the whole operation from the beginning."

DeMontana's brow creased and sorrow filled his eyes. "That would be a tragedy, for me most definitely, but also for the women yet to meet me. That would be unthinkable. We must do something!"

In spite of the gravity of the situation, I laughed, and when I glanced over at Glenna, she was shaking her head in the unmistakable female expression of *what do I do with this man?*

As an icebreaker, it was most effective. DeMontana nearly fell over himself in his newfound purpose of satisfying the women of the world. It was indeed an ambitious undertaking, if not an admirable one. It is important to have purpose in one's life.

I studied our new associate with a critical eye, trying to understand his legendary success with women. He was about five foot eight, with the build of an overweight wrestler. For wont of a better word, he was a bear of a man. He wasn't Clark Gable or Cary Grant or Gary Cooper or William Holden. But then again, neither was Humphrey Bogart. Angelo DeMontana simply radiated—no, that wasn't the right word—he exuded testosterone and confidence and an insatiable love for living. He was one of a kind. I'm married, not dead. Angelo DeMontana was a sexy man — an extremely sexy man — and he knew it. He also knew how to turn a problematic situation into something that would benefit him. It was a gift, an innate talent, and it had made him a wealthy man.

"So!" DeMontana said. "You do not wish money of me." He looked first at Adam and then at John. "You," he pointed to Adam. "There is more to you than I thought, Professor. By the way, what did you do with the money I paid you yesterday? It would appear you are in more difficulty with the authorities than I, unless, of course, you *are* one of the authorities. You are working with this Detective Ellsworth." He held up a hand. "Do not deny it. It would be a lie."

It was Adam's turn, and he drew to an inside straight. "I turned the money over to the British Red Cross for the war effort. It didn't make sense to leave it in an impound account. And I donated it in your name."

De Montana considered this. "That was most generous of me. If you do not want more money, then you must want my art." He paused to consider. "No. Not my art. The stolen art!" His face was triumphant. "That is easily accomplished. Follow me!"

To say we were dumbfounded would have been so far from what we were experiencing that it defied comprehension. After all the searching, was the answer finally here?

We followed, as instructed, down the stairs to the basement and a climate-controlled storeroom. Unlocking the double-doors, DeMontana stepped aside, bowing with a flourish.

"The forgeries," Adam began. "No, I apologize," he said, "the *copies* that I saw yesterday. These are not the same paintings. You still had the originals."

"Of course. *Signore,* I am an artist. I create works of beauty. And I make copies of other works of beauty, improving them just a bit." He smiled proudly. "It is my talent. But, *signore,* I am not a traitor to my adopted country who gave me shelter from that son of a mother's dog, Mussolini, may he rot in hell forever. And that cretin Hitler as well, may he also rot."

Adam's mouth was hanging open at a most unattractive level. "You son of a bitch!" he said.

"No, no, *signore.* I must take exception to that. My mother was a faithful woman, God rest her immortal soul and may she fly with the angels. My father, on the other hand, dropped his seed freely and without regret throughout the countryside, or so I am told." He looked at John and me, his expression angelic. He bowed before us, gesturing towards our windfall. "These are my gifts to you, courtesy of Angelo DeMontana!"

I wondered. If one receives one's own property, how is that a gift? It didn't matter. Then, I had a thought. "If Ronin commissioned you to make copies and gave you the stolen art to use as models, when he comes to collect both the originals and the copies, there will only be one set. How were you planning on explaining that?"

"That?" He snorted. "Please. I made two sets of copies. I work quickly, and it wasn't a problem at all. He'll have his two sets. 'It is double pleasure to deceive the deceiver' my countryman Machiavelli once said, and I now will be sure not to be anywhere around when he comes to collect them. I have come to believe it would not be wise." He bowed again in my direction. "I am most appreciative of your warning and also most interested in how you will resolve this situation. You must let me know how it all plays out. Oh. Just one moment." He moved to the next door, unlocked it, and pointed to a shelf on which lay four parchments. "I have no more need of these. You will want these, as well." He glared at Adam, daring him to challenge his words. "These are the originals, as your inspection will attest. On my mother's grave, may she rest in peace and fly with the angels in heaven with all the saints and the Blessed Virgin Maria the Mother of God."

I stifled a laugh and turned it into a cough. If we stayed much longer, the litany to DeMontana's mother could have become another chapter in the Bible.

"And now if you will excuse me," he said, "I will organize the inventory for my patron and then take my leave. You may handle the affair after that. I wish you luck. From what you say, however, you are prepared." DeMontana opened the door to yet another storeroom, and he and Glenna removed its contents, the second lot of copies of the twenty-nine paintings, transferring them to carts which they then wheeled outside to join their companions awaiting transport to God knew where. One final bow, and DeMontana and his women took their leave.

With the originals back under lock and key, John, Adam, and I were left to play the waiting game.

We hadn't been waiting more than an hour when the sounds of an automobile approaching, horn tooting, brought us to attention. The Italian Cavalry, or more accurately, Navy, had returned in the form of Angelo DeMontana, his five women consorts, and another, younger woman.

"I have prepared *Carpe Ventum* for an impromptu voyage," he said. "With that accomplished, a man never leaves a woman in danger." He bowed to me. "Angelo DeMontana is not a coward! We will protect the art while you pursue this Ronin. Perhaps you will intercept him before he arrives, eh? And when you have completed the task, you will take this woman off my hands. She is also a thief, as are we all, but she's not any good at it. I can't trust her. I wash my hands of her." He rubbed his hands together and then shook them, to emphasize his words.

The women, Glenna being the only one I knew by name, had emerged from the automobile armed to the teeth. It was as if a company of Amazons had been conjured from thin air.

"Pirates," DeMontana confided. "The South Sea is awash with pirates." He smiled. "We never have any problems with them when we sail in those waters. And, conveniently, we have conducted many burials at sea, God rest their larcenous, murderous, souls."

Someday, I told myself, when the war was over, I was going to write all this down. In the meantime, we took DeMontana at his word, I gave the young woman a curious look, and we left him and the armed women in charge. I stole a look back as we made for Morris, and they'd already fanned out. If Ronin did arrive, he wouldn't get them all before one of them got him.

. . .

"He's going to be coming from the south," I said, as the three of us made for our automobiles. "According to Margo, he is on Canvey Island every year on the 15th of July to visit the graves of his wife and daughter. Never misses." This brought a couple of skeptical looks from John and Adam, but it was all we had. "A van will be easy to spot if that's what he's driving."

"And if he's not, he'll be looking for one. He'll need something sizeable to carry all the art, some pieces of which are the size of the Sistine Chapel," John said.

"Then it's going to need to be a big van. Something the size of the horse box we used." Then I had a thought, and it wasn't a good one. There weren't any used van stores about, so the only way he was going to get one was to steal it. He'd be driving around, looking for something suitable. If one didn't show up parked on the street, he'd need to broaden his search to garages and barns. *Colleen*. Oh dear Lord.

CHAPTER TWENTY-SIX

Canvey Island to Port Hope to Colchester

Where the hell was everyone? First Margo, now the Schneiders. The house was closed up. The draperies drawn and doors locked and not a sign of life anywhere except for the stables. The horses were still there. The bitch wouldn't have left them to starve. Or would she? More importantly, the horse box that should have been loaded and waiting for him by the barn was also missing. Speer ran his hands through his hair as he made one last circuit of the property. There was only one logical reason for this, and the anger welled up inside him. He'd been played and played royally. Anger turned to blind rage. He'd find them. No matter how long it took, he would track them down and they'd regret what they'd done. More than regret. They would die for it. Returning to the Austin, he sat and drummed his hands on the steering wheel, thinking, planning. They would be moving the art to the docks just as he had planned to do. They had to have left last night or early this morning. They knew he'd be here today. That was cutting it close. He turned the Austin around and retreated back down the drive, stopping until an old man and his dog got out of the way.

"G'mornin', Sir. If you be lookin' fer the Taylors, you're out a luck. The coppers got 'em. They was all over t'place last night." The old man walking the scrawny dog that looked as old as his owner, stopped to watch his dog attend to business. "You missed a fine show, you did. Can't say as they'll be much missed. Good riddance to 'em." The old man leaned forward, his eyes bright in his lined face. "Nazis, they was. They got more of t'em too!" The old man spat on the ground. "They got those other odd ducks over in Ipswich. Suspicious, we all was. They're gonna hang the lot of t'em." He bent to give the dog a pat on the head and then straightened. "I never seen you about here afore, Mister." He tilted his head, considering, then shrugged and ambled off on their morning walk.

Speer looked left and right and then reached for his pistol. No point in taking any chances. That sort talked. But the arrival of an automobile forced a change of plan. A young woman slowed and parked, waiting to go up the drive. "Good morning," she called out. "If you please, I'm here to feed the horses." Speer waved and pulled onto the road, narrowly avoiding a collision with a tractor that seemed to have appeared from nowhere. Too many witnesses to deal with. He cursed. Too late. He was too late to get the art. It was in the hands of the government. Had they arrested Margo, as well? Why? She'd have been working with them. He cursed again. DeMontana was his last chance to salvage something out of this botched affair, but first he needed a vehicle big enough to hold what remained. He watched the tractor creeping up the road. Other places besides the Schneiders had horses, and that meant horse boxes for trucking them about or some other vehicle the right size. He turned left to begin the search.

. . .

Morris and I left DeMontana's just ahead of John and Adam. I was bound for Colleen's home, and they to the Schneider residence, or the *former* Schneider residence to be precise, in Adam's automobile. As I drove, I tried to catch a glimpse of the driver's face in every vehicle that passed going the opposite direction. Without knowing what Ronin was driving, any automobile, bus, van, or truck was a possibility, and with Morris's predilection for slow-going, I didn't pass anyone, but then, no one passed me, either.

I found Colleen sitting on her front porch, reading. There was the expected tea cup and a plate with a biscuit. "I thought you'd be back in London, by now," she said. "Come have a seat."

"Colleen, listen carefully," I said. She started to speak, but I held up my hand. "Here is the key to Morris. I want you to drive to Bill and have him get back here with reinforcements. There's no time to explain." I handed her the key. "Now, go! Hurry!"

To her credit, Colleen did what I asked without any questions and was on the road in admirable time. She should arrive at the station in fifteen minutes, give or take. With a quick look up and down the road, I hoofed it to the barn to let the air out of the tires of the horse box. If Ronin showed up, I wasn't going to make it easy for him. And, if he opened the horse box, as I expected he would, I wanted him to see the art. It would keep him here until John and the rest of the Allied Forces arrived. All I needed was time.

.   .   .

The tractor turned left off the main road and onto a driveway that made a wide circle of the house, passing by a garage with two bicycles and an ancient automobile up on blocks, and finally came to a stop at a stone wall that separated the property from the neighbors. No barn that might yield what he was looking for. With the tractor's engine off, the elderly man driving it finally noticed the automobile that had followed him. Before he'd taken his third step, Speer had his pistol in hand and fired. He'd turned the Austin around and was returning to the road when the farmer's wife came screaming out of the house. He fired again as she reached her husband's body, and she fell by his side.

The next home, a kilometer away, had a barn visible from the road. The doors were wide open and the interior was empty. Speer moved on. He was getting closer to town, and that meant fewer opportunities and a greater chance of being seen. He'd drive through town and resume his search on the other side, unless this one last home on the other side of the road had what he needed. The home was of an older vintage with a fair-sized barn in the back. He made a left turn across the road and onto the gravel driveway.

．　．　．

One lesson from spy school came to the fore:

You are always the hunter. You are never the hunted.

If you are charged with apprehending someone, you are not focused on escape, although sometimes that's an unintended consequence worth grabbing. When your mindset is that of a hunter, you remain controlled and deliberate in thought and action. The hunted's only motivation is escape motivated by fear.

It was a lesson I had committed to memory. It may seem to fly in the face of common sense, when to all appearances, the situation seems reversed, but the mind/body connection is powerful. Harnessing that power gives you the psychological advantage, regardless of appearances.

I was in the barn. And now, so was Ronin. And while time was on my side, time was his enemy. The reinforcements would arrive. He was trapped. Should he leave while he was able, he risked losing his treasure, but his own chances of survival decreased each second he remained.

I was expecting him. Having seen the tea cup and plate on the porch, he'd probably have knocked on the front door. When no one answered, he'd have forced an entry, just to be sure no one was about. He would have next checked all the rooms and the basement, wasting valuable time in a fruitless search. Ronin is methodical and that means he's predictable. With the interior secured, he'd approach the barn and enter through the first open bay. Then, he'd move to cover, wait, and listen.

By now, he'd have seen the horse box and that would be enough to cause the slightest mental relaxation. From his hiding place, he'd scan the rafters and the walls, before moving into the open to check underneath the vehicles. Having found no one hiding there, he'd likely approach the horse box to see if anyone were in the front seat or crouched on the floor. Satisfied there was no one there, he'd make a circuit of the entire vehicle. He wouldn't be able to see into the rear compartment. The windows were set high and were partly open, probably to keep condensation from forming inside. They let in plenty of light, however, so the interior was not dark.

This script played out in my mind as I waited inside the horse box, pistol in hand, flat against the side escape door bolted from the inside. Focused on my breathing, I was hidden from view behind a large piece by Gainsborough—not one of my favorite artists to this point, but should I survive this, he was destined to rise to number one in my preferences.

My earlier estimation that it wouldn't take much to open the padlock proved to be correct. My pick locks had accomplished the deed in slightly under fifteen seconds. It wasn't my best time but adequate to the task. I wanted Ronin to open the back doors and see what the horse box held. It would hold him here while he thought of a way to get out with his cache. When the time was right, I'd confront him, knowing that he would need to kill me, but I had no intention of allowing that. If it came to that, I would kill him first.

If this were a film, the orchestra would be ramping up the sinister music, building to the climax, but this wasn't the movies. The only sound, and granted, it was ominous enough, was the drip, drip, drip of oil coming from the tractor engine and hitting the metal collection pan underneath. I'd done everything by the book, but my heart hadn't gone through the training and its small voice called out, "*John, wherever you are, please, hurry!*"

. . .

Four flat tires. Not by accident, of course. Someone knew he'd be coming and wanted him to know it. *Who?* This house wasn't part of the network. A search of the tools hanging from a rack above a work table produced nothing helpful, and a further check of a small store room was just as futile. They'd taken the air pump. There was no way to inflate the tires. Frustrated, he kicked the dirt and a cluster of rocks went flying, pinging against the tractor. Then, one more troubling thought intruded. Whoever had done this wanted him to stay here. *Why?* Realization hit hard and fast. He was trapped, or that was the hope. Rage boiled up from deep within. He'd been a fucking fool. There was a distant sound of a car engine, and it grew louder, then a second from the other direction. Then, both died abruptly. They hadn't passed by. They'd parked. Any other time, it would have been normal traffic, but he knew better. There were at least two out there, possibly more. He'd waited too long.

.   .   .

By my estimate, any minute now all hell would break loose inside Colleen's barn. They say God watches over fools and children, and, while not a child, sometimes I can be a bit foolish. I hoped that counted. I heard the sound of something bouncing off metal, so I knew Ronin was still here. I couldn't figure out what he was doing, and curiosity won, as usual.

Sliding the bolt to unlock the escape door wasn't a problem, but a bit of rust on the bottom door hinge was a worry. Another drop of oil hit the pan under the tractor. My kingdom or queendom for a spot of oil, I thought. I glared at the hinges. They needed a bit of spit and polish, for sure. The top one looked all right, but the bottom, no. Spit and polish. I grinned. There wasn't any polish hanging about, but if a bit of spit would help, that was easy.

When dealing with potential noise makers, slow and easy is not the way to go. It's quick and decisive, and so, after giving the remedy a chance to set and rubbing it in with my cuff, I took a deep breath and broke free. Slipping around the back of the horse box, I sought my target. It took a second or two. He was to the side of the open bay, his back against the wall and his pistol raised, ready to fire. That answered my unspoken question. John and Adam, possibly Bill and others were out there, but firing at Ronin would have risked hitting someone outside as the bullet continued on its path. There was only one course of action.

"It's over, Ronin," I said, still somewhat sheltered by the horse box. "You can't win."

He never took his eyes from the entrance, but he remembered my voice. "Where's your partner?" he asked.

That took me aback. There was no way he could know about John. They'd never met and he'd never seen me with him. "Explain," I said.

"Your partner. My sister." He said that last word as if it left a bad taste in his mouth.

I nearly relaxed my hold on my pistol. This was a strange conversation. He was looking away from me, about to kill my husband and God knew who else, we were both holding lethal firepower, and yet, something was wrong. Granted, the entire scene was wrong, but it was a hell of a lot more ordinary than the words being spoken. Anger almost took hold, but instead I fired back with words. "You ought to know, you son of a bitch. You're the one who killed her."

He turned towards me, for an instant forgetting everything else except what I'd said.

"Margo."

If I hadn't seen it for myself, I wouldn't have thought it possible. The eyes are the mirror of the soul, they say, and for a brief moment, there was denial and then pain—such pain—in his. He shook his head and returned his attention to the doorway, but there was a tremor in his hand that hadn't been there before. "That explains it. I didn't mean to. I didn't know," were the last words he spoke, before leaving the wall and moving towards the open, his gun still drawn. I had no way of knowing how many were waiting outside the barn doors, nor did I know where they were positioned. I did know, however, that when Ronin made his move to charge the doors, he made the final decision of his life.

I took one step away from the horse box, aimed, and fired.

. . .

I fell into the easy chair, put my feet on the hassock, and closed my eyes. John took on the bartending, and I accepted my glass of whiskey—two cherries included—gratefully. Shortly, his own drink in hand, he sat down in his own chair, and there we were, looking for all the world like an old married couple too tired to go out to the pub. Which we were.

I held my glass, the coolness of it contrasting with the warmth of our flat. I'd opened the windows to air the place out. Everything needs a breath of fresh air from time to time. From the first warning Margo had given me about her brother, I'd known somewhere deep in my soul that one day our paths would cross one too many times, and the last time would mean that just one of us would be alive to continue on our journey. I had no doubt. He had warned me himself. Without remorse or regret. Those were the words I remembered. Stripped to the core, Ronin had committed suicide. It just seemed such a waste of a life. Regardless, however cold it sounded, Ronin now belonged to the past and to God.

. . .

As I was taking my glass to the sink, I spotted the gift Adam had left for me on the hall table that first evening he had shown up on our doorstep. I couldn't think of a better time to inject a little cheer into my mood, so I brought the package back with me to my chair. The floral giftwrap tied up with a red velvet ribbon was exquisite. Inside, nestled in pink tissue paper lay a crystal paperweight, a red rosebud encased in the crystal. Adam had said I'd love it, and I did, setting it on the side table where I could admire it. And not too long after, as if answering a silent cue, Adam showed up at the door. I thanked him, of course, but he was struggling with a rather large piece of art and the thanks got lost in the struggle.

"If you would really like to thank me, get your husband and both of you come down to my auto. There are three more like this, and they're awkward to handle, to say the least," he said, wiping beads of perspiration from his brow after setting the cumbersome piece down in the hall.

The story behind this collection had to wait until we had done as bidden, and only after they were lined up against the far wall and John had found a lovely Merlot for Adam who had taken his accustomed place on the sofa, did we hear it.

. . .

"I stopped to inform DeMontana and his harem that Ronin had been killed and would no longer be a threat to them or anyone else," Adam said. "DeMontana was most interested in an account, so I gave him the abridged version. I told him that you were the heroine of this mission, and that's when he told me to stay right where I was. He had something for me."

He took three of his women into the house, and when they reemerged, each was carrying a painting. These," Adam said, with an expansive wave in the direction of our lineup. "He said that you should have the honor. He then wrote a letter to you, which I had to wait for." Adam lifted his eyes heavenward. "He is as longwinded when writing as he is when invoking the name of his dear, sainted mother. Anyhow, he finally finished it, placed it in an envelope, sealed it, and handed it to me with precise instructions that you, and only you were to open it. So," he said, raising his glass, "there you have it."

I motioned for him to flip the envelope to me, and he did a credible job of launching a rectangular facsimile of a paper airplane that careened across the room before landing more or less in my lap.

Slitting the envelope with a nail file that I keep by me for emergency repairs, or if the need to stab someone on short notice materializes, I extracted a sheet of paper and began to read:

"Bellissima, I entrust these masterpieces painted by me, Angelo DeMontana, to your safekeeping. They are to be delivered to Christie's Auction House tomorrow prior to noon. Please ensure that the instructions for payment are followed immediately following the conclusion of the auction. Other than that, all has been arranged. There is nothing further required of you, although, it would be in the interest of your government to have a discreet presence at the proceedings, along with the capability of taking the attendees into custody at the conclusion of the sale and after the funds have been processed. You will find their identities most worthy of investigation. Again, my dearest, my

undying gratitude. The world thanks you! Your devoted servant, Angelo DeMontana

P.S. Upon the successful apprehension of the buyers, the paintings may be examined by an expert who will find the exercise most enlightening, as it will indicate the attendees' true reason for bidding on my art. The sacrifices one makes for patriotism! However, the one minor change I have made in the number of the Swiss bank account where the money is to be deposited will suffice to ease the burden of sacrifice.

PPS. Please have an agent of your government claim the woman who is currently in the locked bedroom on the ground floor of my estate. Do not trust her!

. . .

"He really is a dear," I said. John groaned and Adam sniffed. "No rest for the wicked or the tired," I said. "Anyone hungry? I'm starved!"

"You two go enjoy yourselves," Adam said. "I have other plans." He gave a rare smile. "I'll say my adieus tonight. Tomorrow, I'm off to Canterbury and other points of interest."

. . .

Tonight's dinner was too special an occasion to trust to my culinary shortcomings. At Wilton's once again, the dapper lobster greeting us on the overhead sign and a celebratory feast before us, we toasted each other, and I said a silent prayer of thanks for one more mission completed, one more reunion. A promise made and kept.

There are always unanswered questions at the end of a mission. One only sees a small section, an isolated moment in time in the lives of the people we meet. Sometimes, that's for the best; other times, it's bittersweet, knowing that someone who would have become a friend, will never be. But then there are those like Ronin, a man so consumed by hatred that his spirit had died years before a physical death claimed him. I'd been the shooter, but he'd really committed suicide, supposedly the one unforgiveable sin. Learning he had killed his sister, his only surviving family, had finally pushed him over the abyss. Whether angels had caught his soul or the devil had claimed it as his own, I'd never know.

Winston Churchill had given us one week to find Britain's missing art, including the copies of the Magna Carta, as well as locating and neutralizing any German spies operating in our assigned areas.

Sometimes, you just get lucky.

FINAL NOTES

"Hide them in caves and cellars, but not one piece of art shall leave this island." Winston Churchill's directive to Kenneth Clark, the director of the National Gallery. This quote was the genesis for *Whirlwind*.

Initially, England's art was dispersed throughout Wales to protect it from bombings. Deeming this unacceptable, the caves at Manod, Wales, were chosen to house the art and extensive alterations were made to effect this.

All historical figures in this book have been portrayed as faithfully as possible. All historical events mentioned in this novel, with the exception of the thefts of the Magna Carta and specific thefts of art from Britain, are true.

Port Hope is a fictional town.

Adolph Hitler's blueprint for the invasion of Britain was Operation Sea Lion, and Operation Lena was intended to send Nazi spies to Britain to weaken British resolve. The spies sent were inept and ill-trained.

Admiral Wilhelm Canaris, head of the Abwehr (German Military Intelligence) remains an enigma. His portrayal in this story is consistent with both his motivations and his actions. Canaris supported Hitler early but came to see him for what he was. From that point, Canaris did everything he could to sabotage Hitler's war efforts, including sending clumsy and inept spies to Britain in Operation Lena. All these spies were quickly rounded up by British authorities. A principal in the plot to kill Hitler, Canaris paid the ultimate price for his courage and was executed by the Nazis in the waning days of the war.

The Battle of Britain began on July 10 and continued until October 31, 1940. The RAF gave the Luftwaffe a lesson in how difficult control of the skies over the English Channel would be, with the result that Hitler ultimately abandoned the idea of an invasion.

England did send a copy of Magna Carta to the New York World's Fair in 1939, with hopes it would encourage a change in thinking of America and result in America joining the fight against Hitler. A bomb exploded there on July 4, resulting in the death of security guards attempting to detonate it. No responsibility for the bomb has been attributed, although speculation has implicated Sir William Stephenson, a British intelligence officer, among other theories.

Adolph Hitler's Führermuseum was his obsession. Even in his final days at the bunker where he committed suicide, he studied the blueprints for the complex he designed himself. Intended to become the largest art center ever constructed, it was to be furnished with art masterpieces bought and stolen. These thefts were conducted on an international scale. Caches of this stolen art are still surfacing today. To the best of my knowledge, none of the Magna Cartas has ever been stolen.

Winston Churchill's persona and legacy are too large to be contained on the printed page. Numerous biographies have been written about him, and they only begin to do him justice. He was the last hope of Great Britain and Europe in a time of darkness. It is a certainty that, without his intelligence, persistence, and inspirational leadership, Britain would have fallen before Hitler. *"Never, never, never give up!"* he once said. And he never did.

Fictional Characters

Captain Martin Brunner and his wife retired to the family estate in Yorkshire. He bought the local pub and is said to enjoy an occasional pint and a supper of bangers and mash. He sleeps well.

Alese Farmer was buried in the church cemetery. There is a modest gravestone there, but at her home, there is now a stone wall that surrounds her rose bush and a bronze marker that reads:

Alese Farmer died in service to King and Country, June 16, 1940.

Jeanne Feltham became manager of Braithwaite Stables and trainer to Onyx who became a champion eventer. Upon his retirement from competition, he was at stud until his death at the age of 32. His bloodline has produced hundreds of champions and his legacy lives on.

Margo Speer was buried in her family cemetery next to her sister-in-law and niece. Under the direction of Katrin Nissen, the gravestones now bear the names of all interred there. Trees were planted, along with hardy perennials, and the little cemetery is now a peaceful, beautiful garden with a decorative iron fence and a gate, perpetually open. Her brother, Erdmann Speer, the spy known as Ronin, is also interred there. It was left to God to judge him.

Jan Wotjkowski spent the rest of the war eating as much as he wanted, learning English, and attending flight school where he did learn how to land an airplane. He later became a flight instructor for the RAF.

Jim Aldercroft eventually earned the rank of Detective Chief Inspector, and upon the retirement of Bill Barton assumed the leadership of Port Hope's Constabulary. **Bobbie Aldercroft** gave birth to twins, a girl and a boy, the first two of their eventual five children.

Bill Barton and Colleen Richardson remained close friends and occasional lovers. She continued to assist him with his more difficult cases.

Mildred Botherwell continued her friendship with Jeanne Feltham and perfected her winemaking, earning numerous awards. Occasionally, the wine was tart.

Anna Schneider was tried, convicted, and executed under the Treachery Act as a foreign agent during wartime and pronounced guilty of the deaths of three British citizens, the third charge added after the body of Duncan Fitzgibbon was unearthed during plowing to prepare the ground for the Dig for Victory Program.

Douglas Hyde-Stuart and Miranda Haines were tried, convicted, and executed for aiding and abetting a foreign government in wartime under the Treachery Act.

Maisie Dougherty, the not-to-be trusted skinny woman was taken into custody and given the choice of penal servitude or enlisting in the Women's Land Army. She chose the latter and became an expert mechanic.

Gerhardt Schneider eluded capture and his whereabouts remain unknown at this time.

ABOUT THE AUTHOR

Karen K. Brees is the Amazon #1 best-selling author of *Crosswind* and *Headwind* (*The World War II Adventures of MI6 Agent Katrin Nissen* series) and the award-winning author of *The Esposito Caper*. She is also the author and co-author of seven nonfiction titles in the health and general interest field, including *Preserving Food and Getting Real about Getting Older*. She holds a master's degree in history and a doctorate in adult education. She has been a bookmobile librarian, teacher, cattle rancher, goat herder, and an obsessed gardener of anything that will take root. She currently resides in the Pacific Northwest.

PUBLISHING HISTORY FOR
KAREN K. BREES, PH.D.

2006 (contributing author) *Raging Gracefully – Smart Women on Life, Love, and Coming into Your Own* (Adams Media)

2007 (co-author) *The Complete Idiot's Guide to the Power of the Enneagram* (Alpha Books)

2008 *The Everything Health Guide to Depression* (Adams Media)

2008 (co-author) *The Complete Idiot's Guide to Secrets of Longevity* (Alpha Books)

2009 *The Complete Idiot's Guide to Preserving Food* (Alpha Books)

2009 (co-author) *The Complete Idiot's Guide to Arthritis* (Alpha Books)

2010 (co-author) *The Complete Idiot's Guide to Pain Relief* (Alpha Books)

2010 (co-author) *The Complete Idiot's Guide to Pain Relief* (Alpha Books)

2013 *The Esposito Caper* (Museitup Publishing)

2018 (co-author) *Getting Real about Getting Older* (Sourcebooks)

2022 *Preserving* (new edition of *The Complete Idiot's Guide to Preserving Food* (Penguin, DK Books)

2022 *Crosswind: The WWII Adventures of MI6 Agent Katrin Nissen (Book 1)*-
(Black Rose Writing)

2023 *Headwind: The WWII Adventures of MI6 Agent Katrin Nissen (Book 2)*-
 (Black Rose Writing)

2024 re-release of *The Esposito Caper* (Black Rose Writing)
Coming August 2024 from Black Rose Writing: *Whirlwind: The WWII Adventures of MI6 Agent Katrin Nissen (Book 3)*

NOTE FROM KAREN K. BREES

Word-of-mouth is crucial for any author to succeed. If you enjoyed *Whirlwind*, please leave a review online — anywhere you are able. Even if it's just a sentence or two. It would make all the difference and would be very much appreciated.

Thanks!
Karen K. Brees